ALSO BY FREIDA MCFADDEN

The Crash
The Boyfriend
The Teacher
The Coworker
Ward D
Never Lie
The Inmate
The Housemaid
The Housemaid's Secret
The Housemaid Is Watching
Do You Remember?
Do Not Disturb
The Locked Door
Want to Know a Secret?
One by One
The Wife Upstairs
The Perfect Son
The Ex
The Surrogate Mother
Brain Damage
Baby City
Dead Med
The Devil Wears Scrubs
The Devil You Know

THE
TENANT

FREIDA McFADDEN

Copyright © 2025 by Freida McFadden
Cover and internal design © 2025 by Sourcebooks
Cover design by *the*BookDesigners
Cover images © Valeria Ciardulli/Arcangel, Bartol_art/Shutterstock

Sourcebooks, Poisoned Pen Press, and the colophon
are registered trademarks of Sourcebooks.

All rights reserved. No part of this book may be reproduced in any form or by
any electronic or mechanical means including information storage and retrieval
systems—except in the case of brief quotations embodied in critical articles or
reviews—without permission in writing from its publisher, Sourcebooks.

No part of this book may be used or reproduced in any manner for the
purpose of training artificial intelligence technologies or systems.

The characters and events portrayed in this book are fictitious or
are used fictitiously. Any similarity to real persons, living or dead,
is purely coincidental and not intended by the author.

All brand names and product names used in this book are trademarks,
registered trademarks, or trade names of their respective holders.
Sourcebooks is not associated with any product or vendor in this book.

Published by Poisoned Pen Press, an imprint of Sourcebooks
P.O. Box 4410, Naperville, Illinois 60567-4410
(630) 961-3900
sourcebooks.com

Library of Congress Cataloging-in-Publication Data

Names: McFadden, Freida, author.
Title: The tenant / Freida McFadden.
Description: Naperville, Illinois : Poisoned Pen Press, 2025.
Identifiers: LCCN 2024046463 | (trade paperback) | (hardcover)
Subjects: LCGFT: Thrillers (Fiction) | Novels.
Classification: LCC PS3613.C4365 T46 2024 | DDC 813/.6--dc23/eng/20241004
LC record available at https://lccn.loc.gov/2024046463

Printed and bound in the United States of America.
LSC 10 9 8 7 6 5 4 3 2

*For my first roommate,
who would set her alarm for three in the morning
to wake up and study and then would put it on snooze.
Twice.*

I forgive you.

AUTHOR'S NOTE

Even though my books are thrillers, a genre that traditionally has dark elements, I do my best to keep them as family friendly as I possibly can. You're not going to come across any graphic scenes of violence or S-E-X. (Mostly because I know my family members will be reading!)

However, people have emotional responses to different things, and some of my books delve into more controversial topics. So for this reason, I created a list of content warnings for all my thrillers, which can be found linked off the top of my website:

freidamcfadden.com

This is a resource that can be used by readers who need to protect their mental health as well as for adults whose kids are reading my books. Please also keep in mind that in a few cases, these content warnings are major spoilers for twists that take place in the book.

With that in mind, I hope you safely enjoy this journey into my imagination!

PART 1

CHAPTER 1

BLAKE

Six months ago, someone stood in this exact spot—on the twenty-fifth floor of the high-rise building that houses Coble & Roy, the Manhattan marketing firm where I work—and tried to jump.

Unfortunately (or fortunately) for him, the window only tilts open to allow a gap of about three inches, which isn't enough for a grown man to squeeze through. He attempted to wrench it open enough to contort his body into the space, but it didn't quite work. Security stopped him before he plummeted twenty-five stories to his death, and now he's at some retreat in upstate New York, picking daisies or singing songs or getting shock therapy or whatever crap they do at those places.

And now I've got his job.

I wanted the job. I've wanted it since I started working here. It's a *great* position. Everyone was vying for it after Quigley tried to take that nosedive. And now it's mine.

And my new office? It's phenomenal. The leather

desk chair perfectly contours to the shape of my spine and cost more than my first car. The brown leather sofa matches the Peruvian walnut bookcase, which in turn is the same shade as the desk in the center of the room, like someone built them from wood harvested from the same tree.

But the best part of all is the nameplate on the desk, spelling out in gold lettering:

Blake Porter, Vice President.

I stare out the window at the view of the skyline of New York City, dotted with its legendary skyscrapers. When I was a kid growing up in Cleveland, I wanted to see the Empire State Building more than anything, and now I get to look at it every day. Then I drop my gaze to the street below, where, twenty-five stories down, people mill around like ants and the vehicles look like the toy cars my mother used to snag for me at neighborhood yard sales.

What kind of chump tries to jump out the window when he's got an office like this? What an idiot.

He couldn't handle the pressure. I can.

My phone buzzes from where I left it on my desk. I swivel my head so I can make out the name *Krista Marshall* flashing on the screen, and I snatch it up. There are calls I duck and calls I take, but I *always* answer when Krista is on the other end of the line.

"Hey, babe," I say.

"Hello, Mr. Vice President," Krista giggles.

Man, I won't get sick of that for at least another week.

"So how are you holding up?" she asks.

I eye the piles of paperwork on my desk, which are only rivaled by the hundreds of emails waiting for me in my inbox. If I take a bathroom break, I've got twenty messages waiting for me when I get back. And I piss fast.

But you know what? That's perfectly fine. I landed the promotion to VP of marketing last week because I could handle it. Because I *earned* it. You got a week's worth of work I need to blow through in an hour? Great. Bring it.

"I'm good," I say.

"Will you be home in the next few hours?" she asks me. "Do you want me to grab Chinese food?"

It's nearly six, and no, I'm not anywhere close to finished. But also, I've been stumbling home at bedtime to eat cold takeout or a protein bar every night for the last month. I close my eyes and imagine my fiancée waiting for me in the living room of our Upper West Side brownstone, her strawberry-blond hair pulled into that sexy, messy bun she always wears piled on top of her head, her black leggings fitted to her waist just right.

I popped the question two months ago with a diamond that I hoped would make her head spin, and I've barely had a minute to catch my breath since then. We haven't had the engagement party she wanted; we haven't even had an engagement *dinner*. She deserves much better than this.

"No takeout tonight," I say. "I'm leaving early."

"Really?"

The fact that she seems so astonished tugs at me. "Yes, and I'm taking you out to dinner."

"Blake," she says softly. "You don't have to do this. If you need to work, I understand…"

"You're more important." My voice is firm—it's the voice people don't say no to. "We are going out to dinner, and it's going to be someplace really nice, so save your appetite. I'll be home by seven thirty."

She sounds so happy. And all this work will be here tomorrow. Also, I've got a laptop I can crack open after she's gone to sleep.

I'm loving domestic life with Krista. When I was twenty-five, the idea of living with a woman would have been unthinkable, but it's been great. It's been going so well we even decided to get ourselves a pet, which we tacitly agreed was a practice run for when we have a child together. We thought about getting a cat or dog, but we couldn't handle that much responsibility, so we ended up with a goldfish. Her name is Goldy. Granted, I know goldfish aren't particularly cuddly, but I'm already attached.

But I need to learn to balance my work and home life. I needed this promotion to give Krista and me the life we want—the life she *deserves*, which will hopefully be better than what my mom had. I needed it to pay for the brownstone, because the mortgage was eating up my whole paycheck.

I came from nothing and hated it. My dad owned a small hardware store and was always struggling to keep it afloat, so I've taken steps to ensure that *my* life is going to be different. I never want to have to worry about the lights being shut off.

I shove my phone into the pocket of my crisply tailored pants. I'll tie up a few loose ends here, and then I'll take off. But before I turn back to my desk, I take one last look out the picture window. I can vaguely see my own reflection in the glass—I'm on the taller side, close to six feet, with brown hair that I always keep clipped very short because it has an annoying tendency to curl, the hint of a cleft in my chin, and dark brown eyes that are a little too close together but have been called "intense," which I take as a compliment.

"Blake?"

I tear my eyes away from the window. My boss's secretary, Stacie, is standing at the open door to my office, her fist poised to rap on the doorframe to get my attention. And she's got my attention. In that skirt—yes, holy crap, she has my attention.

"Hey," I say. "What's up, Stacie?"

"Wayne wants to talk to you."

I glance back at my watch again. It's late in the day for a meeting. "Now?"

"Right now, he said."

She's not meeting my eyes like she usually does. She's looking down at the oriental rug on the floor, like it's the most interesting thing she's ever seen. And I think to myself, *That's strange*.

"Okay," I say. "I'll be right there."

As I turn away from the window and follow Stacie out of the office, it doesn't even occur to me that in the next five minutes, my whole life will come crashing down.

CHAPTER 2

Wayne Vincent has been my boss for the last decade, ever since I graduated from NYU.

He was the one who hired me. Everything I know about marketing, I owe to Wayne. He taught me how to develop a campaign. He taught me how to organize a budget. He taught me how to analyze the competition and the market. In the time I've known him, he's gone through two wives, gained and lost about forty pounds, and together, we have consumed the equivalent of a truckload of alcohol.

And right now, he looks *pissed*.

He is sitting behind his mahogany desk—about 50 percent larger than mine—and he glowers at me as I enter the room. When I hesitate in the doorway, he points a single finger at the chair in front of his desk and barks, "*Sit.*"

I don't know what this is about. I've had this job for one week, and I'm doing it well. No, I'm doing it *great*.

So whatever this is, it's bullshit. I feel my hackles rise preemptively.

But even if he's wrong, he's still my boss, so I lower myself onto the cushion of the chair in front of him. "Everything okay, Wayne?"

He folds his beefy arms across his barrel chest, only partially concealed by the expensive suit he's wearing. "You tell me, Porter."

He called me by my last name. He never calls me by my last name.

"I'm on track with the Clemente campaign," I say. "I'll have a mock-up by Friday. Thursday, if you need it." I can get it done a day early. Who needs sleep?

Then he says something that shocks me: "You shared the Henderson campaign."

"I… What?"

His scalp turns pink under his receded hairline. "You showed our campaign—*everything*—to our competitors. You let them steal it from us, you thieving asshole."

What? My mouth falls open. "I have no idea what you're talking about."

"I know you did it, Blake." His jaw ticks. "All I want to know is who the contact was and how much they paid you."

"Wayne…"

"*How much*, Porter?"

"Wayne." A misunderstanding—that's all this is. I clear my throat. "I swear to you, I would never—"

"Bullshit." A fleck of his spit hits me in the face with this enunciated word. "You're fired, Porter. Pack up your office and get out."

What?

"Wayne!" I leap out of my seat, my heart jackhammering in my chest. "You can't possibly think I would do something like that to the company—to you. I don't know why you think I would—"

"I said, get *out*."

I can tell from the sneer on his face that this isn't some kind of elaborate joke. Nobody is going to jump out of the closet with a surprise cake to congratulate me on my promotion. He is dead serious. He wants me out. After a decade of loyal service, I'm *fired*. Just like that.

A cold sweat breaks out under my armpits. "Can we please discuss this?"

"Get. Out." He picks up the receiver on his desk, his other hand punching numbers on the keypad. "I'm calling security to escort you from the building."

This is really happening. I've lost not only my promotion but my *job*. What the hell is going on? This has got to be some sort of misunderstanding.

"Okay." I hold up my hands. "I'll go, but…maybe we can discuss this later."

The look on Wayne's face indicates we will never discuss this ever again. "Just get out. And forget about a severance package after what you pulled. Don't even think about applying for unemployment. I'll prosecute you for theft, you piece of shit."

I can only shake my head, unable to conjure up the words to respond to that.

Even though it's six in the evening, practically everyone is still at the office, and all of them just heard every word of what happened. I pass Stacie's desk on the way out, and once again, she won't look at me.

"Stacie," I say.

"Sorry, Blake," she mumbles, not lifting her eyes from her computer screen. "There's nothing I can do."

Okay, so that's how it's going to be. Well, to hell with them all. I'll find a job ten times better than this one.

I make the walk of shame back to my office while my coworkers buzz about me from ten feet away. Chad Pickering will be the happiest of all—he thought the VP promotion was his before I snagged it. But he won't be the only one celebrating.

What can I say? If you want to get ahead, you have to make a few enemies.

When I get back to the office, *my* office, I realize there's very little I'll be able to take with me. The framed photo of Krista. The pen my grandpa bought me as a graduation gift—he was so proud that I was the first in our family to ever finish college.

And I'm sure I can take the nameplate that says *Blake Porter, Vice President*. Nobody here has any use for that.

Impulsively, I snatch the nameplate off my desk and hurl it at the wall with so much force that it dents the paint. The nameplate falls to the floor, fractured in half. The office has gone completely silent, watching my little performance. Fine—let them watch. At least I didn't break my hand punching the wall like that dumbass Craig Silverton did after he lost the Roberts account.

I walk over to the window to get one last look. I lean my forehead against the cool glass, not caring anymore about smudges.

And for the first time, I understand my predecessor. Because I wouldn't mind if this glass broke and sent me plummeting to my death 350 feet below.

CHAPTER 3

I have been unemployed for sixty-two days.

Not that I'm counting.

I'm on my way back to the brownstone now after running for two hours, following an hour of lifting weights. I've got another two months left on my gym membership, and I'm damn well using it. Krista has hinted that it's unhealthy to spend hours every day exercising, but how could that be? It's *exercise*. It's healthy by definition.

Besides, I have to keep my energy up for when I find another job.

I am soaked with sweat when I get back inside—my T-shirt is sticking to my skin. August in New York is the worst time to go for a run due to the stifling humidity, but I do it anyway. I like to see how hard I can push myself. What's the worst that can happen? I drop dead?

We can't really afford to run the central air, but I'm glad it's blasting as I catch my breath in the living room. The aroma of cinnamon hits my nostrils, and my stomach rumbles. All I've eaten today is a power breakfast (three whole hard-boiled eggs), and I'm starving.

I wander into the kitchen, where Krista is pulling a tray of cookies from the oven. She casts a glance over her shoulder at me and smiles. "Snickerdoodles?" I ask.

She nods as she rests the tray on the kitchen counter, next to the antique metal clock we bought at a flea market last summer. Snickerdoodles are her specialty—her signature cookie. That's what she does when she's happy or bored or especially stressed: she bakes.

Let me tell you a little about Krista's snickerdoodles. When you put them in your mouth, the edges are crispy but the center is soft, and they melt instantly, spreading a perfect combination of cinnamon and sugar and butter. She baked them for me on our first date, and those cookies were part of what made me fall in love with her. I knew there was something really special about a woman who could bake something that tasted that good.

She learned how to make cookies from her mother, who I met once when she flew in from Idaho and is exactly the kind of woman who you'd expect to make great cookies. When I asked Krista to marry me, I imagined her someday baking cookies for our children like her mother did for her.

That's the life I want. With her.

I reach for a cookie, but she swats at my hand. "They're burning hot from the oven!" she scolds me. "Take a shower, and they'll be cool when you're done."

She hates it when I'm sweaty from a run, which is fair. "Fine."

I head upstairs and strip off my T-shirt and gym shorts. I turn the faucet in the shower to ice cold and step into the stream. I've heard ice-cold showers are for psychopaths, but I'm addicted—I've been doing it since college. It's an extra rush of adrenaline after I've come down from the high of my workout.

When I'm clean and dressed, I head back downstairs, the rumbling in my stomach more insistent this time. On the way down, I pass Goldy, who is swimming contentedly in her bowl. I slip her a few pellets, even though Krista says I'm overfeeding her. I hate the idea of her being hungry.

Krista emerges from the kitchen carrying a plate of the snickerdoodles. She carries them to the sofa, and I follow her like an eager dog. She lowers the plate onto our glass coffee table and settles down on the sofa, tucking one leg under her like she always does. I sit next to her and grab a cookie.

It's freaking amazing, like always.

"Any luck on the job front?" she asks me.

It was dumb to think I'd score another job in marketing right away. After Wayne talked shit about me all over town, you can imagine nobody was champing at the bit to hire me for any choice positions. I was grossly overqualified for the last job I applied for, and it paid a quarter of my prepromotion salary. I didn't even get a reply.

"Not yet," I say, trying not to sound as dejected as I feel.

Krista notices the catch in my voice and leans in to wrap her arms around me. "Is this about right?" she whispers in my ear.

"Level eight," I say.

She squeezes me tighter. This is a little convention that the two of us have developed. In the early days of dating, Krista had a rough day at work, and when we met up that night and she told me about her terrible day, I leaned in to hug her. When she complained I wasn't hugging her tightly enough, we came up with a ten-point scale to determine how tight of a hug we needed given how shitty we were feeling at that exact moment. I know—we're so cute, you want to vomit.

For a good minute, we stay in the hug, which is around a level eight or nine. She's so good at knowing exactly how to hit the right number that I need.

But of course, the hug has to come to an end. When she pulls away, she has a worried crease between her eyebrows. "So do you have enough money in your checking for the next mortgage payment?" she asks gently.

I do—barely. But after that, I am screwed. I won't be able to pay the mortgage, and I'll lose the brownstone. And even though it's in my name and not Krista's, she'll be homeless too. I'm trying not to think about it. "It's tight," I admit.

"I could contribute more," she tells me, even though I know she doesn't have much to begin with.

Krista manages the dry-cleaning store a few blocks away. It's how we met. I brought in a suit, and when I saw her behind the counter, I suddenly realized I wasn't getting my suits dry-cleaned nearly often enough. I came in two to three times a week, spending a small fortune on laundry just to get to talk to her for a few minutes while dropping it off and picking it up.

I didn't make a move right away, because I had a girlfriend. I had been dating a girl named Gwen at the time, but it hadn't been going that great and was only getting worse. So the day after it ended with Gwen, I walked right into the dry cleaner and asked Krista out to dinner.

"I'll find something," I promise.

She lifts one of her light brown eyebrows. "Will you?"

I frown at her. "I'm not going to be unemployed forever, Krista. Something will turn up."

I'll find something eventually—I have to—but it's not going to pay what my last job did or even a fraction as much. I'm going to have to widen my net.

Damn, I still can't believe it. Sixty-two days ago, I had everything. How did it all fall apart so easily? I've called Wayne a dozen times, but he hasn't called me back. I think my emails are going into his spam folder.

"I'm going to suggest something," she says, shifting her weight, "and I don't want you to say no right away."

Oh great. What amazing idea has she come up with? Does she want me to sell a kidney? How much can you get for a kidney in today's market? "Okay…"

"I think we should take in a tenant until you get back on your feet."

I stare at her. Is she serious? "No. No way. I'm not living with a stranger."

"Why not?"

That kidney donation idea is sounding better and better, although I might not get top dollar for it because of how much alcohol I've consumed over the last decade or so. "Because I'm not a twenty-year-old college student?"

Krista crinkles her nose. "You know, I had a roommate before we moved in together."

"And you *hated* her!"

Krista's former roommate was a day care director by day and an amateur singer by night. During my visits to her achingly tiny two-bedroom apartment near Inwood Hill Park, her roommate would burst into song while showering, cooking, and sometimes in the middle of a sentence.

"So we'll find someone more normal," Krista says.

"In Manhattan?" I grumble. "Nobody is normal here. You won't find anyone normal."

She laughs and reaches for my hand, which is only partially covered in snickerdoodle crumbs. "I found *you*," she points out.

No comment.

She slides closer to me on the sofa, resting her head against my shoulder. I brush the rest of the snickerdoodle crumbs off my T-shirt, then throw my arm around her shoulders to pull her close to me. What does she put in her hair that makes it so damn soft? There must be some secret ingredient in that girly shampoo she uses, because it's just incredible.

"I don't know what to do, Blake," she murmurs into my neck. "I know you're going to find something eventually, but... I'm worried."

You and me both, babe.

"Maybe..." She holds out her left hand, where the diamond of her engagement ring sparkles under the overhead lights. "Maybe I should sell the ring. That will buy us some time."

I suck in a breath. No. I do *not* want her selling that. I mean, yes, it would buy us another two months of breathing room, but I don't care. My dad with his struggling hardware store—passed down from my grandfather—got my mother an engagement ring with a fake diamond that was *still* embarrassingly tiny. I was so proud that I got Krista not only a real diamond but one that all her friends could be jealous of. If I made her sell that ring to keep us afloat...

No. I won't let her do it.

I swore I would always take care of Krista, in sickness and in health. No, wait, that's what I *will* swear when we get married. And if I don't figure a way out of this situation, that's never going to happen. She won't marry me if I make us both homeless.

"Fine," I say. "Let's get a tenant."

CHAPTER 4

Single upstairs bedroom available immediately in Upper West Side brownstone on a quiet tree-lined street. Bedroom is fully furnished and has two large windows and lots of closet space. Large shared kitchen, dining area, and living room. Subway adjacent. No pets, no parking provided.

We have two prospective tenants coming to look at the spare room in the next hour.

I'm not optimistic. Since Krista posted our ad all over town and on the internet, we have had about a dozen people look at the room, and all of them were *awful*. I'm not exaggerating. "Awful" is a charitable word for what they were.

One of them was a self-professed kickboxing fanatic. He then demonstrated by kicking a hole in our wall. So now we have to get that fixed. Another woman showed up with the most ferocious animal I've ever seen. She claimed he was a dog, but I'm not convinced it wasn't a wolf or worse.

The worst one by far was two days ago—a short guy with a scraggly goatee wearing a white Linux hat. He grilled me relentlessly for twenty minutes about the internet capabilities of the place. After I did my best to answer his questions, he reached into the sack he was carrying and pulled out a *drill*. He said he needed to drill through the wall to check the wiring, and I had to physically stop him, or else he would have done it. I didn't need a second hole to patch up.

Now we have a woman named Elizabeth coming in about five minutes, then another woman named Whitney in half an hour. I'm sure they'll both be awful. But in case they're not, we have cleaned the house from top to bottom. I even sponged off the inside of the refrigerator in case they look in there.

Krista places a plate of freshly baked chocolate chip cookies on our small dining table, and when I try to grab one, she swats at me. "That's for *guests*."

"Krista, this isn't an open house. There are two people coming and, like, twenty cookies on the plate."

She shoots me a look, and I withdraw my hand. Her gaze sweeps over me as she does one last check to make sure I'm wearing pants today, which I *am*. I've even shaved, which makes me look significantly less like a homeless person.

"Do I meet with your approval?"

Her lips twitch. "I suppose."

"You know," I say, my eyes dropping lower, "you've got flour all over your shirt."

Krista drops her eyes and gasps when she sees the flour speckled all over her maroon tank top. She attempts to brush it off, but that only seems to spread it out more.

"Hey, let me help you with that," I tell her, and she's not even the tiniest bit amused when I fondle her breast. But hey, it's not like these prospective tenants will be any good. May as well have some fun.

"Blake!" she scolds me, although she's suppressing a smile. "Cut that out. They're going to be here any minute."

As if on cue, the doorbell rings.

"Shoot," she says. "Blake, that must be Elizabeth. Can you let her in, and I'll join you in a minute?"

Before I can answer, Krista hurries off to change her top for the benefit of this woman who we will surely never see ever again. I go to answer the door, but not before grabbing a chocolate chip cookie to stuff in my mouth. Man, there's nothing like good home-baked cookies.

When I throw open the front door, a woman about the same age as my mother is standing there, dressed in robes. Yes, you heard me—*robes*, like the plural of a robe. There are at least three robes that I can identify. She has long white hair, frizzy from the humidity, which is covered by some sort of silver hat. I'm not saying she's wearing a tinfoil hat, but I'm not entirely sure it's *not* a tinfoil hat.

"Uh, hello," I say.

"Drake?" she asks me.

"No, Blake," I say.

She looks disappointed.

"And you must be Elizabeth," I say.

She shakes her head. "No, it's *Quill*izabeth."

"Quill…lizabeth?"

"That's right," she says, like it's a common name I ought to know.

"Okay," I say. "Well, please come on in…Quillizabeth."

Quillizabeth looks down at the threshold of our home

and crinkles her nose. Then she reaches into one of her many robes and pulls out—I kid you not—a salt shaker. She sprinkles salt liberally at the entryway.

"It's an important thing to do," she says sagely, "to keep any evil spirits from entering the premises."

"Uh-huh," I say. Great. Now I'm going to have to clean up a bunch of salt after she leaves.

"I'm sorry about this." She continues to spread salt around and even says a few words to herself. "But I tend to have a very strong connection to the spiritual world, especially if I don't take the proper precautions."

"Huh," I say. I have a piece of chocolate stuck in one of my back molars. "To be honest, I don't believe in that stuff."

She straightens for a moment and fixes me with a calculating gaze. "You're a Scorpio, aren't you?"

"I don't know," I admit.

She looks at me like I admitted I don't know my own first name. This is going to be a long thirty minutes.

Finally, after our doorway has been sufficiently seasoned, Quillizabeth follows me into the brownstone. Her sharp eyes are taking in every nook and cranny, lingering on the photos of me and Krista on the mantel, studying our dark brown sofa, judging the sixty-two-inch TV in the corner of the room.

With each new object her gaze comes in contact with, she clucks her tongue like we have committed some cardinal sin. It's *really* annoying. If I didn't think Krista would be mad about it, I'd ask her to leave right now. I don't need this crap.

"My girlfriend made some cookies," I finally say.

Quillizabeth takes in the plate of chocolate chip

cookies. They're still warm enough that the chips are slightly melty. I'd grab another one if Krista weren't about to burst into the living room any minute now.

"Blake," Quillizabeth says, "are you aware that the sugar in cookies is both toxic and highly addictive? If sugar were introduced to the market right now, the government would never approve it for consumption. You may as well lick the sidewalk outside your house."

Has she *seen* the sidewalk outside our house? But fine. Don't have a cookie then.

"Also," she adds, "cookies are *loaded* with saturated fats and empty calories."

As she says those words, she looks pointedly at my abdomen. I glare at her and decide to go ahead and take another cookie for myself.

"Anyway," she says, "you said in the advertisement that you have a single furnished room available?"

"Yeah," I confirm between bites of the cookie. "But actually, we may have someone already. So…uh…you know, I don't want to waste your time."

Quillizabeth licks a finger and holds it up in the air. "It's quite drafty in here, isn't it?"

"Uh, I hadn't noticed."

"You know what that is, don't you?" Her expression is deathly serious, like she's telling me the secrets of the universe. "It's all the past owners who have lived here before you. They create quite the draft, milling about. I can help you get rid of them with a simple channeling ceremony once I move in. That will get rid of the draft"—she snaps her fingers—"just like that."

Krista chooses this moment to come out of our bedroom, wearing a brand-new shirt that looks almost identical to the one she had on before, except no flour this time. Why does it take women so long to change clothes? I could change my shirt in five seconds, maybe less.

"Is that Elizabeth?" she calls out as she sprints down the steps.

"Quillizabeth," I mumble under my breath.

Krista descends the last of the steps, and when Quillizabeth looks at her, it's with the only shred of approval I've seen since she stepped into the house. "My dear!" Quillizabeth exclaims. "You are such a pretty girl!"

"Thank you," Krista says as her cheeks go pink. The woman has good taste, I'll give her that. Krista holds out one of her pale hands. "My name is Krista. It's so good to meet you, Elizabeth."

"Quillizabeth," she says.

They shake hands, but a split second after their palms make contact, Quillizabeth yanks her hand away as if she's been scalded. She stumbles back, her hands trembling.

"I..." Quillizabeth's voice has gone suddenly hoarse. "I actually have to go. This place...it's too small. I won't be renting it after all."

Thank God. Maybe I'll nab another cookie. "Okay, it was nice meeting you," I say, trying not to sound too pleased.

But Krista frowns. "Is everything okay? You haven't even seen the bedroom yet."

Quillizabeth shifts her gaze to look at me, and there is real fear in her eyes. When she turns back to Krista, her tone is urgent. "Could I...speak to you outside, Krista dear?"

Krista looks at me for permission, and I shake my head no. "What is it?" Krista asks.

Quillizabeth takes another step back. "Outside. *Please.*"

Her watery eyes are locked with Krista's. What the hell is wrong with this lady? I'm sorry I even invited her in. Once the salt shaker came out, I should have slammed the door in her face.

"Look, Quillizabeth," I say. "We have another prospective tenant coming soon, so…"

"He's going to kill you," the older woman blurts out. "Blake is going to *kill* you, Krista. You have to get away from here."

CHAPTER 5

What. The. Hell?

Did this lunatic just come into my own home and tell my fiancée that I'm going to *kill* her? This is horseshit.

Quillizabeth is standing rigidly in our living room, her entire body shaking. It's almost like she's having a seizure. I'd call an ambulance, but then we'd never get her out of here.

"He's going to stab you with a kitchen knife." Quillizabeth points a shaky finger at the rug beneath our feet. "It's going to happen right *here*. I saw a vision of him crouching over your body, watching you bleed to death."

I look over at Krista. All the color has drained from her face. Is there a chance she's taking this woman seriously? *She's literally wearing a tinfoil hat.*

"Okay then." I place a hand on Quillizabeth's back to lead her out of the living room, but she leaps away like I just seared her with a hot poker. "You need to go."

"Please believe me, Krista." Quillizabeth reaches out a

gnarled hand for my girlfriend. "Be careful. My visions… they are never wrong."

"I'm sure," I say through my teeth as I step between Quillizabeth and Krista. "But I'm not planning to murder her today, so I think you're good to go."

I will pick this woman up and *throw* her out if I have to.

Quillizabeth lets out a cry of protest, but finally, Krista shakes her head. "I'm fine," Krista assures her. "You…you should go."

It is Krista who leads Quillizabeth back to the front door. All the while, the older woman is pleading with her and grabbing on to her arm. I hear her repeat the word "dangerous" and then "get out." It takes several minutes of quiet conversation before Krista shuts the door, and by that point, Quillizabeth is practically sobbing.

Jesus. I should have let Krista sell the stupid ring.

I allow myself to collapse onto the sofa. Krista returns to the living room, although she looks several shades paler than she did before.

"Wow," I say. "That woman was out of her mind."

"Yeah," Krista mumbles.

I look up at her. She's wringing her hands together the way she does when she's upset about something.

"You didn't really believe her, did you?" I ask.

"No, of course not." But Krista hesitates a beat too long before saying it. And when she sits down beside me on the sofa, she leaves a little more space between us than she usually does. "But you have to admit, it was a little… jarring."

"Not really. She was nuts."

The left side of Krista's lips quirks up. "You're just skeptical of everything because you're a Scorpio."

I am?

"Look," I say, "skeptical or not, I'm not going to stab you in our living room. I mean, you don't really believe I'm capable of doing anything like that, do you?"

"No," she says, although again there's that weird *hesitation*.

"I've never done anything to make you distrust me," I point out.

And that's true.

Well, as far as she knows.

"I'm a good guy." I reach for her hand, and I can't help notice that, like Quillizabeth, she is shaking. "You know I am. I wouldn't do anything to hurt you or anyone. You *know* that."

Krista looks down at her lap. She takes a breath. "Blake, where did you get the money for the down payment on the brownstone?"

"What?"

She raises her blue eyes slowly. "When you bought this place six months ago. You told me you didn't have enough cash for the down payment. But then all of a sudden, you found the money."

What is she saying? Does she think that I did the awful thing Wayne Vincent accused me of? Does she think I'm some piece of crap who sold out my company to get the money to buy this brownstone? Is that what she's implying?

"I cashed in my retirement," I say through my teeth. "That's how I got the money." When she doesn't say anything, I add, "I'll show you the receipts if you don't believe me."

"No," she says softly. "I believe you."

Does she though? Krista and I have been together for two years, but our relationship is still relatively young. It's apparently early enough that a New Agey quack in robes and a tinfoil hat could say the right things and sow doubts in her head. And let's face it, it's not like I'm batting a thousand lately.

I rack my brain, trying to think of what I can say to reassure her. But before the words can come to me, the doorbell rings.

Oh God, it's another one.

CHAPTER 6

Krista answers the door this time while I brace myself for whoever is on the other side. Who knows what this prospective tenant will be? A convicted murderer in chains? A cannibal? A fire-breathing dragon? At this point, nothing would surprise me.

But the woman standing in the doorway looks… normal.

She doesn't have piercings going through every bit of loose skin in her face, she isn't wearing any robes or tinfoil hats, and she isn't trying to drill a hole in our wall. She's got straight light brown hair that hangs loosely around her face and simple hoops in each of her ears. She's around our age—maybe thirtyish—and she's dressed in blue jeans and a hoodie.

"Hi." She flashes an endearingly nervous smile. "My name is Whitney Cross."

Krista beams back at her. "Hi, Whitney. I'm Krista, and this is Blake."

Whitney sticks out a hand, which we both manage to

shake without her having any psychic visions of a blood-bath in the living room—a good sign. This is already going much better than any other interview. "It's great to meet you both," she tells us politely.

"So we're looking for someone to move into the single room upstairs as soon as possible," Krista says. "Would that timeline work for you?"

Whitney bobs her head. "Yes, my lease ended at my last place, and I'm…um…in between apartments right now. I saw the ad you put up at Cosmo's Diner, where I work, and it was like a godsend."

"You work at Cosmo's?" I ask. It's a Greek diner about ten blocks from here that I've walked by many times but never entered.

"Yes. I'm a waitress." She smiles politely. "What do you both do?"

"I manage a dry cleaner," Krista says.

Now Whitney is looking at me, waiting for my answer. Even before my promotion, I used to be proud of what I did. Now I just mumble, "I'm between jobs."

Krista, the master of subject changes, says, "Would you like to try a cookie? They're homemade."

Whitney scores major brownie points by accepting one of the chocolate chip cookies on the dining table and gushing about how delicious it is. She then follows us to the living room and makes all the appropriate oohs and aahs as we show her around.

"This is our fish, Goldy," Krista says proudly, like she's our child who just graduated from Harvard. But I can't say I don't have a bit of pride over how Goldy does those little loop-de-loops around the bowl. Do all fish do that? I think Goldy might be gifted.

"Cute!" Whitney says, leaning down to look closer.

Krista moves the tour to our kitchen, which is pretty standard, although the way Krista talks about it, you'd think it was a prize on *The Price Is Right*. She missed her calling in sales.

"Oh my God, a dishwasher would be heavenly," Whitney sighs.

"You don't have one now?" I ask, surprised.

Krista shoots me a look, but it's a reasonable question. Who doesn't have a dishwasher in this day and age? Is that a red flag?

Whitney hesitates for a moment, then shakes her head. "No, just the sink."

"I didn't have one until we moved in together either," Krista confides. "Blake here doesn't understand how the other half lives."

The two of them share a laugh at my expense. But I don't even care, because Whitney seems *nice*. First impressions can be misleading, but she seems so harmless. Not a cannibal—I'm, like, 99 percent sure.

Maybe this will actually work out.

After we show her around the first floor, we head upstairs. The stacked washer and dryer are at the top of the stairs, and Whitney's eyes fly open at the sight of them. "Is that what I think it is?"

"You got it!" Krista says. "It's a washer and dryer. Compact but still way better than lugging your clothes to the laundromat."

"Oh my God, *yes*." Whitney rubs her hands together. "The last time I was there, someone took all my clothes out of the dryer and threw them on the floor! It's a jungle in there."

I'm not thrilled about the idea of sharing my small washer and dryer with yet another woman. Krista already washes what seems like a month's worth of clothes in a single week. Still, we can't rent out the room and expect the tenant to take her clothes to the laundromat two blocks away when there's a machine ten feet from her bedroom door.

There is one bathroom as well as two bedrooms on the second floor of the brownstone—the master bedroom that Krista and I share, plus another smaller room. I had fantasized about filling our extra bedrooms with children, but that seems like a lifetime ago. Now we have to hand over one of those bedrooms to a stranger, and if I don't find a job soon, the other one might be up for grabs as well.

We show Whitney the small bathroom with the shower that we will apparently all be sharing, since we only have two bathrooms, and the one downstairs is a half bath. Finally, we make our way up the narrow stairs to the top floor of the brownstone.

The third floor has lower ceilings than the rest of the house. I always feel like I need to duck down even though we measured the ceiling height at six feet five inches—a full half a foot greater than my height. This floor contains one furnished bedroom as well as a wide-open space that Krista and I argued we could one day turn into either a playroom or a man cave. (Guess who argued for the latter.)

The furnished bedroom has been serving as a guest room until now, although we haven't yet had one guest. It contains a double bed, a dresser, a half-size bookcase, and a large closet.

"We also have a room that's unfurnished on the second floor," Krista adds, "if you'd prefer that."

"No." Whitney's gaze rakes over the furniture that I spent far too much on, back when I had money to burn. "This is *perfect*. I don't have any of my own stuff."

What thirty-year-old woman doesn't have a scrap of furniture to her name?

Whitney's eyes are shining as she walks over to the closet and throws open the door. It's not a walk-in closet, but it's a decent size. As I watch her make plans for our spare bedroom, another thought hits me:

Whitney is pretty.

Okay, it's not like I didn't notice when she first walked in. I mean, I'm a thirty-two-year-old guy, and I have eyes. But now that I can see her in the light from the large window in the guest bedroom, I realize she's even prettier than I thought. In jeans and a hoodie, without makeup on, she's a nice-looking girl. If she made even the slightest effort? Well, she'd be really hot. And she's just my type too.

I glance over at Krista, wondering if the same thought has occurred to her. Is she worried about a really pretty girl moving in with us? Is it the kind of thing that might give her pause?

But no, she doesn't look worried. She's smiling. She trusts me.

Even though fifteen minutes ago, she looked concerned I might stab her to death in our living room.

She *should* trust me though. It's not like I'm going to mess around with the girl we live with right under my own fiancée's nose. I'd have to be not only the world's biggest asshole but also a complete idiot.

Whitney turns to us, her face glowing. "I love it. I don't know if you have anyone else interested, but *I'm* interested. Very interested."

Krista arches an eyebrow at me. She's asking my permission to offer Whitney the room.

I take a deep breath. I don't want to rent this room to Whitney, but that has nothing to do with Whitney herself. I don't want *anyone* to have this room. I want my old damn job back so I can pay the mortgage myself, without having to open our doors to a stranger. But that's not ever going to happen, so I have to be realistic. If we don't bring in some cash soon, we're going to lose the brownstone entirely.

And Whitney is nice. You can just tell. She's not a weirdo, she doesn't seem like the type who would blast heavy metal in the middle of the night, and she's polite. She's head and shoulders better than anyone we've interviewed so far.

So I look back at Krista and nod.

"Actually," Krista says to Whitney, "we haven't found someone yet. We'd love to offer you the room."

"Really?" Whitney's face turns pink with happiness. "Oh my God, that's amazing. Thank you! I've got a check on me so I can give you the first month's rent and the security deposit and—"

"Nope." I hold up a hand. "Before you move in, we need to do our due diligence. We need your Social Security number to do a credit check, and we'd like at least one reference."

The smile instantly slips from Whitney's face.

That bothers me. Is there a *reason* why she's worried about a credit check? Why wouldn't she be able to provide a reference? A little alarm bell sounds in the back of my head.

If she can't give us a Social Security number, she's out of here. I don't give a shit how nice or pretty she is.

"It's just a formality," Krista adds quickly. "It's not a problem, is it?"

The smile quickly returns. "Of course not," Whitney assures us. "I can give you whatever you need. I'm just *so* excited to live here, and I want to move in as soon as possible."

I let out a breath. Okay, she's just eager—that's all. She's going to give us her social, and we'll run a credit check *and* a background check, and it'll be fine. God knows we need the money. If she can pay us the first month's rent and security in advance, that will give us some breathing room.

Except… Why does this voice in the back of my head keep telling me to get rid of her right now, while I still can?

CHAPTER 7

Whitney Cross is moving into the brownstone today.

I paid to run the background check myself, and it didn't reveal anything concerning. No arrests, no warrants, no sex offenses—no red flags at all. Whitney is a law-abiding citizen from a small town in Jersey and has a decent credit score. And her boss at the diner assured us she's a model employee.

So we asked her to move in.

She's borrowed a friend's car, and she's driving over here with all her belongings. Because I am unemployed and also the one who carries the heavy items in our relationship, Krista volunteered me to help her move in. Which is fine. May as well make myself useful to *someone*.

I started scoping out parking spots an hour before Whitney was supposed to arrive. Parking is hard to come by on our street (or anywhere in Manhattan), which is why I don't own a car. I tried to keep my car the first year I moved here, but I spent half my commute to work stuck in bumper-to-bumper traffic, so when a taxi rear-ended me and my car was declared totaled, I decided to stick with the subway from then on. No regrets.

Twenty minutes before Whitney's arrival, a spot opens up right in front of the house, so I grab one of our garbage bins and plant it there to save it. I then have to physically guard it, because a car will almost certainly mow down the bin if I'm not here to keep it from happening. Good thing I don't have a job.

While I'm waiting for Whitney on the steps of the brownstone, a girl I've seen a bunch of times on my running trail through Central Park passes by wearing a pair of pink shorts that barely conceal her underwear. She winks at me, and I smile back as blandly as I can. A few years ago, I would have been all over a girl like that, but not anymore. It's okay to take a subtle look but *never* touch, and even looking is something I'm trying my best not to do anymore.

My phone vibrates in my pocket. I pull it out, and the word "Dad" flashes on the screen. I consider letting it go to voicemail, but when I try to remember the last time I talked to my father, I can't. He's been lonely in the last few years since my mother succumbed to breast cancer, and I feel guilty that I've been avoiding him. But we don't have much in common, so most of our conversations are just awkward.

I check my watch. Whitney will be here any minute, so that will be an excuse to get off the phone. I take the call.

"Blake!" Dad says, and then he starts coughing, which makes me feel even more guilty. "How are you doing?"

"Fine," I lie. "How about you?"

"Oh, I'm great." But then he coughs again. The last

time we talked, he said he was getting over a cold, and it seems like he still is. "How is the job search going? Find anything yet?"

"Still working on it."

"Because I was just thinking," he says, clearing his throat, "that with Jeff quitting last month, I could really use some extra help at the store. And if you ever want to take over…"

"Dad…"

"The timing is perfect," he says with growing excitement. "I need the help, and you need a job. And, Blake, the store is your legacy. My father passed it down to me, and now you should have it."

Just what I want as my inheritance—a struggling hardware store in Cleveland.

As if reading my mind, my father adds, "A new housing complex just went up a couple of blocks away. Business has been good."

"Dad…"

"You could sell that expensive tiny brown house of yours," he goes on in a rush. "Move back here, and you can get a house five times the size for a fifth of the price. I bet Krista would be really happy here. And if you take the store—"

"Dad, I didn't get a degree to work at a hardware store!" I burst out.

My father goes instantly silent on the other line, and now I feel like a huge jackass. He's just trying to help, and God knows he won't be around forever—I found that out the hard way when my mom died. He wants his only son to take over his business. It's not a terrible thing to wish for, even though it's the last thing I want.

"I'm sorry, Blake," my father says meekly. "I just thought…"

Before he can finish his sentence, a rusty red Ford Pinto pulls up to the curb with Whitney behind the wheel. I rise to my feet, brushing off the seat of my pants because I don't want to think about the crap that's on the steps. "Dad, I have to go."

"Okay," he says. "I love you, son."

"Love you too, Dad," I say just before hitting the red button to end the call.

I have to move the garbage bin to the side so Whitney can fully pull into the spot. Once she's parked, she climbs out of the car, her light brown hair pulled back into a high ponytail that swings behind her head. She's wearing another pair of blue jeans with a skimpy tank top that's appropriate given the heat.

Yes, I *looked*. So sue me. I'm only human.

"Hey," I say.

Whitney grins at me, clearly delighted at the prospect of moving into our tiny spare bedroom. "Hey, Blake. Thanks so much for helping me."

"No problem," I say, like it wasn't all Krista's idea. "Let's see what you've got."

Whitney leads me to the trunk of the car, which she pops open using the car keys. I peer inside at the two large boxes and one giant duffel bag.

"This is it?" I ask in astonishment.

"I've got another big bag of clothes in the back seat."

I stare into the trunk, trying to make sense of the fact that everything this girl owns doesn't even fill the back of a Pinto. When I moved, I got a whole *truck*, and that was just for me. And Krista… I'm pretty sure she could fill that duffel bag with just her belts. (She's really into belts.)

"I'm not that into clothing," Whitney says, a touch defensively. "And I've been moving a lot, so I've had to pare down."

Still. *Still.* Once again, those alarm bells are going off in my head, although they're more like sirens at this point.

I can still turn her away. She hasn't moved in yet. Of course, we have deposited her check and used it to pay bills. And Whitney has presumably given up her current living situation. It would be a dick move to turn her away at this point just because of a "bad feeling." That's something Quillizabeth would do.

"Well," I say, "this will be quick then, won't it?"

Whitney's face relaxes into a smile as I reach into her trunk to pick up one of the boxes. It's not even that heavy. Barely full. I could carry five of these boxes without breaking a sweat.

She attempts to grab the large duffel bag in the back seat of the car, straining with the weight of it.

"Hey," I say, "just leave it. I can carry all the bags up for you."

She grunts as she frees it from the back seat. "No, I got it."

"But I can do it."

"Are you calling me a weakling?" She flashes me a teasing smile. "I bet you five bucks I can carry more bags than you can."

She adjusts the strap of the bag between the curves of her breasts, and I have to look away. Whitney is even sexier than I thought she was, and that is not a good thing.

Don't even think about it, Blake.

"Hey, Porter!" a gruff voice calls out.

I rest the box on the edge of the trunk and turn around. My neighbor, Mr. Zimmerly, is hunched on the sidewalk in front of his own brownstone, wearing pajama pants and fuzzy slippers. I don't think I've ever seen the man in actual shoes the whole time I've lived here. I'm not sure he owns a pair.

"Hi, Mr. Zimmerly," I say as politely as I can.

I have tried to be nice to Mr. Zimmerly, but he hasn't made it easy. I don't even know what his first name is because he never told me. I know it starts with H because when his mail accidentally gets delivered to me (and I'm nice enough to bring it to his door), it always says *H. Zimmerly* on it, but that's all I've managed to learn about him in the six months I've lived here. Also, he hates me, and I don't know why.

"Porter," he barks at me, even though I told him *my* first name the first time we met. "Why are your trash bins out on the sidewalk again?"

Due to the rat infestation in the city, we are no longer allowed to put black plastic garbage bags on the curb and must instead put our garbage in bins: one for trash and one for recycling. During the week, I keep my bin locked up under the stairwell. (You wouldn't think a bin reeking of refuse would be in danger of theft, but that's New York for you.) Then on garbage day, I haul it to the curb for the garbagemen to empty.

Zimmerly's biggest gripe about me is that I leave the trash bins out too long on pickup day. He wants me to watch for the garbage truck and grab the cans off the street the very millisecond after the trash is taken away. I have failed to do this repeatedly, and every time we see each other, he reminds me of that fact.

It's not entirely his fault though. I don't know how old Zimmerly is, but based on the deep wrinkles on his face and the tufts of white hair on his scalp, my best guess is eighty-something. He bought this place ages ago, when real estate in the city was still relatively cheap, and he expects everything to be done the way it was when he first moved in, back when dinosaurs roamed the earth.

"I'm sorry," I say. "I was just using it to save a parking spot. I'll put it back now."

He mumbles something under his breath and licks his lips, still not managing to clear away the glob of toothpaste encrusted there. He looks like he's about to go back inside, but then he freezes when he notices Whitney standing next to me and the boxes in her trunk.

"What's going on here?" he demands, as if I'm trying to prank him.

I force a smile. "This is Whitney. She's going to be staying with us for a while." But hopefully not *too* long.

"Another woman?" Zimmerly grumbles. "My God, how many do you need, Porter? You're turning the neighborhood into a brothel!"

Okay, I have had *one* woman living with me the entire time I've been here, which clearly falls short of a brothel. But there's no point in explaining this to my neighbor.

"It's very nice meeting you," Whitney says politely. "Mr. Zimmerly, is it?"

Zimmerly is nice enough to Krista, but he doesn't seem to feel the same way about Whitney. He grumbles something under his breath and then stomps back up the steps in his slippers.

"He's always like that," I say to her apologetically. "Don't take it personally."

Whitney seems unconcerned by Zimmerly's rude behavior. I don't know why, but it drives me nuts that my neighbor doesn't like me. I didn't care when my coworkers didn't all love me, but this bothers me.

One of the old man's bottom steps has crumbled slightly—probably eroded after years of snowstorms—and for a moment, he stumbles on it. He catches himself, but it's a close call. An idea hits me, and I dash over to the steps before he can get inside.

"Mr. Zimmerly!" I call out.

He turns around, his sour expression unchanged. "What now, Porter?"

I kick the damaged step, and a little more cement comes loose. "I can fix your step if you'd like. So you won't trip on it."

He narrows his eyes at me. "How much?"

"No charge," I say quickly, even though I could use the money.

He snorts as he looks me up and down. "You don't look like you could do the job. They don't teach you how to fix steps in *college*."

"I know how to fix a concrete step," I say defensively. It's the kind of thing I used to do with my father when I was a kid. Although I admittedly haven't done it in years, I remember how to do it. It's like riding a bike. And if I get stuck, my dad is only a phone call away, eager to help.

For a moment, Mr. Zimmerly looks like he's considering it. But then he waves a hand at me in disgust. "You'll probably just make it worse. You can't even manage your own trash!"

With those words, he turns around and goes back into his house and slams the door behind him.

Well, I tried.

Since Mr. Zimmerly clearly doesn't want my help, I return to Whitney's car. I heave the box back into my arms and also throw one of the duffel bags on my shoulder. Whitney follows behind, carrying the bag from the back seat, even though I told her I'd get it. I left the front door open, so it's a quick trip to get her stuff up the flights of stairs to the top floor. She sets about unpacking while I grab the final box from the car.

When I get back to her room, Whitney has already unpacked about half her clothes. She smiles up at me. "Thanks, Blake. Just drop it on the floor."

I still can't get over the fact that Whitney managed to squeeze her entire life into two boxes and two bags. "Are you sure there isn't anything else?"

"Actually..." She steps over to the door and shakes the doorknob, which rattles loudly, threatening to fall right off. "Do you think we could get this knob fixed? I have this fear about the doorknob falling off and getting trapped in my room."

Prior to losing my job, this was the kind of thing I would have called a repairman to fix because I was just too busy and also because I *could*. But much like the broken step, a loose doorknob is something I can fix. I've got a tool kit, and I'm perfectly capable of fixing this and anything else that's broken in this house. My father taught me well.

"No problem," I say. "Anything else?"

She shakes her head. "I just need to make a trip to the drugstore to get some toiletries."

"If you're too tired to go out after unpacking," I say, "you can use our soap and stuff in the meantime. Or our laundry detergent. And you're welcome to use whatever you want in our kitchen too. Pots, pans…ketchup, mustard."

"Thanks." She sets her eyes on me. I previously thought they were brown, but now I can make out flecks of amber. "I really appreciate everything, Blake. You're a good guy."

She's just being nice when she says that. She doesn't know if I'm a good guy. She doesn't know me at all.

"It's really a beautiful room," she says as she folds a pair of jeans identical to the ones she's wearing and slides them into an open drawer. "You did a great job decorating."

"Actually," I say, "Krista did all that. She picked out the furniture because she wanted a really nice guest room."

"Well, your wife has great taste."

I manage a lopsided smile. "Krista and I aren't married."

"Oh!" Her eyelashes flutter, and she touches a hand to her chest. "Oh, I'm sorry. I thought—"

"No big deal," I say. "I mean, we're engaged. So, you know, we *will* be married."

"Did you set a date?"

No. I was working superhuman hours after my proposal, and once I got fired, I didn't feel like planning a wedding I couldn't even afford. But I'm not sharing any of that with Whitney. "Not yet."

She stares at me for another few beats—long enough to make me squirm—but then she goes right back to unpacking her belongings. As she refolds her clothing and places it in drawers, it hits home that it's too late to turn back.

Whitney lives here now.

"So…uh…" I rub the back of my neck. "I'll leave you to it then. But…" I feel like I have to say something else before I go, so I add, "We should have dinner sometime."

Whitney lifts her eyes from the box she'd been ripping open with her bare hands. "Dinner? With *you*?"

"And Krista," I say, in case it wasn't obvious. Christ, I don't want her to think I'm hitting on her five seconds after moving in.

"Oh, sure," she says. "That sounds great!"

Her enthusiasm makes me feel a little better about everything. Yes, we are bringing a stranger into our home, but Whitney seems really nice. Maybe the three of us will have a great time together.

But even if we become the best of friends, soon I'm going to find a job that's even better than the one I lost, and then we'll show her the door.

CHAPTER 8

My plans for the morning include changing the water in the fish tank.

Krista used to handle this particular chore, but now that I have more free time than she does, it's on me. Actually, I've taken on most of the cleaning duties in the house, and I don't mind it. My mother was always a stickler for a clean house, so I've learned to take satisfaction in vacuuming the floors and scrubbing the countertops until they shine. I even make the bed on mornings when Krista wakes up before me. For some reason, she finds this hilarious and teases me mercilessly about it (something about "Mr. Suzy Homemaker").

Cleaning the fish tank is one of the more involved chores in our household. I can't just pour out all the water and then fill it up again, because apparently, that would kill the fish. So I have to extract 20 percent of the water—no more, no less. Oh, and I can't pour tap water in to replace it, because that would *also* kill the fish. I have to mix the tap water with a dechlorinator. After that, I have to remove the debris from the bottom of the tank using a siphon.

It's a ridiculous amount of work, but at the same time, I can't let anything happen to Goldy. She's our practice *child*, and if we let her die, that seems like an ominous harbinger for the future. (We call the fish "her" because it goes with the name, but we have no solid evidence to support the idea that she's female.) After I'm done with Goldy's tank, I'll go to the gym and work out. I feel like I have to keep moving all the time these days, or else I'll sleep all day and lie awake all night.

While Krista is in the shower, I head downstairs to clean the fish tank. I've got all the supplies ready, but then I get weirdly mesmerized by the sight of Goldy swimming back and forth across her small tank. Before I know it, I've been standing there for five minutes, not moving.

"What the hell happened to me?" I ask Goldy.

Goldy swims in a circle until she's facing me.

"What if I never get another job? What if I lose the house?"

Goldy looks at me. She doesn't have much to say on the matter.

Okay, now I'm having a conversation with a fish. Maybe my blood sugar is low. I need to eat some breakfast.

When I get to the kitchen, I am startled to find Whitney there. Not that there's anything wrong with that. She's lived with us for two days now, and it's her right to use our kitchen. But I'm still getting used to this stranger occupying my house.

Also, Whitney isn't dressed. I mean, she's not *un*dressed, but all the other times I've seen her, she's been wearing regular clothing or once a bathrobe when I caught her coming out of the shower. But now she's wearing a skimpy tank top with what looks like a pair of tiny pajama shorts.

Also, I can see her nipples through the tank top. Which is bad news, considering I'm wearing boxer shorts.

"Good morning, Blake," she says cheerfully as she stares into the fridge, oblivious to how *cold* it is in there.

"Hey, Whitney." *Don't look at her erect nipples. Don't look at her erect nipples.* "Did you sleep well?"

She turns from the fridge empty-handed. "Wonderful. The bed is super comfortable."

It should be. We paid enough for it.

She picks up an apple from our fruit bowl, inspecting it for bruises. "Is this apple mine or yours?"

"I think it's mine, but you're welcome to it."

"Thanks. I'll go shopping soon."

I slip past her, trying my best not to brush against the thin fabric of her pajamas. I reach over the kitchen counter and grab a box of Frosted Flakes. There's no time for a power breakfast right now. I'll make myself a bowl of cereal and get the hell out of here.

"Oh, I love Frosted Flakes," Whitney comments.

"Yeah?" I grin at her despite myself. "It's my favorite cereal."

She takes a bite from the apple in her hand, and a bit of the juice spills down her chin, but she wipes it away quickly. "It makes me nostalgic to look at the box. I ate it every day from ages six through nine."

"Every day?"

"Well, I had to. If you collected enough box tops, you could mail them in for a secret decoder pen."

"The secret decoder pen!" My eyes light up at the shared memory. "I remember that! Did you ever get one?"

"Damn straight." She flashes me a smile with a hint of a dimple on her left cheek, which keeps my attention away from her nipples. "When I want something, I never let anything get in my way."

I bob my head. "Same."

"Anyway, I miss Frosted Flakes!" She eyes the box with a look of longing. "I haven't eaten anything that crunchy and coated in sugar in years."

I hold out the box to her. "Hey, go for it."

She hesitates. "I don't want to steal your cereal. I'm already using all your dishes and eating your apple."

"You're not stealing it. I'm offering it to you. You can't just have an apple for breakfast. And anyway, nobody should be deprived of grr-eatness."

That gets a laugh out of her. She has a nice laugh that sort of matches the rest of her: sweet, clean, and friendly. As much as I hate the idea of needing a roommate, I don't entirely dislike Whitney Cross.

In fact, I sort of like her.

CHAPTER 9

Krista usually has dinner with her best friend Becky once a week, but because she's sick of my self-imposed isolation in the house, she's dragged me along with her to Becky's place tonight to make it a double date with Becky's husband, Malcolm.

I'm not looking forward to what feels like an adult playdate. And it doesn't help that Malcolm also works at Coble & Roy, and he'll be the first person I've seen from the company since I was fired.

But here we are, standing in the hallway outside Becky and Malcolm's tenth-floor apartment. I'm clutching a bottle of wine from Porto that Krista loves, and we've also got the oatmeal raisin cookies she baked last night. Krista is wearing that short blue dress with the low back that makes her look incredible, especially with her strawberry-blond hair loose and running down her bare shoulders. She hasn't applied enough makeup to cover up the smattering of freckles across the bridge of her nose, and when she flashes me a smile, I get that fluttering in my chest.

She's a knockout, and if I don't get my shit together soon, she's going to dump me.

Krista is looking up at me, scrutinizing my face. "Are you okay?"

"Yeah, sure."

She knows when I'm lying though. She throws her arms around me and presses her small body against me. She squeezes just enough to make the evening seem less awful without creating a tent in my pants. "Level six?" she asks.

"Maybe seven," I reply, and she squeezes just a little tighter.

We break off from the hug much too quickly, but we're already five minutes late. Krista is the one to ring the doorbell, and a few seconds later, Becky throws open the door for the two of us. My nostrils are immediately assaulted by the floral perfume that Becky always wears too much of. I don't know how Krista can stand it. It's all I can do not to breathe through my mouth whenever I'm near her.

Becky hugs Krista first, then after a moment of contemplation, I get a hug too. Great. Now I'll smell like her.

"Blake." Becky steps back to look at me, and her nose crinkles slightly, even though I'm wearing a nice dress shirt and I shaved and I don't smell like the inside of a flower. It's especially insulting because in the past, she's always flirted with me in a way that felt very inappropriate, given I'm her best friend's boyfriend. "How are you doing?"

"I'm great," I say, although if she's talked to Krista at all, she surely knows that's a lie.

"Blake is starting a new job next week," Krista says.

I cringe. The temp office job I'll be starting on Monday is the last thing I want to talk about. It's humiliating that I had to resort to a job that I was overqualified for *ten years ago*, with zero benefits and a paycheck to match. But work is work.

"That's wonderful, Blake," Becky says. "I knew you'd find something."

Christ, when can we crack open this bottle of wine?

Naturally, dinner is nowhere near ready. Becky made a lasagna that still needs another half hour in the oven. While it cooks, Becky directs us to the living room with the promise of a platter of crackers and cheese waiting for us on the coffee table. Malcolm is already in the living room, and he stands up from his armchair when we enter the room, waving enthusiastically.

"Blake." He cocks his head to the side in a sympathetic gesture I've learned to despise. "How are you doing?"

"Fine," I say tightly.

"Good good good."

I'd almost forgotten his annoying habit of repeating words multiple times. "How are things at…at Coble & Roy?" I manage to spit out.

He looks a little embarrassed by my question, as he should be. I was the one who got him the job there a year ago, as a favor to Krista. He was decidedly mediocre, but somehow, he's still there, and I've been fired.

"It's not the same without you," he says.

I don't know what to say to that.

"Can I get you anything to drink?" Becky asks me and Krista.

Thank God. "I'll have a glass of red," I say too quickly.

Becky fetches the two of us glasses of wine while we

settle down on the sofa. I reach for a cracker from the table mostly to kill some time, but then Krista swats at my hand. She's been doing that a lot lately, like she thinks I'm snacking too much—which, to be fair, might be true. "Don't spoil your appetite," she scolds me.

I flash her an exasperated look. "They put the crackers out for us to eat."

Malcolm chuckles. "Don't feel bad, Blake. I'm not allowed to eat them either."

I lean back against the sofa and scratch my forearm. I don't know why, but this shirt is itching my arms. I unbutton the sleeve and roll it up, and sure enough, the underside of my forearm is red and irritated. I've been out of work barely three months, and I've already developed an allergy to dress shirts.

I pull down my sleeve and get it buttoned again just as Becky returns with our wine. I accept the glass gratefully, downing half the contents in one gulp. She brought the bottle out and left it on the coffee table so all four of us can self-serve, which is dangerous. I wonder how much I can get away with drinking tonight before either Krista notices or I start slurring my words. It will be an entertaining experiment. I'll do it for the science.

"So," Becky says, "the new roommate has moved in?"

Krista nods. "Whitney moved in last week."

"Is she nice?" Malcolm asks.

"Really nice," Krista says. "She's so sweet. And very quiet. Honestly, she's just about perfect."

"Is she pretty?" Becky asks.

She's looking at me when she asks the question. Actually, everyone is suddenly looking at me. I'm looking at the crackers I'm not allowed to eat.

"Not really," I say, because I'm not a complete idiot.

Krista rolls her eyes. "Actually, she's really gorgeous. A natural beauty, you know?"

"Uh-oh." Malcolm elbows me in the ribs. "Sounds like trouble, right right right?"

"I hardly ever see her," I mumble. That's a lie. I see her all around the house, sometimes in only her sheer pajamas and once in nothing but a towel.

Krista laughs and drops a hand onto my knee. "I'm not worried."

Well, that's good. I think.

My stomach rumbles as the aroma of melting cheese and tomato sauce wafts in from the kitchen. I gaze longingly at the cheese and crackers, but Krista already made a fuss over not having any. So I dutifully polish off the rest of my glass of wine and pour myself a second.

"Anyway," Krista says, "you should see some of the people we interviewed when we were looking for a tenant. Honestly, it was a bit frightening. We got very, very lucky with Whitney."

"Oh yeah?" Malcolm asks, settling into his chair. "Sounds like there's a good story there."

"My favorite was that woman who almost ate Goldy," I speak up, finally starting to get a little buzz from the wine on an empty stomach.

Krista smacks me in the knee. "She didn't almost eat Goldy!"

"She did!" I insist. "She stood right near the fishbowl, and she was telling us how good fresh goldfish tasted. She was basically giving us instructions for how to *cook* Goldy."

"Well, she did mention Goldy might taste good with a side of chips," Krista says.

"Or beer battered," I add.

Krista is giggling now, also a little buzzed. Her face is glowing slightly the way it always does when she's had a bit too much to drink. She's always been a lightweight. "But that wasn't as bad as that last woman...what was her name? It was like some weird version of Elizabeth, right?"

My stomach churns, the wine suddenly not sitting well. "Uh...I don't know if that's an interesting story..."

Krista's eyes go wide as she looks between her friends. "You wouldn't *believe* this woman. She was some kind of psychic or something. And when she touched my hand, she got a psychic vision."

"Ooh!" Becky clasps her hands together. "I love that stuff!"

Of course she does.

"What was the vision?" Malcolm asks.

Krista takes a sip from her own wineglass, which is nearly empty. "She said that Blake was going to stab me to death in the living room!"

Becky and Malcolm adopt equally stunned expressions. For Christ's sake. It's not like it actually *happened*. It was just some nutjob spouting out nonsense.

"This woman was *not* mentally all there." I scratch my forearm, which is suddenly much itchier. "I mean, she was wearing a tinfoil hat."

"She was?" Krista frowns. "I don't remember that. I thought she was very well dressed."

Becky crosses her legs, leaning forward. "She saw it happening in *your* living room?"

"I think so," Krista says. "She pointed to our floor when she said it."

Becky clasps a hand over her mouth, looking at me

with an expression of horror, like I'm standing over her best friend right this second with a bloody knife.

"That woman wasn't a real psychic." I grit my teeth. "You should have seen her. She was wearing, like, three robes, and she kept pouring salt everywhere."

"Salt is important for warding off evil spirits," Becky says sagely.

Is she *kidding* me?

"Why are you so skeptical?" Becky levels her dark brown eyes at me. "Are you a Scorpio?"

"He is," Krista confirms, nodding.

I glare at the two women, ready to stab both of them. (Not really.) "Look, I don't care what some random woman told us. I'm not going to kill Krista, okay? Do I look *unhinged* to you?"

And then I finish off my second glass of wine.

"No offense intended, Blake," Becky says gently. "Nobody thinks you're a murderer. But some people have that vibe, like they might do something…you know, *unexpected*."

I don't like the turn this conversation is taking.

"And you have to admit," Malcolm adds, "you've fallen apart a bit the last couple of months. Krista says all you do is clean the house and go to the gym obsessively. We've all been worried about you, man."

I don't know what they're talking about. Yeah, it hasn't been so great since I got fired. But there's a big difference between hitting the gym a little too often and going on a killing spree in the living room.

"I'm fine," I say for what feels like the millionth time. "And I've got a job starting Monday, so everything will get back to normal, and Krista won't be murdered."

Krista reaches out to take my hand. For a moment, I don't feel like giving it to her. I mean, what the hell was *that* about? Why did she tell everyone about that nutcase? Now everyone in the room thinks I have a screw loose. But then she coaxes her fingers into mine, and honestly, it's hard to stay mad at her.

"We're just teasing you, Blake," she says. "Obviously, I know you're not going to kill me." She winks. "At least not until the wedding planning starts."

"Ooh!" Becky perks up. "Have you two set a date yet?"

I don't think I've ever been so relieved for the conversation to turn to the lack of a date for our upcoming nuptials. I sit back against the couch, scratching my arm absently and sipping my third glass of wine while the two women discuss the best possible month to get married. (May, apparently?) But I can't help noticing that Becky is studiously avoiding my gaze, and when she speaks to me, she is painfully polite.

What is going on here? Does Becky really think I'm capable of killing my fiancée?

That's ridiculous. I *love* Krista. I would *never* do anything to hurt her.

Never.

CHAPTER 10

After dinner at Becky and Malcolm's house, I can't sleep. It's one in the morning, and I've been staring at the ceiling for the last hour. I got up to take a piss twenty minutes ago, thinking that might help, but it didn't. Krista is not having the same issue. She's passed out next to me, her mouth hanging open, an adorable little puddle of drool on the pillow next to her. (I wore her out apparently.)

As I look at the cracks in the plaster over my head, I keep replaying the events of the evening. It's obvious Becky and Malcolm both think I'm a huge loser. But the worst part of all was the way Becky looked at me when Krista told them what that psychic said. How could anyone think I would ever hurt the woman I love? How could they all turn on me so quickly?

I finally give up on sleep. I climb out of bed and creep down the stairs as quietly as I can so I don't wake anyone up. But when I get to the foot of the steps, I'm surprised to discover that the first floor of the house isn't dead silent, as I expected it to be. There are soft sounds coming from the living room, and although the overhead lights are out, there's a faint glow from the television.

Whitney must be awake.

I walk into the living room, and sure enough, there she is. She's sitting on the sofa, wearing that same skimpy pajama set she sleeps in, her eyes pinned to the screen of the television. When she notices me, she startles and clutches her chest.

"Blake!" she cries. "You scared me half to death!"

"Sorry." I offer a crooked smile. "I couldn't sleep."

"Me either," she sighs.

"Mind if I join you?"

"Absolutely. The more the merrier at the Insomniac Club."

Before I join her on the sofa, I grab myself a glass of water from the kitchen. And while I'm in there, I notice some leftover cookies Krista baked that didn't make it to our little dinner party. I drop a handful of them on a plate and carry them to the living room.

"Oh my gosh, are those Krista's cookies?" Whitney gasps.

I place the plate on the coffee table. "Oatmeal raisin."

"These are insanely addictive." Whitney reaches for a cookie, her straight hair falling in her face. "She should be a professional baker or something."

"Yeah, she's amazing." I reach for a cookie of my own and take a bite. It's just the right amount of soft and chewy. "If you see me eat more than four of them, feel free to stage an intervention."

"You got it," she says. "It's the least I can do after you fixed that drawer for me."

One of the drawers in Whitney's dresser had come off the rail and was on the brink of collapse. Expensive piece of crap. I spent about an hour in her room, reassembling the pieces of the drawer until it slid in and out smoothly. It's the kind of thing I did with my dad a dozen times. Whitney made a big thing out of what a great job I did, and I have to admit it was fun working on it, but part of me was also embarrassed that my greatest achievement in the last three months was fixing a dresser.

"So," I say, attempting to change the subject, "what are we watching?"

Whitney tucks her legs close to her chest. "Well, it's a show where people bake cakes that are supposed to look like things that aren't cake, and you have to figure out if it's cake or not."

"Like what?"

"Like, you see that guitar on the table?"

"Uh-huh..."

"That's cake."

"No way!"

"Way," she says with all the gravity of a detective reporting on a recent homicide.

I smile despite myself. "And this is the sort of thing that helps you sleep?"

Whitney stares at the TV screen; the images are reflected on her pupils. "Actually, I can *never* sleep. May as well be entertained."

In the dim light coming from the monitor, I can just barely make out the purple circles under Whitney's eyes. "Do you take anything?"

"I've tried. Nothing helps."

"I'm sorry."

Whitney lifts a shoulder as if it's no big deal. "It's okay—as long as it doesn't bother you that I'm down here in the middle of the night."

"No way. I'm glad for some company."

That elicits a grin. "So what is keeping *you* awake tonight, Blake?"

Whitney reaches for another cookie from the plate on the coffee table. She is *definitely* not wearing a bra.

I squirm on the sofa. "I don't know. I guess I'm nervous about the future."

She arches an eyebrow. "You mean like getting married?"

"No, I'm not nervous about that at all," I say honestly. "But I'm starting this new job Monday, and…it's hard to start over."

"I know exactly what you mean," Whitney says in a way that makes me feel like she absolutely does.

"Anyway." I let out a sigh. "I can't stop thinking about it."

"You're worried," she acknowledges.

"No, I'm not *worried*. Just, you know…"

"Well, if it makes you feel any better," she says, "you seem like the kind of guy who always lands on his feet, no matter what."

Weirdly, her vote of confidence buoys my spirits. "Yeah?"

"Definitely." She starts ticking off on her fingers. "You're obviously intelligent, charismatic, motivated, handsome…"

Hopefully she's just being polite, because Krista wouldn't appreciate me being alone in the living room in the middle of the night with a scantily clad girl who is now calling me handsome. But she's looking at me in a way that makes me think she isn't just being gracious. Her intense eyes are locked on mine, and I have to grab a throw pillow to place strategically on my lap since all I'm wearing is an undershirt and a pair of boxers.

"I'll tell you what," she says. "I'm so confident that your first day is going to go well that I'm going to bring back some cake from the diner for us to celebrate tomorrow."

"What kind of cake?"

"Any kind you want." She flicks her tongue briefly over her upper lip. "What would you like, Blake?"

And now I'm *really* glad that throw pillow is on my lap.

Still, nothing is going to happen between me and Whitney. Not now—not ever. I'd never do that to Krista in a million years.

Although she *is* very attractive.

"Whatever kind you want." I clear my throat. "As long as it looks like a piano."

My joke breaks the tension as Whitney and I passionately debate whether the drum kit on screen might actually be cake. I'm even able to eventually abandon the pillow. We end up watching TV for the next several hours, exchanging occasional commentary but mostly just sharing the space and eating cookies. I pass out on the sofa around three in the morning, and when I wake up, my neck stiff and aching, Whitney is gone.

CHAPTER 11

Today is my first day of the stupid temp job. I'm dreading it.

But I have to take it seriously. Because the agency suggested that if I do well, this could turn into a permanent position. And it's a reputable company, where I might have a chance to claw my way back into a decent job again. I've got a chance anyway.

So I set my alarm for seven thirty in the morning, giving myself ample time to make it to the office by nine if I forgo my workout. I stumble into the shower, returning to my old ritual of starting my day off with freezing cold water to wake me up.

When I can't stand it another second, I switch the water temperature back to hot, but unfortunately, all I can coax out of the showerhead is a lukewarm stream. Krista is still asleep in our bed, so it must have been Whitney who showered early this morning and used up all the hot water. Damn it. Not a great start.

I reach for the bottle of soap, resigning myself to a barely warm shower. But when I attempt to squeeze a dollop into my hand, nothing comes out.

What the hell?

I squeeze more firmly, shaking the bottle this time. No luck. The bottle of soap is completely empty.

Obviously, Whitney used it all up. Granted, I did give her permission to use my soap, but this bottle was half full only a few days ago. Who uses that much soap? Worse, when I try to squeeze out some of my combined shampoo and conditioner to wash my hair, that bottle is empty too.

I have no choice but to use Krista's girly soap and shampoo. So when I climb out of the lukewarm shower, my hair smells like coconut and apricots, and my body smells like lemon and vanilla instead of just smelling like freaking *clean*.

All right, it's fine. I'll talk to Whitney about the shower products. I was trying to be a nice guy, but clearly, sharing is not going to work out.

I get dressed quietly, trying not to wake Krista. Despite how much I'm dreading this job, it feels good to be going back to work. Even though I was accused of awful things, my career is not over. It's just a temporary setback.

I knot my tie the way I taught myself to during my first year as a marketing intern. I check it in the full-length mirror in our bedroom, and it looks perfect. I don't look like a temp. I look like a vice president.

They say you're supposed to dress for the job you want. It's just a matter of time.

My mother taught me that breakfast is the most important meal of the day, and it's one of the few pieces of advice from her that stuck with me. No matter how big of a rush I'm in to get to work, I always eat something. There's definitely no time for a power breakfast, but before I run out to catch the subway going downtown, I head to the kitchen to have a quick bowl of cereal. Frosted Flakes aren't exactly the breakfast of champions, but the influx of sugar will do me good.

I grab the box of cereal from where I left it and shake it over the ceramic bowl. Nothing comes out, so I shake it again, tilting it to the side until it is upside down, at which point a little pile of sugar and some cornflake dust drops into my bowl.

Seriously?

Apparently, giving Whitney permission to use my products turned into a free-for-all. She used them until they were completely gone. Without even *saying* anything, like, *Hey, we need more cereal, Blake.* I mean, who the hell finishes a box of cereal, then puts it right back on the counter?

And now I've got to leave in about ten minutes, and there's nothing for me to eat.

I grind my teeth in frustration. Impulsively, I grab the empty box of cereal off the counter and hurl it at the floor.

That was not the smartest thing I've ever done. The box bounces as it hits the kitchen floor, sprinkling bits of sugar and cornflake crumbs everywhere.

Crap.

Now instead of spending these last few minutes eating a semi-nutritious breakfast, I'll be spending the time vacuuming up the remnants of Frosted Flakes. But I'm not going to leave crumbs all over the floor. That would drive me out of my mind.

Goldy watches me running the vacuum over the floor. She opens her mouth, and a little bubble of air rises to the surface of the bowl.

"How come you didn't warn me she ate all my cereal?" I ask the fish.

Goldy doesn't have an answer.

"Blake? What's going on down there?"

It's Krista—I woke her up with the vacuum. I feel a stab of guilt. She doesn't have work today, so it was her chance to sleep in. But now she's coming down the stairs, wearing my old oversize Green Day T-shirt that she sleeps in.

"Sorry," I say. "I had a little accident."

That's a nicer way to say that I freaked out and threw the cereal box on the floor and then had to clean it up.

Krista yawns, stretching her arms high above her head. "Did you have breakfast yet?"

"Whitney ate all my cereal," I grumble. "She also used up my soap and shampoo."

Krista's eyebrows shoot up. "She just took all your stuff without asking?"

"Well, no," I admit. "I told her she could use it. But I didn't say she could use *all* of it."

"Okay, so basically, you told her she could use your stuff, and now you're mad that she did it?"

I make a face at her. "I just wanted a bowl of cereal, Krista."

"So have some of mine. It's way healthier than Frosted Flakes."

"Yours tastes like shredded cardboard."

"Gee, sorry." She laughs and pushes past me into the kitchen, grabbing that disgusting health crap cereal she always eats with a cup of low-fat yogurt. "Anyway, if you're going to have a fit over Whitney using your stuff, you should say something to her instead of getting all pissy."

She's right. Whitney's already gone to work, but the next time I see her, I need to let her know that I'm not okay with sharing my stuff. I'm sure she'll understand.

I no longer have time for a real breakfast, but there are some apples in the fruit bowl that haven't turned completely brown yet. I grab one of them, noting a few more fruit flies than usual hovering over the bowl. It might be a good idea to get rid of the rest of the apples before the fruit flies multiply, which they have a tendency to do. I've been cleaning the kitchen every day, hoping to keep it insect-free, but fruit is irresistible to those little bugs.

Krista puts down her cereal box to smile at me. "Good luck today," she says.

"Thanks," I say as I run a hand through my still slightly damp hair. "Do I look okay?"

"Almost…" She cocks her head, assessing my appearance carefully. She reaches out and straightens my navy-blue tie, cinching the knot a bit tighter. "There. Now you look devastatingly handsome." She stands on the toes of her bare feet, lifting her pink lips so I can kiss her, and I wrap my arms around her. "Level nine," she whispers in my ear, and I tighten my embrace. It's enough to make me sorry I have to leave, but it's also a relief to be a productive member of society again. When we finally separate, Krista squeezes my arm. "Knock 'em dead, Blake."

"I will."

It's a temp job, but I'll make the most of it. In another couple of years, I'll be running the place.

I head out the front door, having already planned a route to work involving the subway station three blocks away. It'll be a thirty-minute ride to Battery Park City and another five minutes from the train station. So I should be at work in about forty-five minutes as long as there are no delays. Then Mr. Zimmerly, clad in his trademark slippers, comes out of his brownstone as if he's been waiting for me. Unlike in the suburbs, there's zero breathing room between our houses; his brownstone and mine are practically kissing.

"Porter!" he calls out as he makes his way down the steps of his house.

Christ, what now? "I'm on my way to work, Mr. Zimmerly."

Zimmerly looks me up and down in my work clothes, his lips curling as he rubs the whiskers on his chin. "You finally got yourself a job, huh?"

Before I got fired, there wasn't one day in the last fifteen years when I hadn't worked, and that includes working *two jobs* during college. But I don't feel like getting into it with him. "Yes" is all I say. "So I have to get going and—"

"You need to do something about your steps," Mr. Zimmerly tells me.

I look down at the gray cement below my polished black dress shoes. "My steps?"

"They're filthy!"

I don't know what to say to that. My steps aren't spotless, but no worse than his. "They're outdoors."

"So that's your excuse?" he spits at me. "This is a disgrace to the whole block! I'm not the only one who feels this way."

"Fine," I say. "I'll hose them down, okay?"

Mr. Zimmerly mutters something under his breath, then goes back into his own house. He doesn't seem like he believes I'm going to clean the steps. Which is fair, because there's no way I'm going to do it. I don't even have a hose.

CHAPTER 12

The first day at the temp job goes as well as it possibly could. I mean, considering my job is basically to do filing and data entry for people who are five years younger than me.

After spending the entire day stuffed in an office, I decide to get off the subway early and walk the last mile back to the house. It's not a run through the park, which is what I'd prefer, but that's not an option in my work clothes. Also, the summer is finally coming to a close, and the weather is great. Although my Upper West Side neighborhood isn't nearly as colorful as it was around my very first apartment, which was in Greenwich Village, the walk still clears my mind. I'm in such a good mood that I drop a dollar into the coffee cup of a guy begging for change in front of a liquor store.

After I've been walking about half a mile, I realize I'm only one avenue block away from Cosmo's—the diner where Whitney waitresses. Before I can overthink it, I make a detour, weaving my way through the commuter pedestrian traffic to get to the diner. It's barely five thirty, which means it won't be very crowded at the restaurant. If I want to chat with Whitney for a minute, this would be a good time to do it.

Cosmo's is similar to a lot of the other Greek diners in the city—a medium-size restaurant with booths lining the walls and tables in the center of the room, with a faint aroma of burgers on the grill wafting through the air. The menu posted on the wall of the diner next to the A+ from the health department claims to have such ethnic dishes as moussaka and stuffed grape leaves, but it's clear that 99 percent of the patrons come here for a burger and fries.

I scan the room until I spot Whitney near the back, dressed in another pair of blue jeans and a snug T-shirt with the words *Cosmo's Diner* emblazoned on the chest, her hair pulled back into a sensible bun.

She spots me at the same moment as I see her, and her face lights up as she gives me a cheery wave. She hurries over to where I'm standing, tucking a small pencil into the groove over her ear.

"Blake!"

"Hey, Whitney."

She rests a hand on my bicep, which is very decent given how much I worked out during my unemployment. I don't flex for her though.

Okay, I flex a tiny bit.

"How are you doing?" she asks. "How was your first day at work?"

"Not too bad."

I scratch my forearm. Toward the end of the day, I started to feel itchy again, the same way I was at Becky and

Malcolm's place. I wonder if I've developed an allergy to one of the components of the dress shirts during my time away from work. Does that kind of thing happen? Or is it stress? God knows I've been under enough of it.

"You're going to do great," Whitney tells me, her hand still on my arm. "I promise."

"Uh, thanks."

She glances over her shoulder at the mostly empty dining area. "It's pretty dead right now, as you can see. Can I get you a table? Our lemon meringue pie is to die for."

"Actually," I say, "I wanted to talk to you for a moment. Is that okay?"

"Sure." She frowns, looking concerned. "Is everything all right?"

"Yes." I pause for a moment, rethinking if it's a good idea to discuss this with her while she's working. But I'm already here, so I plow forward. "Actually, no. Not exactly. Look, remember how I told you that you could use my stuff? Like, the soap and shampoo and cereal?"

She narrows her eyes, finally letting go of my arm. "Yes…"

"I actually don't think it's a good idea for us to be sharing anymore," I say. "I had no idea how much you'd use, and honestly, I'm a little shocked. I think it would be better to keep things separate from now on."

She blinks at me. "You came here and interrupted me at work to tell me *that*?"

I scratch my arm again. "It was weighing on me."

"Well," she snaps at me, "I am *so* glad you got that off your chest."

She's not taking this as well as I would have hoped. In retrospect, it was a dick move to come to her work and complain to her here. But in my defense, she's always working double shifts, and I had no idea when she'd be home. I didn't want to have this conversation at midnight.

"Listen," I say, "maybe we should label our stuff to make it easier."

"You don't need to stick a label on your cereal, Blake." She sneers at me. "I won't touch it again. I promise."

"I just think it's easier to keep things separate," I say in an attempt to placate her. "I mean, you're our tenant. It's not like we're friends or anything."

Whitney jerks her head back like I hit her. She pulls the pencil out from behind her ear, and for a moment, I'm scared she might stab me with it. She takes a deep breath.

"You're right," she says slowly. "We are not friends. Good point."

I had good intentions coming in here, but I'm screwing up this conversation big time. I struggle to figure out what to say to make this right, but at that moment, a family comes through the door of the diner.

"Excuse me," Whitney says to me, her tone brisk. "I have to get to work."

Well, that was a disaster. But on the flip side, I said what I had to say. Whitney was somehow offended, but the truth is we're *not* friends. She's just some girl we're renting a room to. And as soon as I get back on my feet, she'll be gone.

In any case, I don't think she's going to be bringing home cake tonight to celebrate my first day of work.

CHAPTER 13

Krista and I are cuddled on the sofa, watching a movie. She's been more amorous in the week since I started working. It doesn't matter that my job is basically being a poorly paid intern. At least I'm earning some money. And there's some opportunity for the position to turn permanent if I impress them.

It's perfect weather to be cuddled up on the sofa too. It's raining hard, and now the room lights up with a bolt of lightning, followed by a crack of thunder. The loud noise prompts Krista to nuzzle closer against me. I've got my arm around her, and I squeeze her tighter (level nine). She lifts her face to look at me, and her lips glisten in the light from the television. Even though we're only halfway through the movie, I lean in to kiss her.

"You smell nice, Blake," she whispers in my ear.

I smell like my ordinary soap and shampoo, which I had to buy more of after Whitney used it all. She hasn't used it again as far as I can tell, having purchased her own bottle of

Dove bodywash. And I don't have to smell like apricots and coconuts, two of the least masculine fruits known to man.

"You smell nice too," I whisper back.

I kiss Krista again, this time more deeply, pushing her down against the cushions of the sofa as her fingers dig into the muscles of my back. My hand snakes under her shirt, and I've nearly reached her bra when we hear the locks turning in the front door, and I jump off her.

Damn it, I *hate* having a tenant living here. I feel like a teenager trying to sneak a feel while my girlfriend's parents aren't around, and not in a *fun* way.

Whitney is in the hallway behind us, stomping the water off her shoes on our welcome mat. I hear her fiddle with her umbrella and let out a sigh. I wish she'd just go up to her room already.

A minute later, Whitney comes into the living room, looking waterlogged, her hair clinging to her scalp. If she were wearing makeup, it would be running down her cheeks. She looks at the two of us sitting awkwardly on the sofa.

"Did I *interrupt* something?" she says in a teasing voice, although there's no humor in her eyes.

Ever since I spoke to Whitney at the diner, our relationship has soured considerably. She barely speaks to me, and when she does, her tone is decidedly unfriendly.

"We were just watching a movie," Krista speaks up, oblivious to the tension between us. "Would you like some popcorn? We made tons."

"Oh no," Whitney says sardonically. "I wouldn't want to use it all up."

Krista misses the undertone in her voice. "Don't worry about it! Take whatever you want."

Whitney doesn't even answer her. She just turns around and stalks off to the kitchen. A second later, I hear the microwave whirring. She must be heating up her dinner.

I reach out to squeeze Krista's knee. "I'm going to get more water, okay?"

"Okay. Hurry back."

I grab my glass off the coffee table, even though it's half full. I don't need anything. But I'd like to have a few words with Whitney Cross alone in the kitchen.

When I get there, Whitney is staring at the microwave as a Styrofoam container slowly rotates. She must have brought it home from the diner. She swats at a fruit fly buzzing around her ear, not looking up at me.

"I'll be out of your way in a minute," she says. "So you and Krista can continue having sex on the couch."

"We weren't—"

"I'm not stupid, Blake."

I came in here to apologize, but instead, I want to throw something at her. "So what if we were? It's *my* house, Whitney. You're just renting out a room."

"Yep. You've made that abundantly clear." She flicks her ponytail over her shoulder. "Don't worry. I don't want to use *your* TV, especially without giving you notice."

Christ, why is she so *angry*? "Look, Whitney," I sigh. "We don't have to be best friends, but if you're going to live here, we need to at least get along. If I did something to upset you—"

"*If?*" she snorts. "Are you really that dense?"

"I'm sorry," I say tightly. "I'm very sorry I upset you. And…maybe we can start fresh."

The microwave dings. Whitney pulls out the

Styrofoam container, which has a burger and fries inside. A reheated cheeseburger and fries don't seem very appealing, but Whitney doesn't seem to mind.

"Do you remember," she says, "when you were all worried about your new job, and I was comforting you, and I told you that I thought you'd do great because you're smart and charismatic and good-looking and shit?"

"Uh, yeah…"

"Well, none of that is true." Her gaze sears into me so intensely that I take a step back. "The reason you'll succeed—the reason you *have* succeeded—is because you're a self-absorbed asshole. You like to pretend that you're a good guy, but deep down, you know you're a terrible person."

I gape at her. Is she really this worked up because I asked her not to use my soap? This girl is out of her mind. "Whitney…"

"Enjoy the movie with your girlfriend." She brushes past me, hard enough to jostle my shoulder. "You better hope she doesn't wise up and figure out what you're really like. But for her sake, I hope she does."

I stand in the kitchen, trying to compose myself as Whitney's feet stomp up the two sets of stairs and the door to her bedroom slams shut. What the hell was that? Okay, I admit it wasn't the nicest thing in the world to show up at the diner and give her a hard time, but did I really deserve that tirade?

I'm not an asshole. Sure, I've done a few shitty things in my life. You don't get a competitive marketing VP job by being a nice guy. But there are worse people out there than me.

In any case, I've got to keep a close eye on Whitney.

CHAPTER 14

If I have to stay in this meeting one more second, I'm going to lose my mind.

In the month I've been at this temp job, my expected contribution to meetings has been made very clear: I take minutes. I am not expected to come up with ideas or talk or think. I just write down what everyone else says and what time they said it. It's important work. (Not.)

I've got a paper and pen out because I haven't been granted a laptop, and for the first twenty minutes of the meeting, I was doing a great job taking notes—I was a temp superstar—but over the next twenty minutes, that has changed drastically. I have become increasingly distracted by an intense itching sensation over my entire chest and arms. It is all I can think about.

I've been noticing it more and more. Not every day, but lately, I've been itchy more often than not. And today is the worst it's ever been.

"Porter?"

I rub my fingers along my forearm, but what I really want to do is rip open my shirt and scratch at my chest for five straight minutes or until I draw blood, whichever comes first. I don't know what's under my shirt, but the angry red is now creeping out from under my sleeve.

"Porter!"

My head snaps up. My boss, a guy named Kenny who is definitely no older than thirty, is staring at me. I grip my pen tighter, pretending I'm writing down whatever boring crap they were just discussing about synergistic solutions. Taking minutes at a meeting is such a shit job. I didn't even know companies did that anymore. "Sorry," I mutter.

"So what are you waiting for?" Kenny asks me.

I raise my eyes to look up at his clean-shaven face. He obviously asked something of me when I wasn't paying attention because I was too distracted trying not to scratch my own skin off, and now I have no idea what it is. All I can do is stare at him blankly.

"Coffee, Porter," he sighs. "Can you grab us a fresh pot?"

I forgot to mention my other important job during these meetings: fetching coffee.

"Right." I leap to my feet. "Of course. I'm so sorry."

I snatch the empty coffeepot from the back of the conference room. As I'm leaving the room, I overhear Kenny saying to someone else, "Some of these temps are better than others, huh?"

Great. So much for this job turning permanent.

Since I have no shot of ever working here, I take my sweet time getting more coffee. I bring the pot to the break room, but instead of filling it up, I leave it there and make a beeline for the men's room.

Thankfully, nobody is inside since everyone is at the meeting. I undo the tiny buttons on the shirt, resisting the temptation to rip it open. When all the buttons are undone, I yank the shirt open. And I gasp.

No wonder I'm so freaking itchy. There's an angry red rash covering every inch of my chest. I take the shirt off entirely and discover it's on my arms and back as well. Even though I know I shouldn't, I stand there for several minutes, going to town scratching every inch of my body that I can reach until my skin is raw and practically bleeding.

Why did I break out in a rash like this? Given it's localized to the area under my dress shirt, I have to assume that's the cause. But this shirt isn't new. I've had it for years, and it never caused a problem. And the itching has been bothering me every day, even when I'm wearing different shirts.

It can't be the laundry detergent. I would love to use a detergent where the bottle features a big burly man holding a sledgehammer against a backdrop of the woods, but instead I buy a detergent that has a stuffed animal on it that is hypoallergenic because I know I'm sensitive to that kind of stuff. But even the burly man detergent never made me break out like this. The only thing that makes me break out in a rash like this is…

Limonene.

I am extremely allergic to limonene, which is a citrus-scented fragrance chemical often found in laundry detergent. I found that out as a kid, when I used to break out in a rash every time my mom used it. So I avoid it. Krista knows to avoid any detergent with limonene listed as an ingredient. In fact, I've asked her not to use it in our machine at all, because even the residual in the machine can irritate my skin.

But Whitney doesn't know this.

It hits me now that I've been noticing the itching sensation since right after Whitney moved in with us, a little over a month ago now. The timeline matches up. Whitney must be using a detergent with limonene in the washing machine, and then when I wash my clothes, they are picking up the residual. And now I have to talk to her about it, which I'm sure will be a fun conversation.

I recognize I can't spend the day here in the men's room, scratching my chest. And I'm not doing myself any favors. On top of the rash, I now have scratch marks running up and down my skin. I have to put my shirt back on, fill up that pot of coffee, and proceed with my exciting day of menial tasks.

I splash cold water on myself, hoping that will soothe my raw, aching skin. It helps a little, although more than that, it makes my shirt slightly damp. When I get back to the meeting, they are going to wonder what the hell I was doing all this time.

It's safe to say I've blown any chance of ever working here. And I better get my act together ASAP before I lose everything.

CHAPTER 15

I stop at a drugstore on the way home and buy a tube of cortisone cream, knowing it's the only thing that has a chance of helping. I don't have any health insurance at the moment, so I better hope the nonprescription strength does the trick.

The itching is as intense as ever by the time I get back to the brownstone. I can barely stand it, and I'm definitely not in the mood when Mr. Zimmerly's front door swings open and he comes clomping down the steps in his slippers. He brushes a tuft of white hair off his forehead as he glares at me.

"Porter!" he barks. "Your garbage cans are on the curb!"

He's right. My empty garbage cans are on the curb, and trash pickup was this morning. I'm almost certain I dragged the cans off the curb before I left for work. I can clearly remember hauling them across the sidewalk while trying not to get any garbage juice on my dress shirt. I definitely did it.

Didn't I?

Yet the bins are clearly still on the curb. Zimmerly isn't making it up. And I can't imagine why anyone would haul my empty garbage bins back onto the sidewalk between this morning and now. I must be thinking of last week.

The last thing I feel like doing after the day I've had is dealing with garbage. But if I don't, I'm in danger of not only my neighbor's wrath but also a ticket.

"Also," he adds, "your steps are still dirty!"

The itching on my chest intensifies several notches. I want to rip my skin off. I also want to pick up this trash bin and smash it against Zimmerly's head until he shuts the hell up. I'd say after about three good hits, he won't have much to complain about anymore.

"Well?" he says.

I glare at him. Without saying a word, I grab the opening of my shirt and yank hard, feeling the buttons strain and finally give. A second later, my shirt is open. I rip it off and throw it down on the sidewalk in disgust while Zimmerly stares at me, his jaw hanging open. The October air sends a chill over my bare torso, which feels pretty good, given how raw and red my skin has become.

"Look!" I grab the trash bin and start wheeling it back to the side of the stairs to lock it up. "I'm doing it! Happy?"

For once, that curmudgeonly old bastard is at a loss for words.

I retrieve my shirt from the sidewalk before going back into the house, crumpling it into a little ball. Much like Zimmerly, I stomp up the steps and let myself inside. The house is quiet, but Whitney's sneakers are on the shoe rack by the door, which means she's home.

Good.

Although I'm dying to slather myself in the cortisone cream, I instead head for the washer and dryer. My special hypoallergenic detergent is on the floor next to it, and I don't see any bottles of detergent. But she's using *something* with limonene. She's got to be.

Without even stopping by my own bedroom, I climb up the second set of stairs, going straight for her room, and I rap my fist against her door. Loudly.

She doesn't answer right away, so I knock again. And again. After another few seconds, the door swings open, and Whitney is standing there in her jeans and T-shirt. Her eyes widen at the sight of me without my shirt on, and for a moment, I regret not grabbing a T-shirt before coming to her room.

"Blake?" she says.

"You need to stop using fragranced laundry detergent," I blurt out. "Look at me!"

Her gaze rakes over my bare chest, where the rash is just as red and angry as it was when I stripped at work. My skin feels burning hot. Amusement flickers in her eyes. "I see…"

"I'm extremely allergic to limonene." I gesture emphatically at my chest. "It's a fragrance in a lot of detergents. Even if it's not in my own load, it still gets on my clothes. I mean, does this look comfortable?"

"No." A smile plays on her lips. "It certainly doesn't. But if I don't use fragranced detergent, how am I supposed to get my clothes smelling fresh and clean?"

"I really don't care," I spit at her. "You can go to the laundromat next door. Whatever you want. But no fragrances in the washing machine from now on. Got it?"

She smirks at me. "I hear you loud and clear."

She doesn't seem to be taking this seriously. I don't get it. Whitney seemed so nice when we first met her. How did she manage to hide this side of herself so well?

"Listen," I say, "if I see or smell limonene in the washing machine again, you're out of here. We have no signed lease or agreement. It's my right to kick you out whenever I want."

The smile immediately drops from her face. "That's not true, actually. In New York, even without a lease, you can't just kick me out. Read the law, asshole."

Of course, she is absolutely right. I did look it up, and in New York State, even without a lease, she has rights as my tenant. The best I could do is give her a thirty-day eviction notice, but I can't forcibly make her leave if she chooses to stay, even after those thirty days. The law is on her side with this one. The last thing I want right now is a lawsuit.

I was hoping maybe *she* didn't know that. No such luck.

With those words, Whitney shuts the door in my face. I flinch, taking a step back. I don't know if she's going to keep using scented detergent in the wash or not, but I have definitely not made the situation any better. If I do have to live with this woman for at least another few months, I need to learn to get along with her. And the truth is we still need her rent money. The salary for my temp job is laughable.

I turn around, clutching my balled-up dress shirt, and that's when I realize that Krista is standing midway up the stairs, frozen, peering up at me. I don't think she has been there long, which is a bad thing, because she probably didn't hear us fighting. But based on the look on her face, she did see Whitney closing the door to her bedroom and then me, with my shirt off.

Shit.

"Krista," I manage as I hurry after her back to the second floor. "This…this isn't how it looks."

"Oh really?"

The hurt expression on her face almost breaks me in two. How could she think I'd cheat on her with *Whitney* though? She knows how I feel about Whitney.

"We were just talking," I say. "Arguing, actually. She slammed the door in my face."

"And your shirt is off because…"

I look down at my right hand clutching the offending shirt. This could not possibly look worse. "I took it off when I got into the house because there's something irritating my skin. I mean, *look* at me, Krista."

The hallway is dim, because for some reason, the bulbs just don't seem to work very well in the overhead light fixtures—probably some electrical issue—but it's bright enough for her to see the rash all over my chest and arms. Her eyes widen as she takes it in.

"My God, Blake," she gasps. "That looks terrible. How did that happen?"

I make a face. "Whitney is obviously using limonene in the wash. It's got to be that. She won't admit it, but it's the only thing that would make me break out like this." I look over at the washer and dryer. "I've got to scrub down the washing machine and run all my clothes again."

Her expression softens. "Do you need help?"

"No, I can handle it." I scrape my nails over my chest. With all the drama, I had forgotten about the itch, but now that things are settling down, it's come back full force.

"But I could definitely use some help putting the cortisone cream on my back."

She winks at me. "You got it."

Thank God Krista believes me. It's bad enough that practically everything in my life has fallen apart, but if I lost Krista, I don't know what I would do. I would completely lose it.

CHAPTER 16

Thump!

My eyes fly open at the noise that echoes through my bedroom. A minute ago, I had been sound asleep, but now I'm awake and disoriented. Did I actually hear something? Maybe it's coming from outside. I roll my head to look at the clock by my bedside. It's 1:18 in the freaking morning.

Thump! Thump!

I lift my eyes skyward and groan. Whatever the sound is, it seems to be coming from right above me. I stare up at the ceiling, willing the noise to stop so I can fall back asleep.

Thump! Thump thump thump!

I sit straight up in bed, grinding my teeth. Krista is sound asleep by my side, but she always sleeps with earplugs because she claims I snore. So she is blissfully unaware of the sound that is tormenting me.

Thump!

It's been a week since I confronted Whitney about the laundry detergent, and while she and I are still cohabitating, I can't say we're getting along well. Every time we pass each other in the living room or on the way to the bathroom, she gives me a seething look. Krista says that I should try to apologize to her, although I don't know what I would be apologizing for. Do I really need to apologize for reacting to her rudeness?

At least the rash seems to have improved. But the price is that I have to clean the washing machine every time I put in a load, because I don't trust her not to use limonene.

Thump! Thump!

And now, apparently, she has found a new way to torment me.

What the hell is she doing up there? A dance aerobics workout? A game of handball? Irish step dancing? And why is she doing it at one in the morning?

Thump!

That's it. I can't take it anymore.

I climb out of bed, nearly levitating with anger. I was sleeping in just boxer shorts, so I throw on an undershirt. I like to sleep in as few clothes as possible, in hopes that I might get lucky, although sadly, things have been pretty slow in that department since Whitney moved in. Getting a tenant was supposed to take some of the stress off paying the bills, but I feel more on edge than ever before.

After I leave the bedroom, I head straight for the stairs to the third floor. But as soon as I get into the stairwell, the thumping stops abruptly. I don't hear it anymore at least. But I don't turn around to go back to my room. Whitney needs to know that whatever she's doing at one in the morning is *not* okay.

I don't stop moving until I reach Whitney's door, where sure enough, the light is still on underneath. I bang my fist against the door repeatedly until it finally swings open. Whitney is standing in her tiny pajama shorts and a tank top with no bra, and I am not even the slightest bit aroused.

"Blake." Her lips curl into a smile. "To what do I owe the pleasure of this late-night visit?"

"You're being too noisy," I spit out. "It's one in the morning, and I'm trying to sleep."

She blinks innocently. "I hate to break it to you, but I was just sitting in bed quietly reading."

I crane my neck to look over her shoulder, although I'm not sure what I'm looking for. Tap shoes? A wild animal she's been sequestering in her room? I still don't know what she was doing in there, and it doesn't matter. It needs to stop.

I grit my teeth. "Just keep the noise level down after eleven, okay?"

"It's not my fault if you're hallucinating noises, Blake."

Hallucinating noises? What the hell is she talking about? I could hear the thumping clearly from our bedroom. I didn't imagine that.

I didn't.

Whitney tilts her head to the side. "You don't look so hot, Blake. Maybe you should try to get more sleep."

"Thanks for the tip." I have to bite back the string of swear words I'm tempted to hurl in her direction. "Like I said, just...whatever you were doing, stop it."

She has an amused look on her face. "You got it, boss. Is that all?"

"Yeah, that's all."

"Fantastic."

Then she shuts the door in my face.

I trudge down the steps back to my own bedroom. My heart is still racing from being woken up abruptly and from my encounter with Whitney. I'll be lucky if I fall back asleep in the next hour. All I can say is that if the noises start up again, I can't be held accountable for my actions.

CHAPTER 17

There is a rotting smell in the kitchen.

I've been noticing it more and more over the last month or so. But today, as I step into the kitchen to grab a beer to help me unwind from another truly awful day at my temp job—during which I almost went to battle with the jammed copy machine—the stench is overpowering. I have to clasp a hand over my nose.

My first thought is *it's Whitney's fault*.

It's been two weeks since I confronted Whitney about the thumping noise in the middle of the night. I heard it one more time a week later, but the sound again stopped the second I got into the stairwell, and instead of having another frustrating encounter with a smirking Whitney, I instead went downstairs to the first floor and passed out on the couch watching television.

Sadly, it wasn't even the worst night of sleep I've gotten in the last month or so. I don't know what's wrong with me, but my sleep has been shit. I've got a permanent pair of bags under my eyes.

So I'm not in the mood to deal with a mystery smell in my kitchen. I look around the countertops, trying to figure out the source. A swarm of fruit flies whirls around my face. That's another thing. The fruit fly situation in the kitchen has become almost unbearable. I asked Krista if she would make cookies a few days ago, and she said she didn't want to because there were too many flies in the kitchen.

I yank open the refrigerator, trying to see if I can find the culprit in there. The smell is definitely pretty bad in here. I crouch down, peering inside. It's the usual mix of condiments, a loaf of bread, some cold cuts, fat-free yogurt, and a dozen eggs. But then I notice a few of those Styrofoam containers in the back of the fridge—the kind that Whitney brings home from the diner.

I take them out, and as soon as I have them in my hands, I have no doubt that this is the cause of the smell. They smell *awful*. Like there's a tiny rotting carcass inside.

I stare down at the containers, not wanting to even touch them without gloves on. Yet I can't stifle a sick curiosity. I need to know what's inside. I need to confirm that these really are the source of the smell.

So I open the first box.

I'm immediately sorry I did. The contents of the Styrofoam box are enough to make my stomach turn. It used to be french fries and a chicken sandwich, but the bun has turned almost completely green with mold. The french fries had also been slathered in some sort of sauce, which has clearly turned, and the fries themselves have also gone green. The stench is unbearable.

Damn it, Whitney.

I don't bother opening the other two containers,

because I'm pretty sure what's in them is just as bad. I toss all three right in the garbage, and then I seal the bag and take it outside. I don't even want this crap in my house anymore.

When I get back to the kitchen, it smells just as bad. There are about a dozen fruit flies on the counter, and I kill as many of them as I can with my bare hand. But I'm not sure how easy it will be to get rid of them.

"What are you doing, Blake?"

Krista has materialized at the kitchen, dressed in her clothes for work. She caught me smashing the life out of a fruit fly that was perched on the refrigerator, using more force than technically necessary.

I turn around, taking a breath to calm myself. "Whitney left rotting food in the fridge."

She crinkles her nose. "Yeah. Wow. It smells terrible."

"No kidding."

She brightens. "I have that air freshener in the bedroom. I could spray it around the kitchen."

I know the air freshener she is talking about because she sprays it in the bathroom sometimes. It smells overwhelmingly of flowers and makes my eyes itch. In general, I hate it, but it's better than the way the kitchen currently smells. Anything to cover up the smell of rotting food. But we have a bigger problem right now.

"I don't want Whitney to live here anymore," I say to her.

"Because she forgot about some rotting food in the fridge? You do that all the time, Blake. Are you sure it wasn't yours?"

"It wasn't mine. Trust me." My jaw ticks. "Why aren't you more bothered by this? It smells like death in here."

"It's not that bad." She shrugs. "Just open a few windows and spray the air freshener. I bet it'll be fine in a couple of hours."

"It's not just that, okay? She's just… She's toxic. She woke me up twice in the middle of the night doing God knows what…"

"I didn't hear anything."

"That's because you sleep with earplugs!" I throw up my hands. "Trust me, she's doing this to torment me. And she keeps looking at me like she wants to slit my throat while I'm sleeping. I'm not comfortable with her here."

"I think she's really nice." Krista blinks at me. "I don't get it. You don't like the way she's *looking* at you?"

I grit my teeth. "She hates me. Do you know what it's like to live with somebody who hates you?"

"She doesn't hate you."

"She does!" A fruit fly dances in front of my face, and I swat at it in frustration. "She *absolutely* hates me. Honestly, I wouldn't be surprised if she left this rotting food in the fridge just to torture me!"

The fruit fly finally gets out of my face and lands on the kitchen counter. I reach out and slam the palm of my hand down, smashing the life out of it. I feel a brief flash of satisfaction.

Krista takes a step back, blinking quickly. "Are you okay, Blake?"

"No, I'm not okay!" I shoot back. "There's a psychopath living in my house, and I want her out!"

And now my stupid eye won't stop twitching.

"The last several months have been really stressful for you," Krista says gently. "I know it was hard on you to lose your job that way, and I know you hate your new job.

And I know you aren't sleeping well. But Whitney is not the cause of all your problems. I promise you that." I start to protest, but then she raises her hand. "And I need to remind you that the money Whitney is paying us for the room is the only thing keeping us afloat right now."

She has a point. We need the money. And it's not like there were any other amazing candidates lining up.

"Fine," I mutter. "I got rid of the rotting food at least. She needs to know she can't do it again though."

"I'll talk to Whitney about the food," Krista says. "You stay out of it. You'll just make things worse."

That's for sure.

"And we can get rid of the fruit flies," she adds. "I was looking it up, and you can build a trap using dish detergent and apple cider vinegar!"

"Fantastic."

I wait for Krista to wrap her arms around me in a tight hug—I could really use a hug right now. At least at level seven or higher. But instead, she goes upstairs to fetch the air freshener. It's hard to imagine that it will do anything to help get rid of this terrible smell, but it's worth a try. We have one window in the kitchen, so I throw it open; then I go into the living room to open some windows, because the whole place is starting to smell. Even poor Goldy looks kind of green in her little bowl. Thank God at least the weather is decent so we can keep the windows open.

I feel sorry for our poor fish, so I toss her a couple of pellets. She must be hungry, because she immediately rises to the surface to gobble them up. Eating is literally the most interesting thing that she does. It's sort of cute. I feel a weird rush of affection for our little pet. It's nice to have something to take care of.

As I idly scratch my chest, which feels itchy again all of a sudden, I hear the sound of footsteps thudding on the steps. I raise my eyes from the fishbowl to the stairwell. Someone is standing at the top, and at first I think it must be Krista with the air freshener. But it's not. It's Whitney.

I don't say anything, and neither does she. She just stands there, dressed in her usual jeans and hoodie, looking down at me. I wonder how long she has been standing there. I wonder if she heard our entire conversation.

Then she tucks her hair behind her ears and smirks. She heard every word.

CHAPTER 18

One of my all-important jobs as the temp is to fetch coffee from Starbucks every morning.

I have to walk around, taking drink orders like I'm a waiter, and then Kenny gives me the company credit card. I trot off to the Starbucks three blocks away to join the line that goes all the way to the door, no matter what time I show up. If I get out of there in less than half an hour, it's a miracle.

Today I have a whopping nine drink orders, which means I am going to be carrying two tiers of drink trays back to the office. Balancing something like that as I walk across two streets is no easy task, but I have sadly become very good at it over the two months I have worked there.

I stand in line behind four other people, inhaling the rich aroma of brewing coffee as I scratch absently at my arm. After I started cleaning out the washing machine prior to using it, the rash went away. But in the last few days, it seems to have come back. It's just present enough to be annoying.

Not only that, but the kitchen still smells. It's not as overpowering as it was, but the rotting food smell is still very much present, now mixed with the scent of Krista's air freshener. And although we constructed a very formidable fruit fly trap using instructions we found online, the fruit flies are still abundant. And the trap works—at this point, the cup looks like a graveyard for fruit flies—but they're still freaking everywhere.

"Blake? Oh my God, is that you?"

I cringe at the sound of my name. The last place I want to be recognized is while picking up drinks for the office at Starbucks. But I obligingly turn around.

Oh great. It's Stacie, the secretary for the guy who fired me. And she looks absolutely fantastic, with those long, long legs and short skirt. She's clutching a macchiato in her right hand.

"Hey, Stacie." I manage a smile that I'm hoping looks at least somewhat authentic. "How are you doing?"

"Good!" She smiles, showing off her mouth of perfectly white teeth. "And you…"

I straighten my spine as she looks over my dress clothes and wish I could do something about the dark circles under my eyes.

"You look great! You got a new job, I see."

"Yep." I don't bother to mention that it's a temp job. I don't need her racing back to the office to let everyone know about my humiliation. "Everything is going great."

"And Krista?" She raises an eyebrow at me suggestively. "You two are still…"

"Yes," I say quickly. "We're engaged. Still."

"Uh-huh." She cocks her head to the side. "I remember. I was just wondering if anything changed."

"Nope."

Stacie reaches out and runs a hand along my upper arm. I take a step back. She's just going to make the itching worse.

"Anyway," Stacie says, "it was good seeing you again, Blake. I was honestly pretty worried about you after Wayne fired you and all. But it looks like everything worked out."

"It sure did," I lie. "I wasn't too worried. I always land on my feet."

"You sure do," she agrees.

I hold my breath until Stacie leaves the Starbucks with her drink. There are plenty of other people from the company I wouldn't want to run into, but she tops the list.

About half an hour later, I am heading back to the office, balancing nine cups of coffee in my arms. Two people on the street shout out snarky comments about the amount of coffee I'm carrying ("You gonna drink all that?"), and when a taxi skids to a halt a split second before mowing me down at a crosswalk, I almost wish it had just hit me and put me out of my misery.

By some miracle and what has become a lot of practice, I make it back up to the office without spilling anything. I deposit the coffee trays on the reception desk, and then I let people know the order has arrived. I suppose I could bring the trays around to everyone, but I just can't make myself do it today.

I do, however, grab Kenny's oat milk mocha latte and bring it to his office. I thought I had blown any chance of ever working here permanently, but in a meeting yesterday, I automatically made a suggestion about one of the big accounts. I spoke out of turn, but my idea and knowledge base seemed to really impress him. After the meeting was over, he asked me more questions and almost seemed to be picking my brain. If I can prove that I'm useful, maybe I really do have a chance of a real job here.

When I get to Kenny's office, he is working on his computer. When I come inside, he looks up, but he doesn't smile at me.

"Here you go, Kenny," I say as I slide his coffee across his desk. His office isn't as nice as mine used to be, but it's a hell of a lot better than the cubicle I occupy right now.

"Thanks." He gives the coffee a strange side-eye. "How many cups of coffee did you get?"

"Nine. It took some mad skills to get them back here."

Kenny doesn't smile. "Hey, Porter. How many sandwiches did you get for the lunch meeting yesterday?"

"Uh, twenty sandwiches. That's what you asked me to get."

"If you got twenty sandwiches, how come we ran out?"

I shrug. "I guess people were hungry."

Kenny is still looking at me, an unreadable expression on his face. It's making me very uncomfortable. I shift my weight and try not to scratch absently at my arm. Why is he quizzing me about how many sandwiches or cups of coffee I got? I'm not a waiter.

"Is there a problem?" I finally ask.

He looks at me for a moment, then finally nods his head. "Yeah, actually. I was so impressed by the insights you showed at the meeting yesterday, and I remembered seeing Coble & Roy on your CV. So I made a few calls…"

Shit. I know where this is going. So much for landing a permanent position here.

"I can't believe you ripped off your own company." Kenny shakes his head. "No wonder you're still working as a temp at your age."

"I didn't rip off my company," I say tightly. "It was a misunderstanding."

"That's not what Wayne Vincent said. I'll bet you made a pretty penny doing that."

I flinch. My chest is itching like crazy, but I can't scratch it. Not now. "What happened to innocent until proven guilty?"

"That's in a court, Porter." Kenny takes the lid off his coffee and takes a sip. "This tastes terrible. You got the oat milk mocha for me?"

"I didn't brew it myself."

"Don't be a smart-ass." He slides the coffee back across the desk. "Bring this back to Starbucks, and exchange it for another one."

I don't want to spend another half an hour at Starbucks to indulge a twentysomething middle manager's power trip. But I can't quit this job. I don't know the consequences of quitting a temp position, but I'm not sure if they'll place me again. Or if they do, it might be scooping french fries at a fast-food joint.

"I've got my eye on you, Porter." He narrows his gaze at me. "You try to steal anything from *my* company, you're not going to work in this town ever again. Even for a temp agency."

I don't know if this guy has the power to make a threat like that, but the truth is I don't want to find out. So I grab his coffee and head back outside. But not before I run to the restroom and scratch my chest for five straight minutes. I scratch until I bleed.

CHAPTER 19

I don't know what is going on with my clothes.

I'm afraid to wash anything anymore. I sterilize the washing machine the best I can before using it, and I don't add anything besides a capful of my hypoallergenic detergent, and still, I'm having a terrible allergic reaction to everything that comes out of it. I'm losing my ever-loving mind.

"What are you cleaning the washing machine with?" Krista asks me as we discuss it while getting ready for bed. It's sadly become one of my favorite topics of conversation. She must be bored out of her skull, but I can't help myself.

"A hypoallergenic cleaning spray made with all natural ingredients," I say, feeling about as manly as an eight-year-old girl. "I don't understand it, because cleaning the machine seemed to work for a while, but now it's just as bad as it ever was."

"Do you want me to bring your clothes to the dry cleaner?" she asks. "I can clean them for you there."

"I don't want you to get in trouble." God knows we don't need Krista losing her job on top of everything else. "Maybe I'll try taking it to the laundromat."

It makes me furious that I have to take my clothes to the laundromat when I have a perfectly good washer and dryer right in the house. I even got the most expensive stackable model they had. And now I can't use it.

"I don't mind," Krista tells me. "Nobody will even know. Really, just let me wash your clothes for you. I can't stand to see you suffer like this."

I start to protest again, but Krista is already picking up my laundry basket. She retrieves a mesh laundry bag from the closet and starts throwing my clothes inside.

"Krista, it's really okay," I say. "You don't have to do this."

She doesn't answer. She's holding up one of my dress shirts, a strange expression on her face.

"Krista?"

"Blake," she says, "what's this on your collar?"

I have no idea what she's talking about. I come around the side of the bed so I can get a better look at whatever's bothering her so much. I still don't quite know what she's so upset about, but then I see it: a bright red stain on the collar of my white shirt.

She rubs her finger against the red smudge, and some of the color comes away. "It's lipstick," she says sharply.

I shrug. "I guess you got some lipstick on my collar. What? That'll come off in the wash."

Krista whips her head around to glare at me. "I do *not* have any lipstick this shade."

My gaze darts between the bright red on the collar and Krista's lips, which show no trace of whatever she had on them today. I look at her blankly, because how would I know what shades of lipstick she owns?

"I only wear pink," she says pointedly. "Because of my complexion."

That could be true. I can't say I recall her ever wearing bright red lipstick in all the time we've been together.

So how the hell did red lipstick get on my collar?

I can't even begin to imagine how it could have happened, but from the look on Krista's face, she has a better imagination than I do.

"Krista." I try to touch her shoulder, and she jerks away. "You don't really think I'm cheating on you, do you?"

"If you weren't cheating on me, how did you end up with lipstick on your collar?" Her eyes widen. "Is that why you didn't want me doing your laundry?"

"No!" I tug the shirt away from her, examining the lipstick on the collar, racking my brain to try to figure out how it ended up there. "I really don't know. Maybe I left my shirt lying around and some of Whitney's lipstick got on it."

"Whitney never wears lipstick."

That is true. She never seems to wear any makeup. But my gut is telling me that Whitney had something to do with this.

"What if Whitney came into our bedroom while we were both out and rubbed lipstick on my shirts?" I suggest. "She was probably *hoping* you would see it. She wants me to get in trouble with you."

"Is that seriously your answer?" Krista puts her hands on her hips as she glares at me. "Whitney came into our bedroom and rubbed lipstick on all your clothes? Seriously? Do you really expect me to believe that?"

Yes, I absolutely do. But I can tell from the way Krista is saying it that the right answer is no. "Listen," I say. "I genuinely don't know how the lipstick ended up on my collar. But I promise you, I was not messing around on you. I would never do that."

"Uh-huh."

"Krista." I try to tamp down the feeling of panic rising in my chest. "You can't possibly believe I'm cheating on you. Please tell me you don't really think that."

Krista sinks to the bed, her shoulders sagging. "I don't know anymore. Honestly, Blake, you've been acting so strangely lately."

"Acting strangely?"

"You must know what I mean," she murmurs. "You barely sleep. You're always ranting and raving about something, including noises during the night that nobody can hear but you. And you are so weirdly paranoid about Whitney. I mean, Whitney seems perfectly nice to me."

Right. Of course she's nice to Krista. Krista isn't the one she has the inexplicable vendetta against.

"Krista." I hold out my arms, still covered in that itchy, red rash. "Anyone would be acting strangely if they were dealing with this. It's driving me out of my mind. Christ, do you really think I'm in any mindset to be having an *affair* right now?" I bend down, trying to make eye contact. "Who would even want me? I look like I should be at a leper colony!"

That coaxes the tiniest smile out of her. I sit beside her on the bed, and she actually lets me hold her hand, although I don't attempt to put my arm around her. A kiss would be out of the question.

"I'm sorry this rash is making me nuts," I say. "I

understand it looks bad that there was lipstick on my clothing, but I swear to you I don't know where it came from. I swear on my life." I chew on my lower lip. "Do you believe me?"

I hold my breath, waiting for her answer.

"I...I guess so," she finally says. "I have to admit, it's hard to imagine you having an affair when you can't go five seconds without scratching yourself everywhere."

I squeeze her hand. "Exactly. I don't want to kiss any other women. All I want is some prescription cortisone cream."

That gets a laugh out of her. "I know you're suffering, and you're trying your best. That's why I wanted to do your laundry for you."

"Okay," I agree. "But only for a little while. I don't want this to be a permanent arrangement."

Only until we get Whitney the hell out of here.

Except I'm beginning to worry that it's not going to happen anytime soon.

CHAPTER 20

When I get a phone call from Malcolm—of Malcolm and Becky fame—I recognize Krista's influence.

It's been two weeks since Krista discovered that lipstick on my shirt. I never confronted Whitney about it, but she gave me a knowing look the day after Krista's discovery that made me even more sure she was behind it. I'm also fully convinced that she did something to the washer or dryer to make my clothes itchy, because after Krista started bringing them to the dry cleaner, I haven't had a problem. The rash is now gone.

As for Krista and me, things have been better, if a little tenuous. Does she believe that I'm not fooling around behind her back? I think so. But I also think she doesn't want to admit how worried she is about me. She's out having dinner with Becky tonight, so the phone call from her friend's husband is suspiciously well-timed to keep me from being left to my own devices.

I'm on my way home from work, about two blocks

away from the brownstone, when my phone starts vibrating in my pocket. I was in no rush to get home, meandering down the residential streets, the weather a perfect sixty degrees. I decide to take Malcolm's call and speed up my steps, figuring I'll have an excuse to hang up when I get home. I swipe to answer, and Malcolm's congenial voice fills my ear: "Blake! How are you doing?"

"Fine," I lie. "How are you?"

"Good good good." His habit of repeating words irks me more than usual, but I try not to show it. "And how's Krista doing?"

"I don't know. Ask Becky."

Malcolm laughs heartily at what was not entirely a joke. "Listen, Blake, I was wondering if you want to get a drink with me sometime? We haven't done that in ages."

I'm not sure we ever did it. Back when we were both working at Coble & Roy, sometimes a bunch of us went out for drinks after work, and we were both there. But just me and Malcolm? Never happened. And right now, I'm not excited to hang out with a guy who works at the company that fired me. Who inexplicably seems to be doing better than I am.

"Maybe," I say, meaning no.

"I think it would be fun," he says. "The girls are such good friends, and I feel like you and I ought to get to know each other better."

I pass a Chinese restaurant on the corner that has excellent dim sum all day long. Despite my eagerness to get home, I pause a second to consider picking up an order of shrimp and chive dumplings before I remember that my budget doesn't allow unlimited takeout like before. "I'm just swamped right now."

"Oh yeah? Everything okay?"

"Yes, everything is fine. I'm just busy. But, you know, good busy."

"That's great to hear. Great great great."

"Anyway," I say, clenching my jaw, "I'm definitely up for a drink, but I need to wait for my schedule to calm down a little. You understand, right?"

"Absolutely," Malcolm agrees, "but maybe we should put something on the calendar now."

"Uh-huh. Okay." I turn onto my block, the brownstone in sight. "The thing is, at the moment, I'm walking home from work, and I'll be going through the door soon, so…maybe we can talk about it another time?"

He laughs again. "You trying to get rid of me, Porter?"

"Not at all. We should definitely get drinks. That sounds great." I sprint up the steps to my front door. "Great great great, you know?" I fumble to get my keys out of my pocket. "But at the moment—"

"How about next Wednesday then?"

It takes me a split second too long to think of an excuse. "Um…"

"Great!" he says. "Let's meet at Hannigan's at eight o'clock. You know it, right?"

Of course I know it. It's around the corner from Coble & Roy. If I have to do this, there's no way I'm going to a bar that's likely to be frequented by my old colleagues. I don't need that.

"Let's meet at Cooper's," I say, which is an Upper West Side bar midway between his apartment and my brownstone. We've been there for double dates before, so I know he knows it.

"You got it," he says. "Looking forward to it!"

"Yep," I say.

I manage to end the call just as I fit the key in my lock. I wasn't entirely lying—the days at the office are long, and they feel even longer. I'm exhausted from being everyone's gopher, and all I want right now is to relax. So my stomach sinks when I shove open the door to find Whitney in my living room. Just who I want to deal with right now.

Whitney is wearing her usual pair of straight-cut blue jeans, although this time she's wearing a nicer top, which is black and chic and sexy. She looks…well, she looks great. I wonder if she has a date. It's somehow hard to imagine Whitney on a date though. If she had sex with a guy, she'd probably have to devour him after the mating ritual was over.

"Hello, Blake," she says.

"Going somewhere?" I ask.

"Maybe."

She winks at me and pulls a compact out of her purse as well as a tube of lipstick. She pops open the compact and applies a layer of lipstick to her top and bottom lips. As the color glides on, I recognize it immediately.

It's the same exact color that was on my shirt collar.

"Where did you get that lipstick?" The question is out before I can stop myself.

She puckers her lips and smiles sweetly at me. "And why is that any of your business?"

I imagine her slipping into my bedroom and rubbing the makeup over my shirt collars, just hoping Krista would notice and I would get in trouble. What is wrong with this woman? What on earth did I do to her to make her hate me this much? Why would she try to sabotage my relationship with Krista?

"You're despicable," I spit at her.

She drops the compact back into her purse, the smile now having vanished from her bloodred lips. "*Excuse* me? I'm despicable because I put on some lipstick?"

"Don't try to deny what you did."

Whitney slips the tube of lipstick back into her purse and zips it up. "Maybe you should focus less on me and more on not screwing up your new gig."

I glare at her. "My job is going fine, thank you very much."

She arches an eyebrow. "Yeah? Hard to imagine. You know, considering what happened at your last company…"

Considering what happened at my last company? What the hell does *that* mean? What does she know?

Whitney glances down at her watch. "Anyway, I better get going. I don't want to be late."

"Wait." I reach for her wrist, but she shakes me off roughly. "What are you talking about? Why did you just say that to me?"

"Oh, Blake," she sighs. "You should be more worried about *yourself*. You look like shit, you know."

With those words, she pushes past me and breezes out of the house. God, I wish I had the money to kick her out for good. Better yet, I wish I was never in a position to need her in the first place.

I rub my fingertips over my eyes. Do I really look like shit? I'm half tempted to check out my appearance in the bathroom mirror, but I have a feeling I won't like what I see. The lack of sleep is really getting to me.

Why did she make that comment about my job? Before she started hating me, Whitney and I had a few nice conversations, but I never told her the reason I got fired. Does she know? Or is she just toying with me? There's no way she could possibly know the details about my termination. Unless…

My stomach drops. Is it possible that Whitney moving into my house isn't just a horrible coincidence? Is it possible that she somehow engineered all this from the beginning?

Has she been out to get me from the second she moved in?

CHAPTER 21

My head is spinning. Could Whitney have moved here for the explicit purpose of turning my life into a living hell?

Admittedly, I committed a faux pas when I yelled at her for using my soap and cereal, and I regret it. But I haven't done a damn thing to warrant the way she's treated me. It does feel suspiciously like she's had it out for me since day one.

Or maybe even *before* day one. Maybe she's the entire reason I lost my job in the first place and needed to take in a tenant.

But how could that be? How would she even know Wayne Vincent? And even if she did—even if such a thing were possible—why? Why would she set me up that way? Why would she want to worm her way into my house?

Is there a reason Whitney Cross has it out for me that I don't know about?

No. It doesn't make sense. I may be a little bit more

paranoid than usual lately, but that's a big jump, even for me. And anyway, before she showed up for her interview, I had never seen her before in my life.

Had I?

I whip out my phone and type the name "Whitney Cross" into the Google search engine. I had done a quick search when we first met her, but when no red flags popped up, I stopped looking. But this time, I do a deeper dive.

The first hit is from an American historian named Whitney Rogers Cross, but she died in 1955, so I'm thinking this person isn't related. I click through at least a dozen pages of results, and none of them are for the Whitney I know. I check social media and find a few profiles for Whitney Crosses, but none of them have a photo or any information that's public.

That's very strange. Most people my age have some sort of social media presence. But Whitney has nothing. There is not one digital footprint of that girl.

It's unsettling.

Why wouldn't she have any sort of social media presence? She doesn't seem like a technophobe—she always has her phone in hand. Is she trying to hide something about her past?

Or maybe she just doesn't like the internet. She's always working, so it could be she doesn't have time to be on social media. It's certainly not a crime.

In any case, it doesn't seem like I'm going to find anything interesting on Google.

Since Krista is having dinner with Becky tonight, I'm on my own for dinner. I don't feel like making anything elaborate, but we've got bread and turkey, so a sandwich it is. I grab a loaf of bread and a package of processed turkey from the fridge and lay them down on the kitchen counter.

The impact of the two items landing on the kitchen counter is enough to propel several dozen fruit flies into the air. I take a step back, stunned. The fruit fly situation is completely out of control. How is it possible we have this many?

Krista and I built a second fruit fly trap on the kitchen counter. I peer into the second trap, and my heart sinks. There have got to be at least one hundred fruit flies in each of the two traps. We are catching fruit flies by the dozen, yet it seems like every time we kill one, two more emerge midair.

I look over at the bread and turkey, now covered in a pulsating layer of fruit flies. I gag at the sight of it. Well, there goes my appetite. I don't know what we're doing wrong. Krista and I have been taking turns cleaning the kitchen every day, and I scrub until my fingers are raw. There isn't one spare crumb and certainly no fruit. What are these stupid fruit flies eating?

I can't get an exterminator for fruit flies, can I? That's not the sort of insect that requires heavy-duty poison. We *should* be able to get rid of them on our own. It's all about eliminating the source of food.

But what is the source? The kitchen is spotless.

I raise my eyes, noticing that many of the fruit flies have gathered around one of the upper cabinets. I don't know why they would be up there. All we have in there are clean dishes.

I tap open the cabinet, and a small swarm of flies emerges from within. What the hell? I crane my neck, trying to get a better look at the contents—it looks like it's clean dishes and bowls. Why are there so many insects? They're all clustered around the top shelf, which I can't quite see.

What in the world is up there?

Unfortunately, I'm not going to be able to see what's in that top shelf without something to prop me up. There's a stool in the hall closet that's about a foot tall, which I think will be just enough height for me to be able to reach that top shelf. Unfortunately, the stool isn't incredibly stable. In fact, the last time I used it to help me change a light bulb, Krista made a remark about how I was going to break my neck.

But it will be fine. I'm not going to break my neck.

I drag the stool out to the kitchen and position it beneath the cabinet. When I step on top of it, it creaks threateningly, but it doesn't collapse. It's fine. I won't be on it for very long.

The cabinet is still open, and the top shelf is visible, although not very well lit. The fruit flies are so dense up here, it almost looks like the shelf is alive. I don't think fruit flies make noise, but the swarm almost seems to be buzzing. And there's an odor. I had noticed a smell in the kitchen, although the truth is I had gotten used to it. But it's much stronger up here with the cabinet open. Overpowering.

I blink a few times, trying to see beyond the fruit flies to what is attracting them. What has been feeding them?

And then I see it.

There's a small paper bag in there. It's very clear that the paper bag is the source of the flies because of the sheer number of them crawling all over it. For a moment, I consider grabbing a paper towel so I don't have to touch the paper bag directly, but I don't want to have to get off the stool, get the paper towel, and climb back up here again. No, I'll just pick it up with my bare hands. I need this taken care of *now*.

I tug at the paper bag between my thumb and forefinger. The flies scatter slightly, although they are still intensely attracted to whatever is in that bag. I breathe through my mouth because of the smell, slowly pulling the bag closer to me until it is at the edge of the shelf. It's just close enough that I can see what's inside. I tip the edge of the bag to my line of sight, and I peer inside.

My stomach turns. Oh God. Oh *God*.

A resounding crack fills the kitchen, and the legs of the stool abruptly give way. But before I go crashing to the floor, all I can think to myself is *I hate Whitney Cross*.

CHAPTER 22

I'm okay.

Against all odds, I survived my one-foot fall without breaking my neck, although the wind got knocked out of me. I lie on the floor for a few moments, gradually taking inventory of my injuries. I smashed my elbow on impact, and there is an electric pain shooting down my forearm, but nothing feels broken. No trips to the emergency room are required.

The paper bag is still on the top shelf, and I'm grateful for that. I look up at the shelf, where the bag is teetering at the edge. I swallow down the bile in my throat.

The contents are seared into my brain forever. I'm not entirely sure what was once in that bag. Apples? Pears? I think they're apples. Either way, it doesn't really matter. Whatever it was has rotted to the point that it is now crawling with maggots. The air is heavy with the sickly sweet smell.

It was bad enough to find something like that in my

kitchen, but what is most troubling is how it got there. I like fruit as much as the next person, but I would never put a couple of apples in a paper bag and stick it on the top shelf where no one could reach it.

No, whoever did that did it intentionally. They did it to ensure that I would not discover the rot in my kitchen until the flies had multiplied, driving me out of my mind.

I started noticing the fruit flies not too long after Whitney arrived. It seems one of her first acts after handing over a deposit was to make sure my home would no longer feel safe and clean.

The worst part is that if I confront her, she will definitely deny it. Based on past experience, she will just hate me even more.

And Krista won't believe she did it. She already thinks I'm losing it. Considering our relationship seems to be hanging by a thread, I don't want to bring her into this.

I look up at the paper bag, now nearly close enough for me to touch without a stool, which is good since our only stool is in splintered pieces all over the kitchen floor. Instead, I grab one of the larger pots that is on the kitchen stove. I place it on the floor and put my weight on it, testing it to see if it will break. It doesn't. I use my left arm to help me balance against the counter, and the elbow that I smacked during the fall screams in pain.

I have just enough height now that I am able to grab the paper bag. Miraculously, I manage to pull it off the shelf without the bottom giving way, and I set it down on the kitchen counter. The thought of what is inside is turning my stomach, but even more than that, I am absolutely furious.

But I can't confront Whitney. I can't kick her out. So what can I do?

And then the answer hits me. I'm going to give Whitney a taste of her own medicine.

I grab a plastic bag from the pantry, because the thought of this paper bag disintegrating and releasing the contents onto the floor is too sickening to imagine. Once it is safely inside the plastic bag, I leave the kitchen and climb up the stairs to the top floor of the brownstone, my elbow throbbing all the while.

Whitney's room is right near the stairs. She has a lock on her door, but it only works from the inside. That means that when she goes out, the door is unlocked. When I place my hand on the knob, it easily turns.

I haven't been inside Whitney's bedroom since she moved in. I have confronted her a few times at the doorway to her room, but I've never been inside. It would've felt too intimate. So now I take a second to look around.

It doesn't look too bad. I don't know what I was expecting. Burning incense? Evidence of some sort of satanic ritual? *I hate Blake* scribbled in blood on the wall? But I don't see anything close to that. The room is neat, with the clothing carefully tucked away in drawers, and even her bed is made. She is a bed maker like me—I give her a little grudging respect for that one. But I find it irritating that she clearly hasn't emptied the wastepaper basket by her bed, and it's filled with crumpled sticky notes.

Out of curiosity, I nudge open her closet. It is painfully boring inside. She has a row of shirts and pants and dresses hung up with an extra pair of sneakers and a pair of pumps on the floor beneath them.

All right—enough snooping. I'm going to do what I came here to do.

I position myself so that I am standing over Whitney's bed. I take one last look into the plastic bag, and then I overturn it.

As the paper bag hits her bed, the bottom drops out of the bag as expected, and the contents spill out. Rotten fruit and maggots splatter all over her clean blanket.

There. Now we're even.

I've never done anything like that before. As I take the stairs back down to the kitchen, where I intend to clean until those flies are gone, I make plans to go out and get a beer to celebrate when I'm done. I love my home, and Whitney has turned it into a living hell. I've just dished a little back to her.

Except I'm pretty sure Whitney won't see it that way. As good as it felt getting a little bit of revenge, I have a feeling that I have just made a fatal error.

CHAPTER 23

Because I couldn't figure out a way out of it, tonight I'm having drinks with Malcolm at Cooper's.

It's been several days since I exploded the rotten fruit and maggots onto Whitney's bed. I'm embarrassed to admit I made sure the door to our bedroom was locked that night when I went to sleep. It seemed like there was a chance Whitney might sneak into our room and slit my throat while I was sleeping. Or throw the maggots into *our* bed, which would be almost as bad.

But strangely enough, Whitney made no move to kill me in my sleep. She didn't mention the episode at all, in fact. When I passed her in the hallway on my way to the bathroom, it was like it never happened, which I found incredibly strange. I'm on edge though. I don't know if she's planning anything.

I arrive at Cooper's ten minutes late. It's a small, dark dive bar with chunky wooden chairs and tables that are almost always sticky, even after being wiped down. Even though smoking isn't allowed in bars anymore in the city, the place smells like an ashtray. I suspect it's from the patrons and staff who slip out to smoke and then come back inside seconds after stubbing out their cigarettes on the ground. The floor is smudged with ash. Gwen, my last girlfriend before Krista, was a smoker, and the smell reminds me of her in an unsettling way. That relationship only lasted a few months, and it did *not* end well.

Malcolm isn't at the bar when I arrive, and I almost walk out. He's the one who bulldozed me into this meeting, and now he's even later than me? But Krista was so excited at the prospect of me and Becky's husband becoming friends—she'll be pissed if I return home without a report of how well the evening went. Given our recent fights, I need to be extra careful not to screw things up with her.

I find a table for two and sit down by myself. There are two girls in their midtwenties sitting at the bar, having what looks like a girls' night out, except their skirts are *really* short. I try not to look, but one of them catches my eye and flashes a suggestive smile. I quickly avert my eyes. Where the hell is Malcolm? I'm giving him five more minutes, then I'm gone.

Four minutes later, Malcolm bustles into Cooper's, a suit and tie on his broad frame, which almost makes me wish I'd kept my own work clothes on instead of changing into a more casual blue jeans and NYU T-shirt. He's got that familiar air of being both exhausted and wired. That's how I used to feel after a long day at Coble & Roy.

"Blake, my man!" he calls out.

As he approaches the table, he holds up his hand, and I start to fist-bump him, but it turns out he's looking for a high five, so I awkwardly convert my fist bump into a high five at the last second. I can't wait to get this over with.

Malcolm's chair scrapes against the floor as he pulls it out. "Did you order yet?"

I didn't. I'd been hoping I might get to leave. "Not yet."

Malcolm summons our waitress with a flick of his wrist. I order a Heineken, and he gets a scotch on the rocks, which I recall with a twinge of bitterness was Wayne's favorite drink.

"So how's the new job?" he asks me.

"Great."

"That's good," he says. "Good good good good good."

"Uh-huh."

"And…uh…" I clear my throat. "How are things at Coble & Roy?"

Maybe someday I'll be able to say it without choking on the words, but that day has not yet arrived.

He shrugs. "Oh, the usual. You know."

I want to ask him if Wayne ever talks about me, but I'm not sure if I want to know the answer to that question. Instead, I ask another question I don't want to know the answer to: "Who did they pick as the new VP? Was it Chad?"

"Chad Pickering?" Malcolm snorts. "Actually, it almost was. But then they caught him doing lines in the men's room."

My eyebrows shoot up. "Whoa. Are you serious?"

"I sure am."

I'm surprised but also not that surprised. Chad worked longer hours than anyone else at the company and never seemed tired—it was almost inhuman. But I've known guys who used coke, and I didn't get that vibe from him. He had a wife and kid, and he seemed pretty straitlaced. I guess you never know what the pressures of the job will do to you.

"So who ended up with the job then?" I ask.

"Actually," Malcolm says, "it's me."

"*What?*"

I say it so loudly that a guy two tables over wearing a hat with a penguin on it turns to gawk at me. The moment is saved when we are interrupted by the reappearance of the waitress, who lays our drinks on the table in front of us. I'm too stunned to even manage to say thanks. *Malcolm* is the new VP of marketing at Coble & Roy? He was barely even competent. Six months ago, he couldn't have even told you what search engine optimization was. What the hell?

I take a gulp of beer, trying to restrain myself from saying something I'll regret. "That's a…strange choice," I finally manage. I sound like a dick, but I don't even care. This is all kinds of wrong.

"I've been working really hard," he says defensively. "Wayne says I'm his right-hand man."

"*Wayne* said that?"

"Yes." His face turns pink. "Hey, at least I don't take drugs or steal from the company."

Now I feel my own face start to burn. "I didn't steal from the company. I'd *never* do that. That was bullshit, and you know it."

"Was it?" He arches an eyebrow. "You weren't exactly Mr. Nice Guy at Coble & Roy. Plenty of people had a lot of shit to say about you. I spent half my time defending you. Before he got busted, even Chad told me you stole his ideas and passed them off as your own."

I snatch the bottle of beer off the table and drain the rest of it in two large gulps. I slam it back down on the table and rise from my seat. "I'm leaving."

Malcolm's expression softens, as it often does when someone snaps at him. He's way too much of a wuss for this job—he'll get eaten alive in five seconds, and Wayne will be sorry he ever let me go. "Hey. Wait, I'm sorry. I didn't mean it like that."

"Yes, you did." I pull my wallet out of my pocket and toss a couple of bills on the table to cover my drink. "We're done here."

He scrambles to his feet, stepping in front of me. "But Becky and Krista wanted us to do this," he protests, confirming my suspicions.

"So we did it," I say. "I'll take a walk before I go home. You can tell Becky how great it went. How we're now best friends." I shrug. "Tell her whatever the hell you want, but I'm not sitting here another second."

I push past Malcolm, and I don't stop until I'm out of the bar. After his half-hearted attempt to stop me, Malcolm has apparently decided to stay to finish his drink. I still can't wrap my head around what he said to me. How could *Malcolm* have gotten my old job? He's grossly unqualified. He must have brainwashed Wayne.

Just before I walk away, I peer through the partially fogged window of the bar to make sure Malcolm hasn't decided to follow me. Or worse—tell Becky about how I stormed out, who will then rat me out to Krista. But he's not following me or talking to Becky on the phone. He's decided to join those two girls who smiled at me when I walked in. Well, I hope that asshole has a good time.

CHAPTER 24

"Blake! Blake!"

The sound of Krista's screams coming from downstairs jerks me awake. It takes a second to get my bearings. It's a Saturday, I'm home in my bed, and Krista is not lying beside me. And it's... Crap, it's only seven in the morning.

"*Blake!*"

She sounds outright hysterical, and my stomach sinks. What is it this time? I'm afraid to find out.

It's been a little over a week since the maggot episode. There still hasn't been one word from Whitney about what I did. I'm actually starting to wonder if I imagined the whole thing. The idea of a paper bag full of rotting fruit stuffed intentionally in my cabinet does seem pretty out there. Could it have been some kind of lucid dream?

But no. You don't imagine a paper bag full of maggots.

Plus, the fruit fly situation is substantially better. We set up a bunch of new cups that have caught, like, 90 percent of the flies. Between that and smashing them with my hand, the infestation has been downgraded to a mild annoyance.

"Blake!"

I rub my eyes, struggling to sit up in bed. "Coming!" I call back.

I throw my legs over the side of the bed. I toss on a T-shirt, but I don't bother to change out of my boxers. I'm not dressing up for Whitney. She can deal with looking at me in my underwear.

I get halfway down the steps before I see Krista, standing in the living room. Her face is bright red, and when I get a little closer, I can see that her cheeks are streaked with tears. She's sobbing.

Oh no. What happened?

"It's Goldy!" she wails. "Goldy is dead!"

I sprint down the rest of the steps in my bare feet. When I get to the fishbowl, sure enough, Goldy is belly-up in the water. I've never seen a dead fish before, aside from at the market, but I have no trouble recognizing that she's gone to a better place.

"I'm so sorry." I put my arm around Krista's shoulders, holding her close to me. "It's…very sad."

Oddly, it *is* sort of sad. Despite the fact that we didn't have a whole lot of hands-on interaction with Goldy, I'd gotten used to her presence. And I've been talking to her a little more than is healthy. I know she was just a fish, but she had personality. A little bit of personality at least. For a fish.

Krista is really shaken by it though. She is clinging to me, sobbing into my T-shirt. I give her a level ten hug as her tears stain my shirt. After a few minutes, she looks up at me with eyes that are bloodshot and puffy.

"I know it's weird to be so upset over a fish," she says, "but I just got attached. And she was our first pet as a couple, you know? It feels like...like her death is a *sign*."

"It's not a sign." I need to nip this line of thinking in the bud ASAP. "They even told us in the pet store that these goldfish usually don't live very long."

"But she seemed so healthy," she sniffles. "I don't understand it. I fed her yesterday, and she looked completely fine! She gobbled the pellets right up!"

"Huh," I say.

She wipes her wet face with the back of her hand. "You changed her water last weekend when I asked you to, right?"

"Of course I did."

"But you didn't change all the water, right? Only twenty percent, right?"

"Yes. That's what I did." More or less.

"And you put in the tablet to get rid of the chlorine, right?"

"Absolutely."

As Krista is quizzing me about what I did when I changed the water last week, I can't help but feel a little bit of relief that I don't have to do this anymore. Changing the fish's water was such a pain in the neck. Although I have a bad feeling that we will probably be making a trip to the pet store soon to get another fish. Maybe I can talk her out of it though. At least until things settle down.

I'll have to do some research on what animals are easiest to take care of. A lizard would be cool.

"We...we have to bury her," Krista says.

"We do? You mean, we can't just...flush her?"

Krista flashes me a horrified look. Maybe that *was* a bit

callous. I feel a little tug in my chest as I look at Goldy's tiny inert body.

"Sorry," I say quickly. "Of course we can bury her. We can have a funeral and everything."

That seems to placate her somewhat. Great. Now I'm committed to a funeral for a goldfish. I can't believe this will be how I spend my Saturday morning.

"I'll go get a Ziploc bag to store her," Krista says. "Can you fish her out of the bowl?"

"Sure."

I feel mildly disgusted at the idea of handling a dead fish, but I guess it's not technically that different from when I'm eating sashimi. That's what I tell myself anyway.

As I am leaning over the fish tank with the tiny net, I catch a whiff of the water inside. And that's when I smell it. At first, I'm certain I must be imagining the smell. But no. There's a very distinct odor coming from the fishbowl.

It's bleach.

Krista comes back into the living room, carrying a little baggie about big enough to fit Goldy inside. Her eyes are still very puffy, and I almost wonder if it would be cruel to tell her that her fish didn't die of natural causes. But she needs to know the truth. She needs to know what we're dealing with here, because she doesn't seem to be taking it seriously.

"Krista," I say slowly. "Someone put bleach in the fishbowl."

Her eyes fly open. "*What?*"

"I smell it." Now that I noticed the odor, it seems to fill the entire room. I can't believe I didn't detect it sooner. "It's a very distinctive smell."

Krista dashes over to the fishbowl. She sticks her nose closer than I would be willing to while there's a dead fish inside. She lifts her face. "I don't smell anything."

"Seriously?" I'd be able to smell it from down the hallway. "It's definitely bleach, Krista."

She sniffs the bowl again. "I don't know. I'm not even entirely sure what bleach smells like."

"It's a chemical smell! It's bleach!"

I don't even realize how loud I am until she takes a step back. "Okay, so why would there be bleach in the fishbowl?"

I've been wondering the same thing. "Whitney must have put it in there."

"Whitney?" Her eyes bulge out. "Why on earth would *Whitney* do that?"

"Because she's a psychopath," I reply, because it's *obvious*. "I know we need the money, but I think we should get her out of here. I mean it."

Krista frowns. "Then how are we supposed to pay the mortgage?"

At this point, I'd almost rather get kicked out than live here with Whitney. I don't trust her. If she's willing to poison a goldfish, who knows what else she's capable of? "Do you really want someone living with us who would poison a defenseless goldfish?"

"I really don't smell anything…"

"Trust me, Krista."

She gives me a skeptical look. It's frustrating. How does she not smell that chemical odor? Is she *hard of smelling*?

"We need to get rid of Whitney," I say more forcefully. "We'll find someone else."

"Everyone else was horrible," she reminds me. "I like

Whitney. She's been nothing but sweet the entire time she's lived here."

"Yeah, to *you*."

She gives me the same look she did when that Quillizabeth woman claimed she had a vision of me stabbing her to death. "Blake, is there any chance that you're…"

"That I'm what?"

And now she averts her eyes. "That you're *imagining* some of the things that you say Whitney is doing?"

"That's ridiculous." Although I don't admit that her accusation leaves me with an uneasy feeling. "I'm not imagining anything. Whitney despises me."

"She never said anything about not liking you when we had lunch together."

I feel like I just got socked in the gut. "You had *lunch* together?"

"Why not?" Krista puts her hands on her hips. "She's not the enemy, Blake. She lives with us."

"She *is* the enemy," I shoot back, although when I hear the words leave my lips, I notice I do sound a little hysterical. The water sloshes in Goldy's bowl. I clear my throat. "And she probably did this to get back at me."

"Why would she want to get back at you? Back at you for what?"

"For what I did to her bed."

Krista inhales sharply. "What did you do to her bed?"

Crap. I shouldn't have said that. I wasn't thinking.

"What did you do, Blake?" She narrows her eyes at me. "Tell me the truth."

I squirm. When I threw that mess into Whitney's bed, I was extremely pissed off. In retrospect, I'm embarrassed that I did it. But it's *her* fault. She's the one who hid rotting fruit in our kitchen. *She's* the evil one.

"You remember how we had all those fruit flies?" I begin. "Well, it turns out Whitney stuck a couple of pieces of fruit on the top shelf in the cabinets, and they'd been rotting there the whole time she's lived here. It was growing maggots." I cringe at the memory. "So…I just gave it back to her."

"Gave it back to her? What does that mean?"

"I left the fruit in her bed."

"Oh my God." Krista starts pacing across the living room. "You seriously put fruit that was growing maggots in Whitney's bed? What on earth is wrong with you? Have you lost your *mind*?"

"She's the one who left it in the kitchen—"

"How do you know that?" she bursts out. "You're the one who is always eating apples. Maybe *you* left it up there!"

"I think I would remember putting a bunch of apples in a paper bag and stuffing it on the top shelf where I can't even reach it without a stool!"

Krista shakes her head. "Were you using that awful stool that's in the hall closet that you won't get rid of? You're going to really hurt yourself one day when it breaks."

"You're missing the point," I snap at her. "Look, I know it was Whitney who left the fruit there. And now she's getting back at me by pouring bleach in the fishbowl."

"How would that get back at *you*?" she shoots back. "*I'm* the one who loved Goldy! You don't even care about her at all! You were about to flush her down the toilet!"

I *liked* Goldy—*love* is a strong word for a fish. But yes, if she gave me the option now, I would definitely flush the fish down the toilet and avoid this ridiculous funeral. But I have to play the part of the sensitive fiancé right now. Because it's becoming increasingly obvious that I am in danger of losing Krista if I don't try to fix things. She's acting like I've become unhinged lately, and that's not true. Given that I lost my job and I've been sleeping like shit (in no small part thanks to yet another thumping episode), I think I'm holding up pretty damn well.

I take a few deep breaths to get my emotions under control. Shouting back at Krista is only going to make things worse.

"Krista," I say softly. "I'm sorry. I did care about Goldy. I mean, I do care. And I really want to do this funeral. She was a good fish."

"She *was* a good fish," Krista sniffles.

She doesn't say anything else about the bleach, which makes me think she doesn't believe that is what killed the fish. Strangely enough, when I smell the bowl again, it doesn't smell quite as strongly. But I'm not imagining it.

Whitney killed our fish. I've never been so sure of anything in my life.

And I have a bad feeling this is just the beginning.

CHAPTER 25

We have a small backyard, which isn't so much of a backyard as a little patch of dirt and grass behind our house, although that's a haven in Manhattan where *nobody* has outdoor space. I had imagined Krista and I might eventually set up a small table and chairs to dine outdoors in the fall, although we haven't gotten around to it yet. Instead, the first use of our backyard will be to serve as Goldy's final resting place.

I fished Goldy out of the bowl, stuck her in the baggie, and then went upstairs to change into actual clothing, because apparently an undershirt and boxer shorts are not "appropriate attire" for a goldfish funeral. I contemplate putting on a pair of jeans, but the last thing I want is for Krista to get upset that I'm not taking this seriously, so I put on some nice khaki slacks and a dress shirt. I draw the line at putting on a tie for a fish funeral. On the plus side, the itchy rash seems to have disappeared since Krista started doing my laundry.

When I return to the living room, Whitney has come home from a half shift at the diner. My heart sinks at the sight of her and Krista talking quietly while Krista wipes her eyes. I wonder what Whitney is saying about me—definitely nothing good. I especially don't like it when she seems to be pointing emphatically in my direction. I can only imagine what they'll talk about during their next *lunch* together. But then Krista waves up at me, and she doesn't seem angry, only sad.

"Whitney wants to join us for Goldy's funeral," she tells me.

I didn't think there was anything that could have made this funeral less appealing, but there it is. "Wonderful," I say.

Whitney's mild brown eyes stare back at me. "It's so sad about Goldy. She really felt like part of the family."

"She really did," Krista agrees.

I glare at Whitney. *You killed our fish, you bitch.*

Whitney turns her head in the direction of the fishbowl. "Let me store that somewhere for you. It must be hard to look at it now that it's empty."

"Yes," Krista says. "You're right. Thank you so much."

I don't want Whitney to get rid of the bowl and the water inside it. I want to prove that there is bleach inside—there must be a way to test for it. But if Whitney gets rid of the evidence, Krista will never believe me.

So before Whitney can get to the bowl, I touch Krista's arm. "Maybe we shouldn't. We don't want to just throw away Goldy's memory, right? We should, you know, preserve it as long as possible."

Krista looks at me like I have lost my mind. "It's dirty fish water. I think we can pour it out."

I start to protest again, but Whitney has already grabbed the fishbowl, and all I can do is watch her disappear with it to the kitchen. There's the sound of splashing water, and any evidence that our fish was poisoned has literally gone down the drain.

Whitney emerges from the kitchen empty-handed. I don't know where she put the fishbowl, but she looks awfully proud of herself. She winks at me so quickly, I'm sure Krista misses it.

The three of us head out to the small backyard for the goldfish funeral. Krista located a large rock to serve as the gravestone, and I grabbed one of the large metal spoons from the kitchen to dig the grave.

"How deep should I make this?" I ask.

"Well," Krista says thoughtfully, "for a person who is about six feet tall, you're supposed to make the grave six feet deep. So for a fish that is about two inches long... I don't know? Just a few inches, I guess."

That's great, because I'm not excited to dig through dirt with a spoon.

After I've dug out a few inches of dirt, Krista tenderly lays Goldy inside. She kisses her fingers, then lays them on the plastic-encased fish. I then use the spoon to cover Goldy's body with dirt, and Krista places the rock on top. As Krista is tearfully kneeling beside the fish grave, I look over at Whitney, who is smirking. I want to reach out and strangle her.

"We should say a few words about Goldy," Whitney speaks up.

Krista gets back to her feet, wiping her eyes. "That would actually be really nice."

"Blake," Whitney says, "would you like to begin?"

I really, really hate her. But I can't screw this up. If I want Krista to continue to see me as husband material, I have to be able to step up in times of tragedy.

"As we gather here today, we would like to say goodbye to Goldy." I bow my head. "We got her at the pet store and…she was the fastest of all the goldfish. She liked to eat little pellets, and she liked to swim in circles and…" I sneak a look at Krista, who is looking at me expectantly. "And she was a good fish."

Was that enough? I can't tell. Krista seems a bit disappointed. But I mean, come *on*. How much can you possibly say about an animal that's been inside a bowl for the entire time we've had her?

"I'll miss Goldy," Whitney says. "Whenever I was in the living room, it felt like Goldy was keeping me company. There were times when it felt like she was smiling at me. When I got home from work, no matter how tired I was, there she was, entertaining me by swimming around. And on the nights I couldn't sleep, she was with me. Even though she's gone, it still feels like her spirit is here. With us." She takes a shaky breath. "And we will certainly never, ever forget her."

Krista's eyes well with tears. "That was so beautiful, Whitney. I agree—it does feel like her spirit is here."

Is she kidding me? We will never, ever forget her? I liked Goldy and all, but she was a *fish*. I'm furious with Whitney for upstaging me. Especially since she is the one who killed her. Krista might not believe it, but I know it's true.

"I really needed to hear something like that," Krista goes on, looking at Whitney. "Thank you so much for those kind words about Goldy. You're such a good friend.

I know this all might seem a bit silly…" She looks pointedly in my direction. "But it really does help."

Whitney holds out her hand, and Krista takes it. A vein throbs in my temple—a dull headache is coming on. The headache only escalates when Krista starts crying again, and instead of reaching for me, she turns to *Whitney*, who puts her arms around her. I can't take it anymore. I just can't.

"All right, enough of this horseshit," I blurt out. "I know you were the one who killed Goldy, Whitney."

Whitney and Krista simultaneously swivel their heads to look at me. Amusement flickers in Whitney's eyes, but Krista is furious.

"Blake!" she snaps at me. "What is *wrong* with you?"

"It's true though," I shoot back. "She murdered Goldy, and now she's pretending to be sad about it. Look at her. She's obviously faking it!"

Krista turns to look at Whitney, who is now miraculously tearing up like she's actually sad about that stupid goldfish. Give me a break.

"Blake is just upset over Goldy's death," Whitney says gently. "He doesn't know what he's saying."

"He's not upset!" Krista cries. "He wanted to flush her down the toilet!"

"Blake!" Whitney gasps. "How could you?"

Again, there's that laughter in Whitney's eyes. She's enjoying this. She loves that Krista believes her over me.

This is exactly what she wanted to happen. I played right into her hands.

"Fine, yes, I wanted to flush the fish down the toilet." As the words leave my mouth, I wince at the expression on my girlfriend's face. "But I didn't hurt Goldy! At least I'm not some psychopath who poisoned our fish with *bleach*! Stop being so naive, Krista!"

Krista seems traumatized by my comments, while Whitney is clearly suppressing laughter. How does Krista not see this?

Krista flashes me a hurt look. "I...I need to be alone right now. I'm going to go out for a walk."

We were supposed to see a movie this afternoon, but I'm going to assume that's off the table since we're in mourning. Whitney and Krista return to the house together, while I am left behind in the newly christened goldfish graveyard. But just as they are disappearing into the house, Whitney turns to look at me, and the smile on her face makes me want to do to her what she did to my fish. I wish I could bury her in the ground.

CHAPTER 26

It's been a week since Goldy died.

For a couple of days after the funeral, things were tense between me and Krista. She refused to believe that Whitney could be behind the goldfish's untimely death. And whenever I brought it up, she didn't want to talk about it.

But she's been cooling off. Last night, while Whitney was working a late shift, we watched a movie on TV and were laughing together, and when it was over, she even decided to make a batch of chocolate chip cookies—something she hasn't done in weeks. And because Whitney was out, we had sex right on the couch—something we haven't done in *months*. So maybe we're good.

Tonight is Saturday night, and when Krista gets home from work, I'm taking her out to dinner at a fancy restaurant, which I haven't done since I lost my VP job. She's going to put on a nice dress, and I'll put on my nicest cologne or some shit like that. I'll turn up the charm and win her over like I did in the first place.

If I don't, she'll be gone. And I really don't want that.

After lunch, I went for a run through Central Park, which I haven't done in a few weeks. I pushed myself till my legs ached and my T-shirt was soaked in sweat despite the forty-degree weather, and then I ran home and took a cold shower. I'll pay for it tomorrow, but when it was over, I felt *good*.

While I'm waiting for Krista to get home from the dry cleaner, I flip on the television and grab a few of Krista's cookies to snack on. The adrenaline from the run has worn off, and I doze off for a bit. I don't wake up until I hear Krista's keys in the front door. I scramble to my feet, brushing cookie crumbs off the dress shirt I changed into specially for our date.

Perfect fiancé. You can do this.

Krista enters the brownstone, her strawberry-blond hair pinned on top of her head, smelling vaguely of dry-cleaning chemicals. She looks great though. The smile that spreads across her face when she sees me makes me realize that we are going to be okay as a couple. Whitney will not rip us apart.

"You don't have to stand on my account," Krista teases me.

"Of course I do." I cross the room to take her warm body into my arms. "I missed you."

She giggles. "I haven't been gone very long."

"Yet I still missed you."

She tilts her head to smile up at me. I love it when she looks up at me like that. "I'm sorry I was late. You got my text?"

I didn't. Usually, my phone dinging with a text message wakes me when I have drifted off. I pat my pockets, feeling for my phone, and it's not there. I glance over at the coffee table, where I often leave it when I'm watching television, but it's not there either.

"Shit." I dig deeper in my pockets. "Where's my phone?"

"In the bedroom?"

"Probably." Except I'm sure I had it downstairs. I remember checking the reviews of a few restaurants for tonight. "Let me go check. But after I find it, we're going out to dinner."

Her eyes light up. "I was hoping you would say that. Anywhere special?"

I grin at her. "Make sure you dress up."

She loves to dress up. Krista and I are going to be okay. That fish ordeal was just a blip.

I go upstairs to look for my phone, and Krista follows me to change into something nice (and hopefully sheer and sexy) for dinner. When I reach the bedroom, my phone isn't readily visible. I usually keep it on the nightstand, which is where I keep my charger, but it's not there. It's not on my dresser either. I even yank the blankets off the bed, searching the sheets, but there's no sign of my phone.

"What the hell?" I mutter. "Where did it go?"

Krista whips out her own phone. "Do you want me to call it?"

"Yeah, you better."

I'm the first listed contact on Krista's phone. She hits the button to dial my number, and after a second, I hear ringing. At least my phone is definitely in the house.

But the ringing is distant. Is it coming from downstairs? Maybe I left it in the kitchen, which would make sense since I'm certain I used it downstairs.

Except when I get out of the bedroom, following the

sound of my ringtone, it's clear the sound is not coming from downstairs. I raise my eyes to look skyward.

It's coming from upstairs. The third floor.

CHAPTER 27

The ringing continues for another second before the phone goes to voicemail. But it's obvious to both of us where the sound was coming from.

Krista stares at me. "Why is your phone *upstairs*?"

"I...I don't know."

I stride down the hallway and up the narrow flight of stairs to get to the third floor. The light isn't on under Whitney's door, which means she's out, although I'm certain she was still here when I went downstairs earlier. I grab the doorknob.

"We shouldn't go in there without her permission," Krista says anxiously.

"Screw that," I say. "What's my phone doing in there?"

Before Krista can protest again, I turn the knob and shove the door open hard enough that the door slams against the wall. The room looks about the same as it did last time I was here, when I impulsively threw the rotting fruit onto her bed. The only difference is that this time, the bed isn't made.

I look around the room. The ringtone has stopped.

"Maybe we were wrong," Krista says. She's clearly not thrilled about invading Whitney's space while she is out, but I couldn't care less. "Maybe you left it in the bathroom. That makes more sense."

"Call my number again," I instruct her.

Obediently, Krista selects my number from her phone again. The ringing starts up again, and this time the source is clear. I pull back the crumpled covers on Whitney's bed, and there is my phone, nestled in the sheets.

I scoop up the phone. There are two missed calls from Krista and a text letting me know she's going to be late. But none of this explains how my phone got in here in the first place.

"Blake?" Krista's confused voice is coming from behind me. "What's this?"

I whirl around—what now? For a moment, I actually hope it's something terrible like a wall of pictures of me with my eyes cut out so that Krista will see Whitney like I do. But all she's got in her hand is a small white tube. I don't even know what it is until she takes off the cap.

It's lipstick.

"It's the same shade as on your shirt collar," Krista says in a shaky voice.

"What?" I say flippantly. "No, it's not."

Except that's a lie. It is exactly the same shade. It's the same lipstick Whitney was putting on the other day, right before I found the rotting fruit in the kitchen.

"Is this why you have been acting so weird about Whitney?" Krista's voice is dripping with hurt. "Are you sleeping with her?"

"No!" I cry. "That's *insane*! I *hate* Whitney!"

Her lower lip trembles. "Then why was her lipstick on your shirt collar? Why is your cell phone in her *bed*?"

"She's setting me up!" I throw up my hands. "Can't you see it? She's doing all these things to make you think I'm cheating on you. But I'm not."

"Why would she want me to think you're cheating on me?"

Damned if I know. I wish I did. I wish I knew why Whitney decided to target me. Because if I knew the reason, I'd make her stop.

"Krista," I say. "I love you. I want you to be my wife. I would never, *ever* cheat on you. I swear."

Krista looks between the phone I'm clutching in my right hand and the lipstick in her left. "I...I don't know what to think."

"Please." I am about five seconds away from getting down on my knees and begging. "You've got to believe me. You *know* me, Krista. I wouldn't do something like that."

She lowers the lipstick back onto the top of the dresser. She chews on her thumbnail, a troubled expression on her face. "It's not just about this. You've been acting weird for months, Blake."

"No, I haven't."

She arches an eyebrow.

"Okay," I concede. "It's been a rough few months for me after losing my job and all. But I'm coming out the other end. I swear."

She plays with a loose strand of her silky hair that has come undone from her bun. "I don't know. I...I think it might be a good idea if we took a little time apart."

No. *No*. She can't mean that.

But she means it. I follow her numbly as she goes back downstairs to the second floor and returns to our bedroom, then I watch in horror as she pulls her suitcase out of the closet.

"Krista, no," I plead with her.

I can't lose Krista. I *can't*. She's the only good thing left in my life.

But now it looks like that's going to happen. In a moment, Krista is back in our room, taking clothes out of her drawers, piling them into a suitcase. I want to yank the luggage away from her before she can fill it up.

"Don't do this." My voice cracks on the words. "Please, Krista."

"I just need a couple of days." She toys with her engagement ring, which is still on her left ring finger. If she takes it off, it will kill me. "I'll stay with Becky and Malcolm."

Great. She is staying with Becky, who hates me, and Malcolm, who isn't a fan either after our failed attempt at drinks. I'm sure the two of them will spend the whole time trash-talking me.

But fine. If she needs a few days away, let her have it. Maybe it will be a good thing to have some time apart. And if I get a little time alone with Whitney, she can fess up about what is bothering her so much about me, and we can work things out.

This will be fine. I always land on my feet, one way or another.

I still can't figure out how Whitney got my phone. She must've swiped it off the table while I was napping. I can't even close my eyes for a second around that woman.

"Blake, what's this?" Krista says.

What now?

Krista is crouched in the closet, presumably figuring out which of her five billion pairs of shoes she wants to take with her. Except she's not packing anymore—she's peering at something in the closet. I have no idea what.

"What is it?" I ask.

Krista straightens up, holding a small white jug. It takes me a second to realize what I'm looking at.

"Bleach?" I'm too shocked to say anything else.

"What's this doing in our closet?"

"I have no idea."

"No idea?" she repeats. "You were the one going on and on about how you thought Goldy died because somebody poured bleach into the fishbowl. And then I find *this* in the closet?"

"Wait." I blink at her. "You think *I* killed Goldy? Are you kidding me? You didn't even think that the bowl smelled like bleach!"

She falters for a moment. "I wasn't sure. I didn't think Whitney would have done that. But...well, it *did* smell a little like bleach." She looks at me accusingly. "Did you kill Goldy to frame Whitney?"

"No! Christ, of course not. You can't possibly think..."

"I don't know *what* to think anymore." She drops the jug of bleach onto our dresser, and it lands with a loud thump. "You've been acting so strangely lately. And now I find your phone in Whitney's bed. And this bleach *in your closet* when you've been going on and on about how you think Whitney poisoned the fish with it."

"Jesus Christ, do you really think I would poison our fish?"

"I don't know. Maybe." She lowers her eyes. "Honestly,

I wouldn't put anything past you at this point. After all, you stole from your own company."

There's a sharp pang in my chest. I can't believe she just said that to me. When all that shit went down at Coble & Roy, there was not a single moment when Krista didn't support me wholeheartedly. What made her turn around like this?

Was it something Whitney said to her?

"I didn't steal from my company!" The volume of my voice is much too loud, but I can't seem to control it. "How could you think that?"

"I feel like I hardly know you lately." She frowns up at me. "You're constantly ranting about ridiculous conspiracy theories involving our tenant. You wander the house at night instead of sleeping. When you do pass out, you talk in your sleep—"

"I talk in my sleep?" That revelation shocks me. "What...what do I say?"

"Gibberish mostly." She shakes her head. "Sometimes you say Whitney's name, which is super weird."

Wow. That's...unsettling.

"I'm beginning to think that psychic woman was right," she says. "If I stay long enough, God knows what you'll do."

"Krista, *no*." I'm starting to panic now. She's really leaving, possibly for good. "I would never cheat on you, and I would never hurt you."

Krista zips up the suitcase, even though it's only half full. She didn't even bring any of her shoes—she's that eager to get the hell out of here. "I think I better go."

"Krista." I step in front of the door, blocking her path. "You've got to believe me. Whitney is setting me up for all this. She's been making weird noises all night to keep me from sleeping. She put the rotting fruit in the cabinet. And she's the one who poisoned Goldy, then put the bleach in the closet to frame me."

"Blake, are you listening to yourself?"

Her eyes meet mine. She doesn't believe a word I'm saying. She thinks I've lost my mind—or worse.

"I'm leaving," she says. "Like I said, I need a few days to clear my head."

I don't want her to leave. For a split second, a thought occurs to me: I'm a lot bigger and stronger than Krista. And it's not like she has a weapon. She might not want to stay, but I could *make* her stay. Make her *see*.

"Blake," she says, and there's a sudden flicker of fear in her eyes.

I quickly step out of her way, horrified by my own thoughts. What am I *doing*? I would *never* force a woman to stay with me. How could that idea have even crossed my mind? I'm not that guy. My mother taught me to *respect* women.

What has Whitney done to me?

But I do follow Krista downstairs. I watch her grab her jacket and slip her feet into her sneakers. She's really leaving. And I have no idea when she's coming back. If ever.

"I love you, Krista," I say. My voice cracks on the words.

She turns to look at me, and the expression on her face almost breaks me. She doesn't seem angry. She just looks miserable.

"I'm sorry." Her voice quakes. "This wasn't what I wanted to happen."

Even though I know I shouldn't, I follow her out the

front door. I don't know what I'm expecting exactly. Yet I can't seem to stop.

"Krista," I say again. "Can we talk about this more? Please?"

She doesn't answer me at all this time. Instead, she sticks out her right hand to hail a taxi.

In the best of times, it takes several minutes to find a cab in our neighborhood, and we usually have to wait for an Uber. So naturally, a second later, a yellow taxi skids to a halt in front of the brownstone, splashing me with the contents of a puddle while leaving Krista relatively dry. She doesn't waste a second before climbing inside.

"Krista!" I shout.

She doesn't even turn to watch me through the window.

The cab zips away a second later, before I even have a chance to say goodbye. I watch it vanish into the distance, wondering if this will be the last time I ever see Krista. The next time she returns to the brownstone, it'll be at a time she knows I'm at work so she can take the rest of her belongings without me bothering her.

No, I won't let that happen. I'm getting Krista back.

No matter what it takes.

"Porter!"

The crackly old voice from behind me sets all my nerves on edge. Not this. Not now. I turn around, my hands already balled into fists. I'm not in the mood for Mr. Zimmerly.

"How many times am I going to need to tell you to take in your trash cans?" Mr. Zimmerly barks at me.

As he says the words, a few flecks of his spittle hit me in the face.

"I'm sorry," I mumble. "It's been a rough day, so I didn't get to it."

"It's been *two days*," he points out.

Has it? Damn.

"Trash day was *yesterday*. You left your cans out here for two days." He hawks up some gross-sounding phlegm. "You think the street is your own personal garbage can, Porter?"

"I'll take them in now," I say through my teeth.

"Oh great," he mutters. "You take 'em in a day late and only when I tell you to. How come you're the only one on the block who can't seem to get it right? Guess they didn't teach you how to tell time at that fancy college you went to, huh?"

You know what? I have had enough of Mr. H. Zimmerly. I've been dealing with him practically every week since I moved here. And now? I'm done.

Done.

"You want me to get my trash cans off the curb?" I pick up one of the metal cans. "Well, here you go!"

With those words, I hurl the can at Mr. Zimmerly as hard as I can. He's got to be close to ninety years old, and it probably would have killed him, but the can misses him by a mile and rolls onto the street beside him. His rheumy eyes widen.

"What the hell is wrong with you, you lunatic!" he shouts at me. "You could have killed me!"

I pick up the trash can where it rolled. "Maybe I should try again then?"

Zimmerly gets the message this time. He scurries back into the house, his slippers scuffing against the ground. He's moving so quickly that he nearly stumbles on that broken step I offered to fix. At his age, a fall down those stairs would be bad news.

A few people heard the commotion and mill about uncomfortably. A bunch of damn busybodies in this neighborhood. Maybe it'd be better to get the hell out of here.

I wave to my nosy neighbors and stomp back inside the house. I wasn't trying to hit Mr. Zimmerly with that garbage can—I missed on purpose. I didn't want to hurt him. I haven't completely lost my mind.

But I can't say the same about what I would do if Whitney were in front of me.

CHAPTER 28

I end up taking a long walk around the neighborhood.

Usually, I'm one of those New Yorkers who always have a destination in mind, my eyes carefully avoiding eye contact with passersby as I walk briskly to wherever I need to be. But today, I have no destination. I walk aimlessly as the sun drops in the sky and the drizzle turns into a rain shower.

And even then, I keep walking. I don't have a jacket, although it's decidedly chilly. My legs are aching from my run earlier, but I don't give a shit.

The whole time, all I can think about is Krista, about how I screwed everything up, and I don't know how I did it. I didn't leave my phone in Whitney's bedroom. That bleach in the closet wasn't mine. I would never do that to Goldy and especially to Krista.

Whitney wanted Krista and me to break up. That was her goal from the beginning.

Except I'm worried that isn't her only goal.

This is just the beginning.

I walk for about two hours. I get back home after eight o'clock, my shirt damp, my legs on fire, my hair plastered to my scalp. It's good though. I want to feel something besides the sharp pain in my gut whenever I think of Krista.

There's a light on upstairs, and for a moment, I feel a flash of hope. Did Krista come back? Did she have a change of heart?

But no. It's Whitney's sneakers by the front door. Whitney is the one upstairs.

As I stare up at the second floor of my house, my stomach lets out a low growl. I hadn't even realized until now how hungry I was. I had intended to take Krista out to dinner tonight, but that's not going to happen. I may as well scavenge the refrigerator for food. At least all the fruit flies are gone.

I throw open the fridge, spotting the Chinese takeout container from last night. Krista and I had finished off the beef with broccoli, but we still have one container of lo mein left. I may as well eat it before it goes bad.

And there's beer. Plenty of it.

I don't bother to heat up the noodles—I prefer them cold, right out of the takeout container. I twist off the cap of the beer, drink about half of it in one swig, then bring the takeout container and the beer back to the living room.

If I'm not going out with Krista tonight, I may as well get drunk.

I flip on the television to a random reality show and settle back on the sofa with my lo mein noodles. I pry the container open, inhaling the scent of day-old Chinese food. I dig my fork into the noodles, spinning it twice. I shove a forkful into my mouth, hoping it will ease the ache in my belly. I start chewing and then…

Suddenly, I'm gagging. I'm practically *choking*.

You know that feeling when you eat something that you realize has a strand of hair in it? The way it winds itself into knots at the back of your throat? You know how gross that is?

Well, at this moment, it feels like I have a mouth *full* of hair. It feels like I'm eating *hair*…wound around a noodle or two. And the hairs seem to be growing longer in my mouth.

I drop the container onto the sofa beside me as I gag again, spitting the food into my hand. My stomach turns as I peer down at what I spit out. And sure enough, I see it. Except it's not just one.

I snatch the container off the sofa where I dropped it and squint inside. I hadn't looked closely in the takeout container before I started eating—why would I?—but now I can see that it is threaded with long, brown hairs. There are almost as many hairs as lo mein. Maybe more.

There is hair in my food. *Plural.*

Oh Christ. I think I'm going to throw up.

I run to the kitchen sink, coughing. In between desperate gasps of air, I end up pulling five intact strands out of my throat, and it still feels like there's more in there, threatening to strangle me. I gag and feel around until my fingers locate one strand that had already made its way partially down my throat, and it scratches against my voice box as I extract a hair about as long as a ruler. Nothing ends up coming up though. Thankfully, I hadn't swallowed anything, or else I really would be sick. But there is *hair* in my food. And by the appearance of it, I'm pretty sure who it belongs to.

A surge of rage like nothing I have ever experienced builds in my chest. I run the water in the sink, gulping down a handful of water. My head is buzzing. If Whitney were standing here, I would grab one of the knives from the knife block and I'd...

No. Stop it. Get ahold of yourself, Blake.

I take deep breaths, but I can't calm myself down. Whitney has infested my home with fruit flies, given me a horrible rash, killed my fish, and wrecked my relationship with the only woman I've ever loved. And for *what*? I can't take one more second of this.

This is it. It's over. She's *done*.

I storm up the two flights of stairs, my anger mounting with each step. When I get to the third floor, I spot the light on under Whitney's door. I am very, very glad she is home.

I slam the palm of my hand against her door. Repeatedly. And each time, the sound gets louder.

It takes a good minute of me pounding on Whitney's door before she leisurely pulls it open. She looks like she's in for the night, dressed in one of her tank tops with the pajama shorts, her brown hair pulled into pigtails on either side of her head. Her shirt is almost see-through, and for a quick moment, that stops me in my tracks. But then I remember how I want to wrap my fingers around her neck until she's dead.

It takes all my self-restraint to keep from doing it.

"I want you out," I hiss at her.

"Good evening to you too, Blake." Her lips twitch. "Where's *Krista* tonight?

My hands ball into fists. "I want you out *now*."

She blinks at me. "Excuse me?"

"You heard me. You need to get the hell out of my house right now."

"It's the middle of the night," she points out. "You can't possibly expect me to pack up my things and go right this minute."

"I don't care what time it is," I spit in her face. "This is *my* home, and I want you *gone*. I've had enough. *Enough.* You hear me?"

Her eyes harden. "Well, that's too damn bad, Blake. You can't just throw me out in the middle of the night without any notice because you feel like it. I *live* here. I have rights."

"Yeah, well…" I glare at her with such venom that it's hard not to imagine her skin sizzling off her bones. I speak slowly. Deliberately. "You might want to leave for the sake of your own safety."

She arches an eyebrow. "Yeah? What are you going to do?"

Is she kidding? I've got at least half a foot of height on her and a hell of a lot more muscle. I could do a *lot*. I could *wreck* her.

I imagine my fist making contact with Whitney's smug face. I imagine my fingers wrapping around her skinny little neck and squeezing until her lips turn blue. It would feel so good.

I take a threatening step toward her, my hands still clenched into tight fists. But Whitney doesn't flinch.

She's called my bluff. As angry as I am, I won't hurt her. I've never laid a finger on a woman in my life, and I'm not going to break that rule for Whitney. Even if I wanted to, I don't have it in me.

I grit my teeth. "Consider this your thirty-day notice."

If she doesn't leave, I am going to take all her crap and dump it on the sidewalk in front of the building. I don't care if she sues me. I'm flat broke anyway.

"Oh, don't worry," Whitney says with a laugh, "I'll be gone long before then."

And then she slams the door in my face. I hear a click as she locks it.

Her words should be reassuring. After all, I *want* her gone. Yet something about the way she says it makes me very uneasy.

It feels like a threat.

CHAPTER 29

As I'm walking home from the train station after a day of work, my phone buzzes in my pocket.

It's been a week since Krista moved out. In the days after she left, I sent her roughly a billion text messages and voicemails. She sent me one single text, asking me to give her some space, and I then proceeded to send her another billion text messages and voicemails. I'm having a lot of trouble playing it cool. I just want her back.

Every time my phone rings, I'm hoping it's her. So I can't say I'm not disappointed when I pull out my phone and "Dad" is flashing on the screen. But I haven't talked to my father in weeks, maybe longer, and it hits me right now that I desperately want to see him and hear his voice. I have no friends at my new job because Kenny told everyone about my history, and nobody from my old job still speaks to me. Which means there isn't anyone I've been able to talk to about what happened between me and Krista. Not even Goldy.

I swipe to take the call, and there's a squeezing sensation in my chest as my father's familiar voice fills my ear: "Blake! You picked up!"

That squeezing sensation gets even tighter. "I always pick up. If I'm free."

"Sure," he says. "It's okay. I know you're busy, Blake."

Great, he knows I dodge his calls. Well, I'm not going to anymore. I'm going to quit being such a shitty son. When my father calls, I'm going to pick up the phone. Most of the time anyway.

"So how is it going?" he asks me. "How is the new job?"

"Fantastic," I lie.

"That's wonderful," he says, and it's a tribute to him that he sounds like he actually means it. "And how is Krista?"

"She's…" I almost lie again, but then I realize this is my dad I'm talking to. Why pretend? Who am I trying to impress? "She moved out."

"Aw, Blake." His voice lowers a few notches. "I'm really sorry to hear that. She seemed like a nice girl, and I know you liked her a lot."

Liked her a lot? She was *the one*. And Whitney *ruined* it.

"Yeah," I manage.

"What happened?"

I swallow a lump that always seems to pop up in my throat when I think about Krista. "She thinks I cheated on her."

And she thinks I murdered her fish. I'll leave that part out though.

"Did you?" he asks.

"No!" I can't believe he would ask me that. "She just

got this idea in her head. None of it is based on reality, but she doesn't believe me."

"Well," he says, "if you didn't even do the thing that she accused you of, why don't you win her back?"

"Believe me, I'm trying." Krista hasn't blocked me yet, but if I keep sending her this many text messages, that is the next thing coming. "She says she needs space."

My father is quiet, thinking this over. I'm waiting to hear what he has to say. The funny thing is, even though I don't talk to my father much, he gives great advice. He's a smart guy. He was married to my mother for nearly thirty years when she died, and even though they had their financial problems and he couldn't give her everything I thought she deserved, they were always really happy together.

Maybe my mom didn't get her dream house and sometimes the electricity went out, but she was content. She gave me a wonderful childhood, full of camping trips and home-cooked dinners and treasure hunts for fireflies in our backyard. And when the cancer finally got the best of her, she died in her own home, with my father holding her hand. Maybe I've been looking at this all wrong.

"If she asks for space," Dad says, "you need to give it to her. She knows you love her. I think at the end of the day, she'll come back to you."

I can't help but think about another piece of advice he gave me after I lost my job. He told me I should come back home to Cleveland and bring Krista with me. If I'd taken that advice, none of this would be happening. I'd be living in my hometown with my soon-to-be bride, and we'd probably be house hunting right now.

I wonder if it's too late for that dream to come true.

"I was also wondering," Dad says, "if you were planning to come home for Thanksgiving this year?"

Oh right. Thanksgiving is in only two weeks, but it's been the last thing on my mind. Most years, I work right through the holidays, and I haven't been back to Cleveland for Thanksgiving in…well, a long time. But I suddenly feel a desperate urge to see my father and my childhood home.

And the bonus is I'll get a break from Whitney too.

"Yes," I tell him. "I'll be there."

"That's great!" I can't see his face, but I can hear his smile. "I'll start working on the menu right now."

My father is rambling something about yams and cornbread stuffing when I turn the corner to get onto my block and stop short. Something I see shakes me to my very core. I blink my eyes, certain this must be some kind of mirage, because what I'm looking at simply isn't possible. I am even more stunned than I was when I found that rotting fruit in my kitchen cabinet. For a moment, I feel my heart stop.

It's the end of the day on trash day, and Mr. Zimmerly's trash bins *are still at the curb.*

"Dad," I say. "I have to go."

"Sure," he says. "Hang in there, Blake. I know you'll get her back."

"Thanks, Dad."

I hang up the phone just as I come to a halt in front of my house. I thought it might have been some sort of mirage, but now that I am closer, I can plainly see Mr. Zimmerly's regular trash and recycling bins still at the curb, even though they have been emptied and it's nearly 5:30.

Oh, I am going to enjoy rubbing this in his face.

I take a minute to drag my own trash and recycling bins back behind my house, just so I can clearly demonstrate that I have the moral upper hand here. Mr. Zimmerly still has not come out to grab the trash, so I march up the steps to his front door.

I ring the doorbell, listening as the chimes echo throughout his house. I wait for his shuffling footsteps behind the door, and when I don't hear them, I ring the doorbell a second time. And then I pound on the door for good measure.

After a good minute has passed, there is still no sign of Mr. Zimmerly. I don't hear anything either. Could he be traveling? I suppose that's possible, but he did put the garbage bins out last night. It seems strange that he would have put his garbage out and then left town.

Maybe he's napping. Old people nap all the time, don't they? And Mr. Zimmerly is very old.

Christ, I hope he's okay.

I almost turn around to go back home, but then on a whim, I try the doorknob. And it turns in my hand.

It's a bad idea to enter his house. Mr. Zimmerly and I are not the best of friends, to put it mildly. But the truth is I'm worried about him. Failing to take his garbage cans off the curb after garbage day is shockingly unusual behavior for him. I could call the police and let them know my concerns, but given that I only saw him yesterday, they might not have cause to investigate yet on the basis of a couple of empty garbage bins. And by the time they do, it might be too late.

What if he's lying on the floor of his bedroom with a broken hip? No, he isn't my favorite person in the world, but the idea of him lying helpless and injured somewhere gives me a pang in my chest. Despite what Krista and Whitney seem to think, I'm a decent person. If Mr. Zimmerly needs help, I should try to help him.

I'm going in.

I crack open the door, pausing for the sound of a dog or some other animal coming at me. Even though I've never heard any barking coming from the house next door, nothing would surprise me at this point. But when I get inside, I am met with only silence.

"Mr. Zimmerly?" I call out.

No answer.

I have lived here for nearly a year now, and I have never been inside Mr. Zimmerly's house before. He never invited me, and I never bothered to try to get to know him. But when I get inside his house, it's clear to me that he doesn't have many visitors. The furniture in his living room looks old and dusty, as if nobody has been in the room for years, even though he obviously lives here. I pass by his mantel, which is full of black-and-white photos in metal frames, also covered in a layer of dust. My eyes linger briefly on what appears to be a wedding photo from a time long before digital cameras. There's also an antique clock that looks remarkably like the one we have in our kitchen, although it seems to have stopped working, the hour and minute hands frozen at eleven and eight.

"Mr. Zimmerly?" I say again.

As I walk through the living room, stepping over a stiff brown rug, a voice in the back of my head tells me that I should turn around and leave. I am essentially trespassing in my neighbor's house. And from the stillness around me, I sense that the house is empty at this moment. If he went out grocery shopping and returns to find me here, he's going to be furious. He might call the police himself.

Yet I don't leave.

My next stop is the kitchen, which is even smaller than mine. Unlike mine, it hasn't been renovated, and the gas stove has a layer of brown crust over it that makes me think it hasn't been used in a long time. But what disturbs me about the kitchen is what is on the kitchen counter.

A glass of water, filled to the brim. And a sandwich on whole wheat bread, carefully sliced in half.

It seems weird for a person to make himself lunch, then leave it on the kitchen counter while he goes out shopping. Or even take a nap. No, my neighbor made himself a sandwich with the intention of eating it. And then for whatever reason, he didn't.

"Mr. Zimmerly?" I call out again.

Shit.

I stumble out of the kitchen, my head spinning. I should definitely call the police at this point. After all, I have ample evidence that something is amiss. I'll have to explain to them what I'm doing here, but it's not like I came here to rob him. I only entered his house because I was worried.

I reach into my pocket for my phone, and just as my fingers close around it, I notice the light is on in the downstairs bathroom.

The door is slightly cracked open, and a wedge of yellow light peeks out. Mr. Zimmerly is not the sort of man who leaves a room without turning off the light. If the light is on in the bathroom, he must still be in there.

I creep in the direction of the bathroom. When I get to the door, I hesitate, listening for any sounds from inside.

No. Nothing.

Although I guess he could be on the toilet.

"Mr. Zimmerly?" I say one last time.

I reach out to knock on the door, but because it's already cracked open, the door shifts. The hinges protest as it swings entirely open, revealing the contents of the small bathroom, and the foundation trembles as I let out the loudest scream this brownstone has heard in years.

CHAPTER 30

I can't stop seeing it.

Even after I run out of the bathroom and dial 911. Even after the paramedics arrive and declare there's nothing to be done. Even after they wheel the stretcher out of Mr. Zimmerly's house with a sheet covering his face.

"You okay, Mr. Porter?" a young police officer dressed in blues asks me.

I startle as the doors to the ambulance slam shut. Of course, when it drives away, there won't be any sirens. There's no urgency. I knew it the second I found my neighbor lying on the floor of his bathroom, a pool of blood around his head.

"Uh-huh," I mumble, even though I'm not. I wish somebody would wrap a blanket around me or something, because I can't stop shaking. It's humiliating.

"These things happen," the cop says with an air of authority, even though he looks barely older than twenty. "He was ninety-three years old. He must've slipped in the bathroom and hit his head. We see it all the time."

Ninety-three. Jesus, I had no idea he was that old. "Uh-huh," I say again.

He squints at me. "You got someone to be with you?"

I have absolutely no one, but I don't need to tell this police officer my life story. "I have a roommate" is all I say.

He nods like that's good enough. I'm sure he has a busy night ahead of him, and the last thing he wants to do is babysit a thirty-two-year-old man. Besides, I'll be fine. Yes, seeing that dead body was a shock. I'm going to have nightmares tonight. But I'll be okay.

Unlike Mr. Zimmerly.

"So I gotta just confirm with you one more time…" The officer pulls what looks like a small iPad out of his jacket. "Why were you in Mr. Zimmerly's house?"

"I was worried," I say. "He never brought his trash bins in, and he's really anal about that. I knew something had to be wrong."

I don't need to tell him that I knocked on my neighbor's door with the intention of giving him hell.

The officer nods sympathetically. "Yeah. I got a neighbor like that too. So…do you have the key to his house?"

"No. The door was open."

"Open?"

"Unlocked, I mean."

"Does he usually leave it unlocked?"

"I have no idea."

"So when you noticed it was unlocked, you went in?"

I nod. "I just wanted to make sure he was okay, but

then I saw there was some food he left on the kitchen counter. And I saw the light on in the bathroom, and I…"

I find myself getting choked up. I don't know why. I didn't even like that bastard.

"It's okay." The officer taps at the screen of the iPad and stuffs it back in his jacket. "I think that's enough."

I nod, unable to speak.

"I'll be giving his daughter a call," he tells me. "I'll let her know what happened."

"Mr. Zimmerly had a daughter?"

"Looks like it," he confirms. "She lives all the way out in California. Guess they didn't see each other much."

I never saw one person coming in or out of Mr. Zimmerly's house in the time I've known him. Certainly not a woman young enough to be his daughter. (Although I suppose given his age, any daughter would be at least in her sixties.) He had a whole family I never knew about, yet it seemed nobody cared about him at all.

Somehow, I think about Krista. And how I imagined building a life with her. Without her, I have nobody. The same way Mr. Zimmerly had nobody.

Great. I'm going to end up bitter and alone and obsessed with garbage until one day, I drop dead in my own bathroom.

As soon as the last of the entourage leaves my block, I take out my phone. I tap out a message to Krista:

Mr. Zimmerly died.

I am heartened by the fact that a few bubbles appear on the screen, indicating that she might be responding. Although I have been fooled by those bubbles before.

But then a response pops up:

I'm sorry. Are you OK?

Kind of shaken. At least I don't have to worry about the garbage bins anymore.

She writes back:

Silver lining.

She's talking to me. This is a really good sign. Maybe she's done having her space and she's ready to come back. While I've got her attention, I type into the screen:

I miss you.

The bubbles appear again. They flash on the screen over and over as I stand there, holding my breath, waiting for her to respond.
But she never does.

CHAPTER 31

I'm at the laundromat.

It's not my favorite place to be, especially after I spent most of last night tossing and turning, having nightmares about finding Mr. Zimmerly's dead body. But I don't have much of a choice. I don't have Krista to wash my clothes at work anymore, and I can't trust my own washer and dryer.

So now I am relegated to using the laundromat two blocks away. It's the weekend, and I don't have anything else to do, so I threw my clothes in the washer, and now I'm sitting in the corner with my phone, the laundry basket and bottle of emasculating detergent with a stuffed animal parade on it at my feet. I've got another twenty minutes to kill until I need to switch over to the dryer.

My life is exciting.

Krista still hasn't messaged me back after I told her I missed her. But the fact that she messaged me at all is a good sign. Maybe I *won't* die alone in my bathroom.

Although at this point, I would give anything just to live in my house alone again.

I didn't see Whitney last night at all. I assume she came home at some point, but she wasn't around when I went to sleep. I expected to get woken up by that loud thumping coming from above me—I was waiting for it—but the top floor of the brownstone was silent the entire night. I'm not even sure she was there this morning. Of course, we're not on speaking terms, so it's not like she would let her presence be known to me.

While I'm waiting for the clothes to finish in the washer, I type Whitney's name into the Google search engine. The first search I did of her name didn't turn up much, but I'm feeling a lot more motivated right now. And bored.

Once again, the results are minimal. I check all the social media outlets one by one, but I don't see any accounts under her name. She's a ghost.

Then I get an idea.

When she was applying to move in, she allowed me to take a photo of her driver's license. I find the image, still saved in my photos, and crop it out of the license. Then I bring up a facial recognition website and upload the photo. I hold my breath as the search engine runs.

Apparently, Whitney has an extremely generic face, because pages of photos appear on the screen. I scroll through the dozens of women who look like Whitney but not like her at all. A photographer named Cherilynn. A software engineer named Alexandra. A PhD candidate named Amanda.

None of them look familiar to me. None of them are women I have wronged in the past. Not that I've wronged a lot of women. I can be an asshole at work when I need to be, but I've generally been decent to all the women I've dated. There have been, of course, a few exceptions. There was that party during my senior year of high school when I made out with a cheerleader in the bathroom while my girlfriend was doing shots in the kitchen. There was that pregnancy scare during my sophomore year of college, and I acknowledge I could have behaved better. Still, I eventually said the right things before she miraculously got her period and we broke up.

Anyway, Whitney isn't any of those girls. I never dated her. I never laid eyes on her before she came to live with us. I'd bet my life.

It's driving me out of my mind trying to figure it out. Who is this woman that I allowed into my home? And more importantly, what does she want from me?

I lower my phone in frustration, and as I stretch out my legs, I accidentally kick the bottle of laundry detergent. I knock it over, and of course, I didn't manage to screw the top on properly, so detergent spills freaking everywhere. This is not my day. Actually, it's feeling like it's not my *year*.

I find the bathroom in the laundromat and grab a bunch of paper towels to clean up the mess. I return to where I spilled the liquid detergent, and I crouch down on my knees. Well, at least this will give me something to do until it's time to move my clothes. It really has come to this.

But as I'm bent over the spilled laundry detergent, the scent of citrus smacks me in the face. I hadn't noticed it before, but now, with the detergent out of the bottle, it's painfully obvious.

Limonene.

There's limonene *in* my freaking laundry detergent.

I grab the bottle, which is now nearly empty. It's the same sensitive skin detergent I've always used with no extra chemicals or fragrances. I check the ingredients, making sure it doesn't contain limonene. It doesn't.

Which means somebody mixed a detergent with limonene with my detergent without me knowing it.

It finally makes sense. I finally understand why I was having an allergic reaction to all the clothes I washed, even though I was obsessively cleaning the washing machine prior to each use. Because I was *washing my clothes in limonene.*

I'm so furious, I want to throw the bottle of laundry detergent across the room. Impulsively, I grab my phone and shoot off a text to Krista:

> Whitney has been putting limonene in my laundry detergent! That's why I've been breaking out in a rash! I told you she was behind all this!

As soon as I send the message, I regret it. Krista already thinks there's something strange going on between me and Whitney. I'm not helping things with this message.

I try to unsend it, but it then gets marked as "read," so now it's too late. Krista read what I wrote. And once more, she's not replying.

Okay, winning Krista back is not going to be as easy as I hoped. But right now, I need to focus on getting Whitney out of my house. My life is never going to recover until that woman is gone.

But before that, I need to go out and buy myself more laundry detergent and wash my clothes. Again.

Time to clean up this mess.

CHAPTER 32

Since Krista is gone and I'm broke, after I finish with my laundry, I hit one of the halal food carts to grab dinner.

Don't judge. The truth is I love those food stands—the tantalizing smells of the roasted garlic and charred meat always get to me. I even kind of admire when they don't list the prices on the cart and then make up a seemingly random number after they've already prepared your order. Unfortunately, ever since Krista got really bad food poisoning from one by the entrance to Central Park, she won't eat from them anymore. But she's not here right now, and this is an entirely different food truck. It's not fair to discriminate against every food cart in the city based on that one truck that made Krista vomit for two hours straight.

I am waiting in the line to get my falafel wrap when I get this prickling sensation in the back of my neck, like someone is watching me. I ignore it for as long as I can, because, hey, the city is crowded and there are always people around, especially weirdos who stare at the folks standing in line for the food cart.

But the sensation doesn't go away, and it bothers me enough that I turn around, just to prove to myself that I'm being paranoid. And I almost do a double take.

There's a man by a newsstand adjacent to the food cart, who is looking right at me.

The man is short and scrawny, with wrinkled clothes and an unkempt goatee. As soon as he catches me looking at him, he looks away, as if he's suddenly very interested in the newsstand's gum selection. Was he looking at me or just considering his dinner options? I'm sure it's the latter. I could almost shrug the whole thing off, except…

He looks extremely familiar.

I stare at the baseball cap on his head, trying to jog my memory. It's a white baseball cap with a picture of a cartoon penguin. It's not the kind of cap you'd expect a grown man to be wearing, and I'm certain I've seen it before.

Then it hits me. He was one of the people who came to look at the spare room before Whitney showed up. The guy who wanted to drill a hole in the wall, so I had to kick him out. And not just that, but I'm certain I've seen him at least one other time since then.

He looks up again, and when our eyes meet, he doesn't look away this time.

I step out of line—which I'm pissed off about because I've been waiting for ten minutes already—and I stride over to the newsstand. The man adjusts his cap and, once again, drops his gaze. "Excuse me," I say. "Is there a problem?"

He doesn't answer me. He picks up a package of Mentos and examines the label.

I clear my throat loudly. "I said, *excuse me*."

At first, I'm sure he's going to continue to ignore me, but then he adjusts his cap again and raises his chin to look up at me. "What you did to Whitney," he hisses at me, "was *disgusting*."

My jaw drops. What the hell? How does this random prospective tenant know Whitney? That couldn't possibly be a coincidence, could it? And what did I do to her that was so disgusting?

"What did you say to me?" I breathe.

"You heard me."

This time, he doesn't break our eye contact. He is staring at me—challenging me.

It's at that moment I realize I am at least half a head taller than this little creep, and I've also got a good fifty pounds on him. I haven't been hitting the gym as hard as I did when I was unemployed, but I've still built up plenty of muscle. I've never thrown a punch in my life, but if I did it now, he would go down. And damn, it would feel *good*.

I take a step toward him, anger coursing through my veins. "*What* did you say to me?"

The little weasel's eyes widen—he knows I'm not messing around and that I could flatten him if I wanted to. He scurries off down the street, reminding me a little of the rats I see when I'm down in the subway.

At least I'm not as paranoid as I thought I was. That man really was staring at me—I wasn't imagining it. But that doesn't make me feel even the tiniest bit better. Because I have absolutely no idea why.

CHAPTER 33

I'm extremely buzzed.

I'm finishing up beer number four. Or is it five? I lost track of it somewhere along the way.

Back when I was working at Coble & Roy, five beers wouldn't have even touched me. But since leaving the company, I haven't had the opportunity to drink as often. I usually only have one drink per night, and only a couple of times a week. So I'm *feeling* these beers. But tonight, I need something to numb the pain. I'm not drunk yet, but I'm getting there.

My life has fallen apart. I lost my VP job. I don't know how I am going to pay the mortgage next month since I have drained my savings, and even Whitney's rent money isn't enough to close the gap. Krista is gone.

And my tenant has a vendetta against me that I don't understand.

After I finish the last of my beer, I stumble in the direction of the kitchen to get another one. I can't help but notice that the fruit flies seem to have returned over the last few days. I don't even want to think about what rotten thing Whitney has stashed away somewhere in my kitchen. I don't have the energy to search for it right now.

I twist off the cap of a new bottle and toss it in the garbage. I take a long swig as I walk back to the couch. But just as I'm returning to the living room, I trip over the rug, dislodging the corner and stumbling to my knees.

I curse under my breath. I might be drunker than I thought. Stupid rug. I don't know how I managed to trip over it, but when I try to smooth the corner back in place, I realize the whole rug is off center. The corner is supposed to fit under the sofa, but it doesn't—that's why I tripped over it.

I don't know how I didn't notice until now, but at some point in the last few weeks, this rug has moved. It used to be mostly under the coffee table, but now more than half of it is *beside* the coffee table, covering the path from the sofa to the kitchen. I remember noticing something seemed a little bit off about the living room, but I couldn't put my finger on it until this moment.

Why would somebody move the rug?

Despite (or maybe because of) my inebriation, I decide to relocate the rug to its rightful location. I shove away the coffee table, which is holding the rug in place, and then I pull it off the floor. But as I pull the rug away, I notice that on the rectangle of hardwood floor where it used to lie, there is a large brown stain.

What is *that*?

Why is there a stain on my floor? I squint, trying to figure out what the hell I'm looking at. It wasn't there when I moved in, but it's been there long enough that whatever it is seems embedded in the floorboards. How do you end up with a stain *under* the rug when the rug itself is clean?

Did somebody move the rug to cover the stain?

I narrow my eyes at the brown stain that is about half a foot in diameter. I don't know what it is. It looks like somebody might've spilled a glass of wine.

I crouch down next to the irregular brown circle and run my fingers along the floorboards. It's long since dried. I wonder if I can get it out.

I make another trip back to the kitchen and grab a handful of wet paper towels, along with some cleaning spray from below the sink. I am going to be so pissed at Whitney if she spilled some crap on my floor and I can't get it off. That's coming straight out of the deposit.

I spray a liberal amount of the cleaning fluid on the floorboards and wait for sixty seconds to allow it to absorb. It's probably not long enough, but I don't want to spend the entire night cleaning the floor, so I do a first pass with the paper towel. To my relief, some of the material on the floorboards wipes off on the paper towel. Except…

I didn't notice this when the stain was dry, but now that it's on the paper towel, it's clear that I got the color wrong. The stain is not brown.

It's dark red.

It's got to be wine. It's the right color. Well, not exactly—it doesn't have that purplish hue that I sometimes associate with wine. But it's got to be. What else could it be? What other dark red liquid could have stained my floor boards?

Okay, there is one other thing it could be.

Yes, it is the exact color of blood. It much more closely

resembles blood than wine. And it has a strange metallic smell. But it can't be that. Because why would there be a bloodstain all over my floor?

While I am staring down at the paper towel, trying to sort this out in my beer-muddled brain, the doorbell rings. I leap to my feet, my heart racing. Is there any chance this could be Krista? I haven't heard from her, but maybe she decided to pop by.

Even if she's only here to pick up some extra clothing, I hope it's her.

After a brief hesitation, I toss the carpet back on the floor to cover the stain. Though some of it came off on the paper towel, it's still very visible. At the very least, I don't want Krista to see it.

But it isn't Krista that I see through the peephole. It's a man dressed in a dark suit, standing in front of my door. I don't recognize him, and for a second, I just stand there, trying to figure out what the hell this strange man would be doing ringing my doorbell at eight o'clock at night.

And then he rings again.

"Who is it?" I call through the door.

"This is Detective Garrison from the NYPD," he speaks up, loud enough to project through the door. "Could I have a moment of your time, Mr. Porter?"

Why is there a detective at my door? I look over my shoulder at the rug that is now concealing what may very well be a bloodstain on the floor of my house. But he couldn't be here about that.

Shit. I don't want to let a detective into my house right now—or ever, really. But what am I supposed to do? Tell him to go away, please come back later? That isn't an option.

Finally, I crack open the door. It's only after the cold

November air hits me that it occurs to me that I am in an undershirt and boxer shorts. Not exactly ideal apparel for talking to a detective. But I'm sure he's seen worse.

The detective is relatively unassuming. Fortyish, dark brown hair and brown eyes. No distinguishing features aside from a couple of grooves in his cheeks that make him look older than he probably is. The only remarkable thing about him is his voice, which is deeper than it rightfully should be for his height and build.

"Blake Porter?" he asks me.

"Uh-huh."

"Detective Garrison," he says, even though he told me his name through the door. "I was hoping I could ask you a few questions. It's about your neighbor."

I'm not thrilled about inviting a detective into my home when there's something potentially suspicious under the rug. But then again, it's covered. And the detective isn't investigating a homicide. I'm not sure why he wants to talk to me about Mr. Zimmerly, but it seems benign. There's nothing too exciting about an old man slipping and hitting his head in his own bathroom.

"Sure." I take a step back, scrunching the paper towel I'd been holding in my right hand. "Come on in."

The detective strides into my house, and I close the door behind him, shutting out the cold air. I shift between my bare feet, wishing I were wearing pants at least. Why didn't I put on pants to answer the door? What's wrong with me?

"Nice house," the detective comments.

"Thanks." I attempt a smile, but it turns out lopsided. "So…what's going on? Everything okay? Mr. Zimmerly is still dead, right?"

I wince. Wow, that joke was in horrible taste. From the detective's face, he thinks so too. But they can't arrest you for having a bad sense of humor.

"Still dead," Detective Garrison confirms.

"I feel bad about it," I say, trying to seem a little more sensitive.

"Oh?" he arches a bushy eyebrow. "Why do you feel bad?"

"Because, you know, he fell and hit his head." I scratch at my forearm with my hand not holding the paper towel, even though it isn't technically itchy. I have officially solved my rash problem since I replaced the detergent and keep it locked up in my room when I'm not using it. "And maybe if I had gotten in there sooner—before it was too late—we could've saved him."

"I don't think so."

"Well, maybe not. But we don't know for sure."

The detective levels his eyes at me. "Actually, the medical examiner feels that your neighbor didn't die from the fall."

What?

"I don't understand." I shake my head. "Why did they even do an autopsy on a guy in his nineties? That doesn't seem like a good use of medical resources."

"It was an accidental death. And it's a good thing they did, because the medical examiner felt that the trauma to his head was not consistent with hitting his head on the sink or bathtub. He felt that it was from blunt force trauma."

I stare at him. "What? What are you saying?"

"I'm saying somebody hit your neighbor on the head." The detective frowns. "He was murdered."

CHAPTER 34

A wave of dizziness washes over me. I have to hold on to the wall to keep from collapsing onto the floor. The four or five bottles of beer I drank are churning in my stomach.

"You been drinking, Mr. Porter?" Detective Garrison asks me.

I don't like the way he asks me that question. It's the middle of the evening, and I'm in my own home. It's my right to have a few beers. Twenty-First Amendment and all that. "A little. I'm just… I'm surprised. Are you sure about this?"

"Very sure," Garrison says. "We also found traces of his blood on an antique clock on his mantel."

The *clock*.

I saw it when I was looking at Zimmerly's mantel. I remember thinking how much it looked like the one in our kitchen—almost identical. Then it occurs to me…

When is the last time I saw that clock in our kitchen?

"So I've been talking to his neighbors," Garrison is saying, "trying to figure out if anyone saw anything."

"I didn't see anything," I say quickly. "I was at work the whole day."

"Right," he says, "but the medical examiner said that he died the night before. So did you see anyone entering or leaving his house the night before?"

"No," I murmur. "I...I didn't see anything."

The night before? That means the sandwich on the kitchen counter wasn't his lunch but was actually a sad little dinner. He was about to eat when somebody came into his house and hit him on the head with that antique clock, killing him.

I'm suddenly desperate to check the kitchen to make sure our own clock is still in its place. It's got to be a coincidence. It's *got* to be.

"...didn't get along with?" the detective is saying.

Somehow, I had tuned him out. My head feels so cloudy. Christ, I need a cup of coffee or something. "What?" I finally say.

Garrison does not look amused. "Do you know anyone that Mr. Zimmerly didn't get along with?"

"Not really," I say. "He mostly kept to himself."

"Uh-huh." He nods slowly. "And how about you? Did you get along with Mr. Zimmerly?"

I don't like where this is going, but I play along. "We weren't best friends or anything. But we got along okay."

"So what were the two of you fighting about last week?"

I suddenly regret so many of my recent life decisions. "It was stupid. Just about the garbage pickup. Dumb neighbor stuff."

"Dumb neighbor stuff," he repeats.

"Right."

He cocks his head at me. "And did you throw a trash can at him?"

Shit.

"I wasn't trying to hit him." I drop my head. "Look, that wasn't about him. My girlfriend had just left me and…"

"Your girlfriend left you?"

Why does he keep repeating everything I say? I run a shaky hand through my hair, which feels extremely greasy. When is the last time I showered? "We're going through some stuff, that's all. Taking some time apart."

"Uh-huh."

The room is spinning. I need to sit down before I collapse. Does this detective actually think that I killed my neighbor? Is that possible?

But somebody killed him. Somebody bashed Mr. Zimmerly on the head with a heavy metal clock. I can't even wrap my head around it.

"Mr. Porter," Garrison says, "I'm wondering if you could come down to the station with me to give an official statement. I can get you some coffee, and we can have a nice chat over there, and then we can be done with all this."

"I…I don't think…"

"Also, it would be great to get your fingerprints on file," he says. "Just to rule you out entirely so you can be done with this headache."

He wants my fingerprints.

That's not good.

My brain is still foggy from all the beer, but I'm still

with it enough to know that I shouldn't go to the police station without a lawyer and start giving this detective information that he can later use to incriminate me.

And also, I've got to get rid of what I'm almost certain is a bloodstain on the floor of my living room, as well as the bloody paper towel crumpled up in my right hand.

"Actually," I say, "I'm not feeling so hot. I don't think I can help much right now. I think…I need to go to bed."

"I'd be happy to give you a ride," he says. "I've got my car parked right down the block."

I have a terrible feeling that if I go to the police station right now, I might never leave.

"I'm sorry," I say. "I just can't right now. Unless… I don't have to, do I?"

Detective Garrison stands there for a moment, and I'm scared that he's going to whip out a pair of handcuffs and slap them on my wrists and *make* me go down to the station with him. But he doesn't do that. He just shakes his head.

"No," he says, "you don't have to. Not yet anyway."

Not yet. That doesn't sound good for me. But it's better than the handcuffs.

"Okay then," he says. "I'll be on my way. Thank you for your time."

I let out a breath as he turns around and heads toward my door. He's leaving. Thank God he's leaving. I dart ahead so that I can get the door open for him.

"I may have some more questions, Mr. Porter," he tells me as I fumble with the locks. My fingers aren't entirely functional right now. "Please make yourself available."

"Right," I manage. "Happy to help if I can."

I'm not happy. I hope he never comes back.

I watch from the window by my doorway, making sure the detective disappears down the block, returning to his car. What the hell was that? Was Mr. Zimmerly really murdered? How could that be? Who would murder such an old man? I mean, another few months and nature would have probably done the job.

Unless…

Is it a coincidence that Mr. Zimmerly was killed so soon after I had a very visible altercation with him on the street? What would that detective have discovered if I let him take my fingerprints?

I nearly trip over my feet hurrying back to the kitchen. The first thing I do is toss that bloodstained paper towel deep in the trash. Then my gaze falls on the far end of the kitchen counter, where Krista had placed that antique clock after we got it at the flea market, back when life was still good.

There's an empty space where the clock had sat.

Shit.

How long has that clock been missing? I don't even know. The entire last week feels like a blur. But it's clear the clock from our kitchen was the same one used to kill Mr. Zimmerly. Then the killer left it on his mantel, knowing that it would be identified as the murder weapon. It's also covered in my fingerprints, I'm sure.

But maybe this isn't as ominous as it seems. It's entirely possible that…I don't know…Krista gave the clock to Mr. Zimmerly as a gift. And it just happened to be the weapon that a startled burglar used to subdue him.

Except somehow, I don't think that's the case.

My heart is pounding as I return to the living room. I pull back the rug again to look down at the stain on the floor. Now that I have moistened it, it is very clearly redder than brown. And when I bring my nose close to the floorboards, it doesn't smell anything like wine.

A key turns in the lock to the front door, and I jerk my head up. I manage to scramble to my feet just as Whitney enters the brownstone, wearing a light jacket. She raises her eyebrows at the sight of me.

"Hello, Blake," she says. "Did I interrupt a special moment between you and the floor?"

Is it possible that *Whitney* is responsible for what happened to Mr. Zimmerly? Did she take that clock from our kitchen and bash him over the head with it to frame me? Despite everything, it's very hard to imagine her doing something so diabolical and deliberate. But not impossible. You never know what someone's capable of.

I point at the floorboards, grateful for my alcohol-induced lack of inhibitions. "What is this stain, Whitney?"

She plays along, stepping over to the spot where I am standing. She looks down at the stain, and a smile touches her lips. "Looks like it's going to be a bitch to get out."

"Did you do this?"

She blinks innocently. "Boy, you're getting very paranoid, aren't you? Perhaps you should cut back on the booze."

"I had *three* beers," I say through my teeth. Okay, four. Maybe five. "Perhaps *you* should quit acting like a manipulative bitch."

"What are you going to do to me?" She folds her arms across her chest, her eyes flashing. "The same thing you did to Mr. Zimmerly?"

My mouth falls open. Is she serious?

"Some detective talked to me when I was on my way

out this morning." She's enjoying the expression on my face. "I made sure to let him know that Herb wasn't your favorite person in the world."

The surge of rage that I feel almost overwhelms me. How *dare* she implicate me with the police? Yeah, he pissed me off sometimes, but I wouldn't come into his house and murder him, for crying out loud. "I would *never* have done anything to hurt Mr. Zimmerly. You can't possibly think I'm capable of that!"

"I'm not sure what you're capable of. You're constantly flying into uncontrollable rages over nothing. You're extremely paranoid. You've basically *threatened* me. And any hour I come home during the night, I find you wandering the house like you're in a trance. God only knows what you're up to."

Is that true? I don't wander the house all night long. Yes, my sleep has been shit. But it's not *that* bad.

Is it?

No, it's not. Whitney is trying to get to me. She's trying to make me think I'm losing it. She's even making me wonder if I could somehow be responsible for what happened to my neighbor, even though I know I'm not. She's an evil person.

All of a sudden, the overwhelming urge comes over me to reach out and wrap my fingers around Whitney's skinny little neck. I'm much stronger than she is. All I would have to do is squeeze hard enough, and I would never have to look at her taunting smile ever again.

It would be so easy…

I can't help but think of that psychic woman who came to our house before we found Whitney. She seemed so certain that I would stab somebody in this very living room. She said she saw me crouching over Krista's dead body. The fear in her eyes was real—real enough that she told Krista to make a run for it. At the time, I thought the whole thing was bullshit.

But what if she got it right? Or at least part of it?

What if her vision was real, but it was the girl on the floor that she got wrong?

I take a step back, shocked by my own thoughts. I'd never stab someone to death. It's out of the question. What is Whitney doing to me?

"I...I'm going to bed," I mutter under my breath.

I'm not tired, but I've got to get out of here. I've got to get away from Whitney before I do something I'll regret.

I race up the steps as fast I can, feeling Whitney's eyes on my back the entire time.

CHAPTER 35

The next morning, I've got a terrible hangover.

My head is throbbing like it used to when I had too much to drink in my early twenties. I haven't had a hangover like this in years, and I used to drink a lot more back then. Since I've been with Krista, I have had no desire to go binge drinking with friends.

I hope she comes back soon.

I'm lying in bed when the doorbell rings. I grab the pillow next to me and put it over my face, hoping whoever is at the door will go away, or else maybe Whitney will answer it. But when the doorbell rings a second time, I realize that's not going to happen. Plus, I've got to get to work. I'm already not Kenny's favorite person.

I finally stumble out of bed, which only makes my headache worse. My mouth feels like it's glued shut. I don't know how I'm going to make it to work today. I might have to call in sick, which I hate doing. I used to be so proud of my work ethic.

As I leave my room, voices float up to the second floor from downstairs. Sounds like Whitney answered the door after all, and apparently, it's somebody she knows. Now that I'm off the hook to answer the door, I hit the bathroom and piss for about five minutes straight.

This time, I put on a pair of sweatpants before I go downstairs. If Whitney has company, I would rather not be in my underwear. Although it's weird, because she *never* has company. She's gone out a few times, but she's never invited anyone here. Not even once. I don't think she has one friend—none that I've seen anyway. Isn't that a sign of a sociopath?

When I get halfway down the stairs, I can see Whitney talking quietly to somebody in the living room. She touches their arm. It takes me a second to figure out who it is, and I have to blink a few times, because I'm not sure I'm seeing right.

It's Malcolm.

He's dressed in a suit and tie, presumably on his way to another busy day at Coble & Roy, doing the job that should have been mine. I sprint down the rest of the steps, ignoring my throbbing head. Why is he here? Is he here to talk to me about Krista? Or does it have to do with Coble & Roy? And why is he talking to Whitney like they're old friends?

Before they see me, I hover in the staircase, straining to hear what they're talking about. But I can't make it out. I take one step closer, holding my breath as I attempt to be as quiet as possible.

"Blake!" Malcolm calls to me. "Hey hey hey!"

Busted.

"Hey." I make it down the rest of the steps, unable to even plaster a fake smile on my face. "What's going on?"

Malcolm and Whitney exchange looks, which I find very strange. Whitney shoves her hands into the pockets of her jacket, flashes Malcolm a smile, and heads toward the door. "I better get to work," she says. "I'll let you talk to Blake."

What was that all about?

"How do you know Whitney?" I ask as casually as possible.

He hesitates for a split second. "She works at that diner, Cosmo's. I love that place."

I guess that makes sense. Except what were they talking about for all that time? I can't exactly ask though. "So what's this about?"

"Listen, Blake." He shoves his hands into the pockets of the trench coat he has on over his suit. "I want to apologize for the way I acted when we got together at Cooper's. I know you've been going through a lot, and I was a jerk."

"Okay..." His apology seems sincere, but the timing is strange. "So that's why you're here? To apologize?"

Malcolm is fumbling around in his coat pocket. At first, I'm thinking he is trying to figure out what to say, but then I realize he's looking for something. After a few seconds, he pulls out a blue velvet box, and my heart sinks.

"No," I murmur. "No."

"I'm so sorry, Blake," he says.

"No." I take a step back, like the velvet box is made of poison. "I'm not taking that from you. This is *not* how she ends our engagement."

"It's not over." He tries to rest a hand on my shoulder, and I shrug him off. "She said she just needs space, and she wanted you to have this back. She said... She thought the money from selling it might help make ends meet."

I hate that she's right. The money I could get from selling that ring could tide me over for another month or two. But then what? I'll still end up losing everything.

"Blake..." Malcolm's face is full of pity. "She still has feelings for you. You just have to give her some time."

I swallow hard. "You need to go."

"Blake..."

"Just...go. *Now*."

I have cried one time in the last ten years, and that's when my mother died. But I'm coming damn close to doing it right now. And I don't want it to happen in front of Malcolm.

He gently places the velvet box on the coffee table. He takes one last look in my direction, and then he slips out the front door.

The second the door clicks shut, I drop down onto the sofa and bury my face in my hands. No. *No*. It can't end this way. I have to see her. I have to talk to her.

I grab my phone from my pocket. Before I can overthink it, I tap out a text to her:

I need to see you, Krista.

Those bubbles appear on the screen, and I hold my breath, hoping she's going to answer me. I hope she tells me that I can see her.

I don't think that's a good idea.

Bullshit. If she thinks she can break up with me via Malcolm, she's got another thing coming. I look down at my watch—there are still another three hours until the dry cleaner opens. She's almost certainly still home. My hands are shaking as I type the next message:

> I'm coming over to Becky's house right now. I have to see you.

I stare at the screen, waiting for her to threaten to call the police on me. I don't know what I'll do if she says that. I don't want to get arrested, especially since I'm already worried that the detective I talked to yesterday is suspicious of me. So I add:

> Please.

I grip the phone, waiting for her reply, which comes a few seconds later:

> OK. Come in an hour.

I have just enough time to shower.

CHAPTER 36

Becky and Malcolm's building is within walking distance, so after I get out of the shower, I put on my sneakers and hoof it.

I reach the apartment building about five minutes before the agreed-upon time. I wait outside, pacing on the sidewalk, and people start giving me funny looks. I take out my phone and use the camera to make sure I look okay, and the truth is I seem a bit disheveled. Even though I recently showered, my hair is wet and windblown from the walk over here, and I also realize that my shirt is inside out.

I take off my shirt, which involves some maneuvering because I'm wearing a jacket on top of it. I manage to flip it, and then I throw it back on over my head. As I'm putting the jacket back on, I realize a woman with white-blond hair is standing a few feet away, staring at me.

"*Blake?*" she blurts out.

Out of context and with her hair looking different from the last time I saw her—shorter? longer?—it takes me a few seconds to recognize my former girlfriend. "Gwen?"

"It *is* you." Gwen seems astonished, even though I think I look roughly the same as two years ago. "What are you *doing*?"

"My shirt was…" I gesture helplessly at my T-shirt. "Anyway…uh…how are you, you know, doing?"

She sticks out her chest, and it's hard not to notice that her shirt is definitely not inside out. And she doesn't smell like cigarettes anymore. I wonder if she quit.

"Great, actually," she says, and there's an edge to her voice that surprises me. "I got a promotion at work, and also, I got engaged last week."

Then she sticks her giant diamond right in my face.

I don't know why she's rubbing my nose in her success, because *she* was the one who broke up with *me* for practically no reason. Well, more like she started a stupid argument that ended with us breaking up. I don't know if she thought I was at fault for the breakup, but by the way she's looking at me, I can tell that she doesn't have warm, fuzzy feelings for me.

"I'm really happy for you, Gwen." I mean it—more or less. I'm not going to start listing my own accomplishments, the highlights of which include getting fired from my job and dumped by my fiancée. "You look like you're doing great."

Her gaze rakes over me. "And you look…"

She doesn't complete the sentence. Just as well.

I glance at my watch—time to go upstairs. "Anyway, it's been good seeing you, but I have to run."

She gives me a strange look that I don't try too hard to interpret. "Yes, so do I. I'll…um…see you around, Blake."

I'm willing to bet a thousand bucks I don't have that I will never see her again.

The encounter with my ex-girlfriend has not put me in a good mindset to see Krista. I was anxious before, and now I feel much worse. What if two years from now, I run into Krista on the street and barely recognize her? The thought of it makes my chest tight.

I'd forgotten Becky and Malcolm's building has a doorman, so my attempts to muscle my way upstairs probably would not have worked. For that reason, I'm grateful that when I say my name, the doorman waves me right in. The whole elevator ride to the twelfth floor, I'm tapping my right foot and resisting the urge to start pacing again.

When I get close to the apartment door, the smell of cinnamon hits me. I have clearly stressed Krista out, because she is making her snickerdoodle cookies. The aroma hits me with a wave of nostalgia—I miss her so much. I'm more determined than ever to win her back. I square my shoulders and knock purposefully on the door.

I fully expect Becky to be serving as the gatekeeper, so it's a little surprising to see Krista standing at the door. Her strawberry-blond hair is pulled back into her patented messy bun, her lips are cotton candy pink, and she looks a little tired and disheveled too, if I'm being honest. But that only makes her more beautiful.

It's been barely over a week since I've seen her, and it feels like a year. All I want is to reach out and give her a level ten hug.

"Krista," I choke out.

I'm not imagining it when her own eyes fill with tears. "Hey, Blake."

The diamond ring is in my coat pocket. I'm ready to give it back to her.

"Can I come in?" I ask.

She sucks in a breath. "Okay, but just for a minute."

When I enter the apartment, the smell of cinnamon grows stronger. I follow Krista into the kitchen, and she pulls out an oven mitt, then pulls a tray of freshly baked cookies from the oven. She places them next to another tray that is already cooling. She made a *lot* of cookies. She's clearly miserable.

"They smell great," I say. "As always."

She manages a tiny smile but doesn't offer me one. "Thank you."

"I miss your cookies."

"Thank you."

"I miss *you*, Krista."

She looks away, her cheeks turning pink. "Blake…"

"Please give me another chance." I attempt to reach for her hand, but she steps out of my grasp. "Nothing happened between me and Whitney. I swear on my life."

"I believe that it didn't," she sighs, "but even so, you're obsessed with that woman in an extremely unhealthy way. She's all you talk about, Blake!"

"That's not true."

"It absolutely is true! You act like she is evil incarnate, but she's just an ordinary person. A *nice* person."

I clench my teeth. "Whitney is a lot of things, but she is *not* nice. In fact…"

In fact, I think there's a chance Whitney killed Mr. Zimmerly.

I think something terrible may have happened in our living room.

I think Whitney might be trying to frame me for murder.

As I say all those words in my head, I recognize how wild it all sounds. Whitney framing me for murder? That sounds ridiculous. I can't say that out loud. If Krista thinks I'm obsessed with Whitney, telling her what I really think will make things worse. Even though it's all true.

"I'm worried about you, Blake." She scrunches her eyebrows together. "I'm worried that you...that you're losing your grip on reality. It's scaring me. You're so paranoid, and you won't listen to anything I say."

Okay, I definitely can't tell her I think Whitney killed Mr. Zimmerly.

"I'm fine, Krista," I insist. "I swear I am. The only reason I'm not fine is because you moved out."

"I needed to do that." She frowns. "I'm sorry, but you're out of control. I couldn't deal with it all anymore."

"Deal with what?" I shoot back.

"Blake..."

"I'm serious! What are you talking about?"

I hadn't even realized I had raised my voice until Becky materializes behind me, her arms folded across her chest. She clears her throat loudly.

"I think it's time you get going, Blake," she says.

I look between the two of them. Becky is glaring at me, and Krista just looks sad. This isn't fair. I didn't do anything wrong. I never cheated on Krista, and I'm not imagining that something is going on with Whitney. Krista might not believe me, but I know that woman has it out for me. She has been targeting me practically from the moment she moved in.

I appeal to Krista: "Can we please just talk a little bit longer?"

"No." Becky's voice is firm.

I don't understand why she gets to be the gatekeeper.

"Time to go. Also..." Becky looks me up and down. "Your shirt is backward."

I look down, and sure enough, the tag is showing on the front of my shirt. Damn. I must've flipped it around when I turned it inside out. How hard is it to put on a damn shirt?

"Fine," I say. "I'll go."

I look over at the tray of cooling snickerdoodles on the counter. Will I ever get to eat any of Krista's baked goods again?

"Wait." Krista must notice the look on my face, because she grabs the spatula from the counter. "Let me give you some cookies—for the road."

I'm pretty sure I will never be able to eat these cookies because they're the last thing I have left of hers, but I let her pack them up for me. I memorize this moment, watching her slim fingers prying the cookies off the tray—her nails are painted a pale pink color that makes her hands look even more fragile. She places about six of them into a Ziploc bag and seals it for freshness. She steps forward and slips the bag of cookies into my jacket pocket.

It's a strangely intimate gesture, and it makes me think that despite everything, there's a chance we might be okay again someday.

If only I can get rid of Whitney.

"Goodbye, Blake," she says.

"Bye, Krista," I manage.

She reaches over to give me a level seven hug, which is tight enough to give me another modicum of hope. I hold her long enough that Becky gives me a look of disapproval. But Becky can go to hell.

One way or another, I am getting Krista back.

CHAPTER 37

When I return to the brownstone, the first thing I do is make sure Whitney isn't home. When I am certain I'm alone, I grab my laptop and bring it to the sofa. I wait for it to start, and then I bring up Whitney's background check, which I had downloaded to the hard drive before she moved in nearly five months ago.

It doesn't have much in it. It verifies that she has never been arrested or incarcerated. There are no active warrants for her arrest. It basically verifies that if Whitney has committed any crime in her life, she has not been caught.

But that's not the information I'm looking for.

The background check also lists the town where she was born. It's a place I never heard of in New Jersey called Telmont. I look it up on Wikipedia, which states that it's a town in Sussex County with a population of fifteen thousand. It's also about a two-hour drive from Manhattan.

I've never been there before. I'm positive of that. But

there's something about the name of the town that rings a bell.

A little more investigation reveals that it's a small enough town that there's only one high school. I bring up the website for Telmont High, which has a number listed.

I stare down at the phone number on the screen of my laptop. I don't entirely know what I'm doing right now. Just because Whitney was born in Telmont, New Jersey, doesn't mean she went to high school there. Back at Becky's house, Becky and Krista were both looking at me like I had lost my mind—like they were *scared* of me— and now that I'm sitting here, googling high schools in New Jersey, there's part of me that wonders if they aren't entirely off the mark.

Yet my gut is telling me that something is going on.

I'd dropped my phone on the coffee table, and now it starts vibrating. I grab it from the table, and my stomach turns when I see who is calling me. Shit—it's Kenny. I completely forgot to call in sick today. I swipe to take the call.

"Porter," he barks at me. "Where are you? You know we have that meeting with Haywood in twenty minutes."

Back at my old job, I would have been running a meeting like that. Now I'm photocopying spreadsheets and pouring coffee. And taking minutes, of course. "I'm sorry. I'm really sick today. I can't even get out of bed."

There's a long silence on the other line. "You're sick?"

"Yeah. It just hit me when I woke up. Fever, chills. Really bad stuff."

"You know," he says, "Davidson saw you standing on the street this morning. He said it was on the west side on his way to the subway."

Is that possible? I *was* on the west side, outside Becky and Malcolm's apartment building. But Davidson is an asshole, and he isn't above making something up to get me in trouble.

"He said you were taking off your shirt," Kenny adds.

Okay, that was definitely me. "Oh" is all I can muster.

"So you're not sick."

"I just…" The last thing I want is to share any of my problems with my boss, who already dislikes me. "It's been a rough morning. I need a personal day."

"What I don't appreciate is the deception." His voice is tight. "You could have asked for a personal day. You could've let me know at the *beginning* of the day, for starters. But instead, I have to call you when you don't bother to show up, and then you lie to me. But after what I heard about you, I guess I shouldn't be surprised."

"I…I'm sorry," I stammer.

"You don't want to come in today? Fine. Don't bother coming in tomorrow either."

"Kenny—"

"We'll mail you your things. Goodbye, Porter."

And then he hangs up on me.

He fired me. I can't believe it. Actually, I *can* believe it, because I've been phoning it in recently, even when I did show up. I can't even hold down a temp job.

He'll let the agency know I've been fired. And then what? I don't know. I suppose they'll find me another degrading job. I'll definitely need to sell the brownstone.

Somehow, Whitney is behind all this. I just don't understand why or how.

I focus my attention back on the laptop screen. Telmont High School. It's still morning, so they will almost certainly be open if I call. This is something I can do.

I punch the ten digits into my phone. Immediately, it starts ringing. I grip the phone, my palm suddenly sweaty. I don't know what I'm doing exactly, but I have to start somewhere. I need more information about Whitney Cross, and this is as good a place as any to begin.

After a few rings, a pleasant-sounding woman picks up on the other line. "Telmont High School," she chirps.

I clear my throat. "Yes, hello. My name is…John Sanders. I'm considering hiring a candidate for a job, and I'm trying to track down a copy of her high school transcript. She told me that you might be able to send it to me."

"Yes, I could certainly do that," the woman says cheerfully, "although we would need a signed release from the student."

Damn, I had a feeling she might say that. "Actually, we faxed that over this morning. Didn't you get it?"

To my relief, she laughs. "Oh, probably. We got a stack of faxes this morning, and I still haven't gone through them all. I'm sure it's in there."

"It definitely is," I assure her.

In the background, I can hear her tapping on a keyboard. "What is the candidate's name?"

"Whitney Cross."

The tapping abruptly stops. "Whitney Cross?"

"That's right."

"Whitney Cross applied for a job?"

"Yes. Is there a problem?"

On the other line, I can hear the sharp inhale of her breath. "Maybe it's not my place to say so, but…"

"What is it?"

"If Whitney is applying to work for you, I would highly recommend you pick another candidate."

I grip the phone tighter. "Why?"

Her voice drops several notches. "Whitney Cross—she's extremely dangerous. If I were you, I would stay far away."

CHAPTER 38

Whitney Cross is extremely dangerous.

That is information that would have been helpful to know *before* I let her move into my home.

"Dangerous?" I squeak out.

"I'm sorry, Mr...."

It takes me a second to recall the fake name I came up with. "Sanders."

"Mr. Sanders," she corrects herself. "I don't want to spread rumors. And it was a long time ago."

"She has excellent references." That's actually true. I personally talked to Whitney's boss at the diner as well as a friend who said she was a former roommate, and they both raved about her. *I have never met a nicer or more responsible person*, her boss told me.

"Oh, I'm sure," the woman says. "Whitney was always very good at getting people to say what she wanted them to say."

"How do you even remember her? It was so long ago."

"I could *never* forget what Whitney did. Believe me."

"So...um..." I squirm on the sofa. "What exactly did Whitney do? Her background check was clean."

"Well, it would be," the woman acknowledges. "Whitney was very good at keeping her nose clean. I can send you the transcript, and you'll see that her grades are excellent. She was exceptionally smart."

"But?"

"She was manipulative," she says in a low voice. "She was one of those girls who were always surrounded by friends, but you could tell none of them were *true* friends. And if anyone did anything she didn't like, she made it her business to wreck their lives."

"Wreck their lives?"

"Well, this is all conjecture, Mr. Sanders." She suddenly sounds reluctant to say any more. "I don't want to start spreading rumors about her. Maybe she's changed."

On the contrary, this woman seems like she *loves* spreading rumors. I just have to get her to keep talking.

"This is all confidential," I reassure her. "But this is an important position, and I need to make sure she is the right candidate."

"Oh! I see."

"So if there's any information I should know, I'd appreciate hearing it. You would be doing me a great service."

"Yes, I understand." She lowers her voice even further so that I have to strain to hear her. "Look, there were a lot of stories about things Whitney did when she was younger, but I never witnessed any of it myself. I never saw what she was capable of until there was a mess with her boyfriend during her senior year."

"Her boyfriend?"

"His name was Jordan Gallo," she says. "Nice enough kid. Football player. He was dating Whitney for about a year. And then, apparently, he cheated on her with another girl—you know how boys are. It was the usual high school drama you see a million times. They broke up, and Whitney made it her mission in life to destroy him."

"Oh." That doesn't sound so bad. Like she said, it sounds like typical high school drama. I'm surprised this woman would even remember it fifteen years later.

"Mr. Sanders, Jordan Gallo jumped off the roof of the school."

I freeze. "What?"

"She *tormented* him," she whispers into the phone. "I remember seeing him a couple of days before he killed himself, and he looked terrible. Like there was a ghost haunting him."

"What did she do to torment him?"

"I only heard the rumors. I'm just the school secretary." Her whisper is barely audible, and I need to press the phone close to my ear. "But right after the breakup, he got busted for cheating when an upcoming exam was found in his backpack, even though he swore he had no idea how it got there. He didn't get expelled, but he was kicked off the football team. Football was everything to him, and he was banking on a scholarship. Which, of course, didn't happen." She pauses, as if caught in the memory. "And then there was the time Jordan opened his locker and found it crawling with insects." I can almost hear her shudder through the phone.

The story of what happened to Jordan Gallo is different from mine yet eerily familiar.

"But that's not all," she adds. "Even though Jordan was

acting strangely before his death, his parents insisted that he never would have killed himself."

"What did they think happened?"

"Apparently, Jordan and Whitney used to go up to the roof together to be alone," she says. "His parents insisted that she pushed him and made it look like a suicide."

"That is..." I cough. "Wow. That's pretty awful. Was she ever charged?"

"They were attempting to get the police to look into it," she says. "But then Whitney took off. I mean, just flat out left town. Didn't even bother to finish high school. Even her parents didn't know where she went—or so they claimed."

"Oh."

"I always thought she left the country," the woman muses. "She seemed like the sort of person who wanted to travel the world. Either way, she had to get out of town because there was too much heat. If she had stayed, there probably would have been charges against her."

"Well, she's back in Manhattan now," I say weakly. "So..."

"Oh gosh, I've been talking your ear off, haven't I?" she sighs. "Listen, I didn't want to upset you. Those were all rumors, and they happened quite a long time ago."

Yet she hasn't changed at all.

"It's fine," I manage. "It's certainly good information to have."

"Do you still want that transcript, Mr. Sanders?"

"Uh, yes. Yes, that would be great."

I read off the virtual fax number I own, which forwards to my email account. The very helpful secretary at Telmont High bids me goodbye and good luck, and I wait for the fax to come in with Whitney's transcript.

After I hang up the phone, my hands won't stop shaking. I go to the bathroom to splash some water on my face, and when I look in the mirror over the sink…I look like a disaster. My hair is sticking up, there are dark purple circles under my eyes, and I look ten years older than I did a few months ago. Even my teeth don't look as pearly white as they used to.

I wonder how Whitney's old boyfriend looked before he plummeted off the roof.

That poor kid, Jordan Gallo. He committed one sin against Whitney Cross, and she made him pay the ultimate price.

And now she's doing it to me. Except in this case, I don't understand why.

I dry my face off and wander into the kitchen. I'm itching to have a beer, just to calm my nerves, but I recognize that it is ten in the morning. I don't want to go down that path. Instead, I pour myself a glass of water from the sink. While I'm filling up my glass, a housefly buzzes in my face. The flies have come back with a vengeance lately, although these are of a larger variety. I wonder if Whitney stashed more of that rotting fruit in my kitchen. I wouldn't put it past her.

This time, I notice the flies are gathered around the crack of space between the kitchen counter and the refrigerator. The gap is about three inches—just large enough to squeeze in a rotting apple or pear, something along those lines. There's got to be something in there. I'm sure of it.

I pull my phone out of my pocket and turn on the flashlight. I shine it into the wedge of space, and sure enough, I can just barely make out what looks like a paper bag stuffed into the gap.

Part of me wants to just leave it there. I don't want to deal with more maggots—not right now. But when I lean close to the space, trying to get a better look, the smell turns my stomach. It smells different and much worse than before.

What the hell is in there?

I crouch down next to the refrigerator. I reach my arm into the gap, trying to grab the paper bag. My arm isn't quite long enough though. I can't reach it. I need a few more inches.

I get up and sift through one of the drawers, and I pull out a serving spoon. I return to the refrigerator, and this time, I use the spoon to nudge the bag closer to the opening. After a few notches, I'm able to grab on to the corner of the bag, and I pull it out.

If I had any doubt in my mind that whatever is inside the bag is the cause of the stench and the flies, that doubt has flown out of my head. Even before I look inside, the sweet, putrid odor is overpowering. The insects are fighting to get close to it, whatever it is.

I have to look inside. I have to know what is in this bag. I don't want to, but I need to see.

Man up, Blake. How bad could it be?

My hands are still shaking. I squint into the depths of the brown paper bag, trying to get a good look without spilling the contents onto the kitchen counter. It looks like there are three small objects, each about three inches long.

What the…

Oh God.

Oh *God*.

This is much worse than I thought.

CHAPTER 39

It's not rotten fruit.

I wish it were rotten fruit. That would be so much better.

It's *fingers*.

It took me more than a second to figure it out. Because the fingers are discolored and swollen, and *also*, you don't expect to open a paper bag and find three fingers inside. Even when you're expecting something horrible, you don't expect *that*.

The painted pink fingernails are what gave it away.

My stomach clenches, and I'm gripped by an overwhelming wave of nausea. Between the bag with the fingers inside and the flies circling, I feel like I'm going to lose it. But I take a few deep, wheezing breaths, and then I'm okay. Well, I'm as okay as a guy holding a paper bag with three fingers in it could possibly be. My own fingers tingle.

After I get control of myself, I reach into my pocket

for my phone. I type in nine, followed by one, but before I can type the final number, I stop myself.

Maybe I shouldn't call the police.

It seems like the obvious thing to do. These fingers belonged to a human being, and I'm pretty sure they have not been stashed in my house with that person's permission. How am I supposed to explain this to the police? *Yeah, I was just looking through my kitchen, and I found these fingers. How about that?*

Also, I can't help but think about Mr. Zimmerly, about his little accident that turned out not to be an accident after all, and how it feels like the evidence is starting to point to the fact that I might have been responsible.

What if these fingers somehow lead to me as well?

I don't know how they possibly could. After all, I don't know anyone who has been murdered or is missing—well, aside from Zimmerly, but I'm pretty sure he had all his fingers. But there's that strange bloodstain on the floor that I still haven't managed to clean entirely. Is it possible that this all comes back to Whitney?

I drop the paper bag on the kitchen counter. I feel like I'm almost in a trance as I bring up my email on my phone, where a new document has arrived in my inbox.

It's Whitney's transcript from Telmont High School.

The name Telmont still sounds familiar to me. I could swear I've heard it somewhere. I scroll through the pages of the document, and just as the woman on the phone promised, it is filled with Whitney's classes and superior grades from high school. But none of that interests me. There's only one piece of information on this transcript that catches my attention.

Whitney's home address.

That's where her family lived back when she was in high school. And there's a decent chance they might still live there. I sensed that there was even more to the story about Whitney Cross than the secretary was able to tell me, and I'm desperate for answers. There is something important I am missing about Whitney Cross, and the place she came from may hold the key.

I have to speak to her parents. I have to know why she's doing this to me.

I could call them, but I have a feeling they are not going to answer the questions I have on the phone. No, this has to be done in person.

I enter the address in the map app on my phone. The drive is a bit over two hours. I glance at my watch. If I leave soon, I could be at this address by early afternoon. Of course, I don't have a car, so that complicates things. Telmont is not the kind of town that is accessible by public transportation. And who knows if Whitney's parents even still live at this address? Maybe they've left town by now, as one does when their daughter is accused of murder.

I should call the police. That's what a normal, law-abiding person would do if they found dismembered body parts in their kitchen.

Except I can't help but think about Jordan Gallo. That poor kid who dared to cheat on Whitney Cross. I have no doubt that she was responsible for his death, and she managed to make it look like a suicide. I have a feeling that if I call the police, I will leave my house in handcuffs.

Screw it. I'm going to Telmont.

CHAPTER 40

The car issue is going to be a problem. Namely, I don't have one, and a rental is pricey.

For the most part, having a car is a liability when you live in Manhattan. The streets are treacherous, parking is scarce, and public transportation is ubiquitous. There's no reason to have a car.

Plenty of my friends back at Coble & Roy had cars. Luxury vehicles they used as status symbols and took for joy rides on the weekends. As someone who grew up broke, I never had it in me to spend a fortune on a Porsche that I was going to stash away in the garage most of the time anyway. But I don't have any interaction with my old friends, so I can't call them out of the blue and ask to borrow their car.

The only person I know who owns a car is Malcolm. He and I are hardly good friends, but maybe after stealing my job and breaking the news that my fiancée dumped me, he'll be feeling charitable. Thankfully, I have Malcolm's number saved in my phone.

Before I do anything else, I stuff the paper bag with the dismembered fingers in it back where I found it in the kitchen. This way, if Whitney returns, she might not realize I've discovered what she's stashed in our kitchen. It makes me feel like I'm one step ahead of Whitney.

Although it occurs to me, in the back of my head, that now my fingerprints are all over that paper bag.

I bring Malcolm's number up on my phone and start to click on it, but then I hesitate, remembering the way he chatted amicably with Whitney this morning. That was so strange. But then again, his explanation about knowing her from the diner made sense. There's no reason not to trust him. I'm second-guessing everyone lately.

Finally, I select his number, and it rings a few times. He might not answer. He is, after all, likely at work. I'm the only unemployed loser here. But at least I have my freedom—for now.

"Hello?" Malcolm's deep voice floats into my ear. "Blake? Is that you?"

I clear my throat. "Uh, yeah."

"Everything okay, man?"

"Yeah, definitely." It might be the biggest lie I have told in my entire life. "But, listen, I need a favor."

"Sure. What is it?"

"I need to borrow your car."

"My car?" He sounds flabbergasted. "Why do you need my car?"

"I have to take a little road trip."

"To where?"

"Not far. Just New Jersey."

"*Jersey?*" He couldn't have sounded more surprised if

I told him I was going to the moon. "Why are you going *there*?"

"I'm visiting a friend."

"What about the PATH train?"

"It's a little...far out there." I'm still holding Whitney's transcript, and it crinkles underneath my grip. "Where is your car? Is it in the garage at your apartment building?"

"Yeah, but..." He hesitates. "I don't know about this, Blake. All of a sudden, you need to go to Bumfuck, New Jersey? And if there's an accident, I'm not even sure my insurance would cover it. Do you have insurance?"

I obviously don't. Why would I have car insurance when I don't even have a car? "I'm a really careful driver. I promise, it will be fine."

"I'm sorry, man." He sighs. "I want to help you out, but... I don't think it's a good idea. But, listen, what if we went out and got a drink again to talk about all this or..."

"I don't need a *drink*!" I snap at him. "I need a *car*."

I shouldn't have yelled at him. I can tell by the silence on the other line that I upset him. If there was any chance at all he was willing to help me, I have blown it.

"Are you sure you're okay?" he presses me.

"Forget it," I mumble. And I hang up.

Okay, Malcolm won't let me borrow his car. But that's fine. I can rent a car. I don't need him.

One way or another, I am doing this. I am getting to the bottom of this if it's the last thing I do.

CHAPTER 41

I end up renting a Corolla.

It costs more than I wanted to spend, but it won't be too bad if I can return the car before the end of the day, which I should be able to. Anyway, it's all on my credit card, and that bill isn't coming for two more weeks. That's a problem for Future Blake.

It's after lunch by the time I manage to get on the road. There's more traffic than I expected, but I go as fast as I dare on the highway. I keep an eye on the GPS on my phone, my heart speeding up with every mile behind me.

It's about 3:30 by the time I arrive in the town of Telmont. As expected, it's a quiet town with small streets and lots of tiny houses with picket fences. It reminds me of the little town outside Cleveland where I lived with my family growing up. I couldn't wait to get out of there and do something with my life, but now I feel a jab of nostalgia. It wouldn't have been so bad living in a place like this as an adult, and I get the feeling Krista would like it too.

Maybe after this is all over, Krista and I can move out of the city. Start over again somewhere new, where the cost of living isn't quite so insane. That is, provided I can win her back.

That's why I'm here. To figure out what Whitney's deal is so I can get Krista on my side again.

And also to figure out whose fingers are in my kitchen.

The GPS directs me to a pale yellow house with a fence partially encircling the front lawn. It's quaint—the sort of house any child would be happy to grow up in, with a bunch of siblings and maybe a dog or two. It's hard to imagine someone growing up in a house like this turning out like Whitney.

I park on the curb near the house. It takes me a few minutes to psych myself up, but then I get out of the car and walk up to the front door. The door is painted a brighter shade of yellow than the rest of the house—too bright. It's almost hard to look at.

I say a little prayer, then press my finger against the doorbell. And I wait.

After a minute, it's clear nobody is coming. I look around, checking to see if anybody is watching, and then I peer through the window next to the front door. The house looks dark inside. Nobody is home.

I walk back down the walkway to where the mailbox is perched. I take one more glance around, and then I open the mailbox. I check the first letter on the pile, noting that it is made out to Jeannette Cross.

That means I'm at the right house. This is where Whitney Cross grew up, and this is where her parents still live.

Well, it took me two hours to drive here, so I'm not

leaving without talking to someone. Unless they took a trip somewhere, I'm guessing they'll be back before the evening.

So I return to my rental car to wait.

I lean back in the seat, closing my eyes for a moment. I'm so damn tired, but there's no chance I'll be able to sleep. That would be impossible, especially since every time I close my eyes, I see those three fingers with the pink nail polish in the brown paper bag. Who do those fingers belong to? It's haunting me.

And then a thought hits me that sends a chill down my spine.

Could the fingers belong to Krista?

No, they couldn't possibly. I saw her this morning; then I went home and found the fingers in the kitchen. Yes, I walked home and wasn't rushing, but there's no way Whitney could have killed Krista, cut off her fingers, and then stuffed them in the kitchen. It's not physically possible.

Is it?

No, no, no. It can't be. The fingers were... I mean, I'm pretty sure they were decomposing. So even if Whitney pulled off the impossible, those couldn't have been Krista's fingers. Although it's not like I got a good look at them. All I saw clearly was the nail polish, which happened to be the same cotton candy pink shade Krista was wearing this morning when I watched her scoop those cookies off the tray.

I grab my phone with shaking fingers and tap out a text message to Krista:

Are you OK?

She doesn't have to answer me. She doesn't have to do anything except look at the message so I can see that little "read" denotation.

But it doesn't appear. The message doesn't even say that it was delivered.

Okay, I'm being paranoid. Yes, I'm pretty sure those were women's fingers, and yes, the nail polish was the same shade Krista was wearing, but I still don't see how it's possible they could belong to her. Krista is fine. I saw her just this morning. She's *fine*.

And if she's not, I will kill Whitney with my bare hands.

CHAPTER 42

I wait in the car for over an hour.

At some point, I get hungry. I skipped breakfast, and all I had for lunch was a bag of chips from the convenience store next to the car rental place. At the end of the first hour, I remember the baggie of cookies from Krista. I had wanted to save them, but my stomach grows insistent enough that I decide to eat a few of them. As the taste of cinnamon spreads through my mouth, I get a lump in my throat. I hope they're not the last cookies she ever makes for me.

The thought almost makes me choke.

Over the course of the hour, I check my phone multiple times to see if Krista has returned my text. She hasn't. I have to believe there's no chance that those fingers could be hers. The timeline is too tight. Krista is just fine. Except…

That shade of nail polish is so similar to what I saw on her this morning. At least I'm pretty sure it is. Every time I think about it, my stomach clenches.

Why won't she answer my text?

It's close to five when a Chevrolet pulls into the driveway of the yellow house. I duck down in the car, watching a woman in her sixties with dark blond hair climb out of the vehicle and walk to the front door. That must be Whitney's mother. She looks a little like her.

I wait another few minutes. I don't want to pounce on her the second she walks in. I'll give her a chance to take off her shoes and relax a bit. Then I'll go knock on the door once she's settled. I eat another cookie.

Once she's had ten minutes in the house, I climb out of the car. Just like before, I stride down the path to the front door, this time knowing that somebody will answer. I just hope she doesn't tell me something I don't want to hear.

I ring the doorbell, and there is a scuffling of feet behind the door. I haven't quite decided what to say to Whitney's mother. I have a few cover stories in the back of my head, but all of them sound weak. If she recognizes that I'm bullshitting her, she will slam the door in my face, and that will be the end of it.

When the door opens, a woman who I presume is Mrs. Cross stands in the doorway. Up close, she looks less like Whitney than I thought—I guess Whitney looks more like her father. I had gauged her age to be in her sixties from afar, but now that I'm close up, I can see the spiderwebbing of wrinkles around her eyes and a haunted look that reminds me of what I see when I look in a mirror.

That's the moment I decide to tell her the truth.

"Mrs. Cross?" I say.

She gives me a wary look. "Yes…"

"My name is Blake Porter," I say. "And…the thing is,

five months ago, I took in a tenant named Whitney Cross. And I..."

For a moment, I can't go on, thinking about all the terrible things that have happened since Whitney moved into my beloved home. The rotting food in the kitchen. Krista leaving me. The murder of Mr. Zimmerly. And now those disembodied fingers belonging to God knows who. (*Please not Krista.*) It's overwhelming. And while driving here seemed like the answer at the time, now I'm not sure anymore.

What if this doesn't fix anything?

Mrs. Cross looks up at my face, and she seems to see the same thing in me that I saw in her. She reaches out and puts a hand on my shoulder, and all I can think is, *This woman gets it.*

"Come in, Mr. Porter," she says. "We need to talk."

CHAPTER 43

Mrs. Cross offers to take my jacket, but I keep it on, feeling like there's a chance I could need to make a quick getaway. She leads me to the living room and sits me down on a flawless white sofa with big, puffy cushions. Like the rest of the house, the living room has a quaint, cozy appearance. I can just imagine sitting here in the middle of winter with the fireplace blazing and a cup of hot cocoa in my hand.

Whitney's mother sits across from me on a matching love seat, keeping her eyes pinned on my face. When she speaks, her tone is measured, her true feelings only revealed by the slightest tremor in her voice. "You're living with Whitney," she acknowledges.

"Yes," I say.

She looks down at her lap, carefully smoothing out a crease on her beige skirt. "I thought she might be dead. I should have known better."

It's shocking to hear a woman comment so cavalierly

on the death of her own daughter. But now that I know Whitney, it's not all that surprising.

"I need help," I say. "She's ruining my life, and I don't even know why."

"That sounds like Whitney." She gives me a humorless smile. "But if she has decided to ruin your life, she has a reason. There is always a reason."

I can't think of what the reason could be. I'd never met Whitney before the day she showed up looking for a place to live. Yes, I was rude to her at the diner, but it doesn't seem like enough. She must have some other reason.

"Let me tell you a little story about my daughter," Mrs. Cross says, sitting up straighter. "I have a younger son. When he was four years old and she was seven, he accidentally broke one of her toys. It wasn't intentional—he was *four*. The next day, I took the two of them to the playground, and she waited until they were at the highest point on the jungle gym, and she shoved him off. Joey told me what happened when they were setting his arm in the emergency room." She crosses her legs. "When I asked Whitney about it later, all she said was, 'That's what happens to you if you're not careful.' I put her in therapy after that, but she didn't like it, so she made it stop."

"Made it stop?"

A haunted look fills her eyes. "She would steal things from me—items that I treasured like my grandmother's diamond necklace or an old letter from my late father. And she would destroy them, leaving the remnants in a place she knew I'd find them."

"Jesus."

"I learned to be very careful around my daughter,

Mr. Porter. And believe me when I say that isn't the worst thing she has done. Not even close."

I swallow. If only I had known some of this—any of this—before I let Whitney move in with us. Now I suspect I have opened a door that can't be closed. "I heard about Jordan Gallo."

She flinches. "Yes, that was a terrible situation."

"Did she... I mean, do you think she was the one who..."

"Did she kill him?" There is a flicker of amusement in Mrs. Cross's eyes, and for a moment, I wonder if the apple didn't fall far from the tree. "Only Whitney knows the answer to that question. Well, Whitney *and* Jordan. If I had to guess, I'd say yes, I think she pushed him off the roof. But I can't be sure. Whitney has a way of making you so miserable, suicide suddenly seems like a viable option."

Her words rattle me down to my soul when I think about the last couple of months. "Yes."

"My husband would still be here if not for her." Her eyes drop. "He couldn't take it. He had a heart attack one month after she disappeared."

"When she disappeared," I say, "where did she go?"

"I didn't know at first," Mrs. Cross says. "I still don't know for certain. The Gallos were making a lot of trouble for her, so I don't blame her for wanting to get away. We reported her missing, but the police considered her a runaway, and since there was no warrant for her arrest, they didn't spend much time looking." She cocks her head thoughtfully. "She definitely left the country at some point. Three years after she vanished, she sent us a postcard from Braga, Portugal."

Braga, Portugal. Like the name Telmont, it sets off

little bells in the back of my head. Why can't I remember? It's so frustrating.

"But I knew she was back in the States," she adds.

"How? Did she contact you?"

"No." Mrs. Cross leans forward as if to tell me a secret. "Because six years later, the girl that Jordan left Whitney for was found murdered."

It takes me a second to wrap my head around this. Whitney's high school boyfriend cheated on her with another girl, and she killed him right away, waited *six years*, and then killed the girl too. Over a stupid high school infidelity.

That takes a special kind of insanity.

"So you have to understand, Mr. Porter," she says, "if you have done something to Whitney, she will never let it go. Not a year later—not ten years later. No matter how long it takes, she will make sure you pay the price."

I bury my face in my hands. I don't understand. I never even met her before she moved in, much less committed some unforgivable crime against her. Why is she doing this to me? Why?

"Are you okay?" Mrs. Cross asks me gently. "Can I get you something? Some water?"

I raise my head and nod. "Water would be great. Thank you."

A deep depression sets in. I had hoped coming here might solve all my problems, but it hasn't solved anything. Mrs. Cross doesn't know how to handle her daughter any better than I do. And I still don't understand why Whitney has targeted me.

Mrs. Cross leaves me alone in the living room while she disappears into the kitchen. I stand up to stretch my legs and wander over to the fireplace, where several framed photos are positioned on the mantel. There is one of Mrs. Cross and a man who I assume is her late husband. Then another of a man in his twenties—presumably her son.

She has one family photo, which looks like it was taken a long time ago. Mrs. Cross looks at least fifteen years younger than she does right now. Positioned between the parents are their two teenage children—a much younger version of the man in the other photo and a teenage girl. I stare at the photo for a second as a sick feeling mounts in my stomach.

What the hell is going on here?

Mrs. Cross returns with a glass of water in her hand. I rip my eyes away from the family photo and turn to look at her. I jab at the picture frame with my index finger. "Who is *that*?"

"That's a family picture," she says defensively. "Just because my daughter has done something terrible, that doesn't mean I have to forget her entirely."

"But…" I shake my head. "Who is that girl in the photo?"

She looks at me like I've lost my mind. "That's Whitney. My daughter."

"But…that's not…"

I turn to examine the photo again, making sure I'm not imagining it. Then I look over at Mrs. Cross. And now I see it—the resemblance.

"Mr. Porter?" Mrs. Cross crinkles her brow. "Are you all right, young man?"

No, I am not all right. I am so far from all right, it's not even funny.

Because the teenage girl in that photo is not the

woman who has been living in our guest bedroom, the one who's been tormenting me. The one who calls herself Whitney Cross. No, the teenage girl in the photograph is somebody entirely different.

It's *Krista*.

CHAPTER 44

My head won't stop spinning.

For a second, I have tunnel vision, and I have to grab on to the mantle to keep from falling. Mrs. Cross seems a bit panicked. Maybe she's sorry she invited me in.

"Mr. Porter?" she says in a worried voice.

"I…" I take a few deep breaths, trying to keep myself from passing out. "I just…"

How could the terrible person Mrs. Cross was describing be *my* Krista? That's ridiculous. It doesn't make any sense.

Although…

In a way, it makes perfect sense.

Oh no.

A terrible thought hits me. I've got to get out of here. This situation has just gone from bad to worse.

"Thank you for talking to me, Mrs. Cross," I say. "But I have to…"

She seems to get it. She leads me back to the door, and

I burst out of there as fast as I can, gasping in the fresh air. But what I really need is to get off my feet. Well, I need to do that, and I need to make a phone call. Right away.

I hurry back to my car. Once I'm inside, I scroll through my phone, searching my contacts. It's not easy, given how badly my hands are shaking. When I find the name Stacie Parker, I click to place a call to my old boss's assistant.

Please pick up. Please.

After several rings, the call goes to voicemail. She's not answering. But it might be okay. People sometimes don't answer their phones during the day.

My head is spinning so much that I can barely think straight. I have to focus to get my hands to work as I bring up the Facebook app on my phone. I find her profile right away, with her pretty smiling face. I click on it, and right away I see that the last post wasn't from Stacie at all. It's from another name that I recognize as belonging to her roommate.

Still trying to locate Stacie. If anybody has any information or has heard from her, please let us know right away! Still hoping she will come home, safe and sound!

Except Stacie is not coming home safe and sound. And whenever they find her, she will be missing three of her fingers with their nails painted pink.

Shit. Shit, shit, shit.

It was one time. *One* time. It didn't mean anything. I was working such long hours, trying to snag that promotion, and she was there, and I just... I slipped.

It was so stupid. I knew it at the time, and right after, I told Stacie it was never going to happen again. I was just thankful that Krista never found out.

Except it turns out Krista knew. She knew the whole

time. I thought everything was *fine* between us. We were getting married, for Christ's sake.

I stuff my phone into my jacket pocket, trying to figure out what the hell to do next. While my hand is inside, I feel a slip of paper in there that I hadn't noticed before. I pull it out and discover a sheet of notebook paper that has been folded several times.

What is this?

I unfold the piece of paper, which is covered in scribbled writing. Somebody has written a letter in black ink. It actually looks a lot like my handwriting. I can tell the difference, but a casual observer probably wouldn't be able to.

> *I'm so sorry for what I've done. I couldn't deal with losing my job, and it was all too much for me. After all the lives I've taken, I can't go on. I've decided it's better to end it all right now.*
>
> *Blake*

Is this a *suicide note*?

Did Krista slip it into my jacket? Based on what she did to her high school boyfriend, it sounds like her MO. Except I'm not dead, so why is there a suicide note in my pocket? It doesn't make any sense. What good would a suicide note be if I'm still alive?

When I get back to the city, will Krista be waiting for me on the roof of the brownstone, ready to push me off? Waiting in the kitchen with a butcher knife? Whatever she has planned, I know her game now. I'm not going to give her the chance to take me out and make it look like a suicide. She has missed her chance.

Except…

I swivel my head to look at the passenger seat. There's a Ziploc bag on the seat, which still has one cookie left inside.

The *cookies*.

Krista knew I was coming to see her. She knew I was on my way, and the first thing she did was start baking cookies. She knew I would eat them—they're my favorite.

Fuck.

I wrench the door of the Corolla open. I leap out of the car and make a beeline for a group of bushes on the outskirts of the Cross residence. Then I shove my index finger down my throat until my eyes start to tear. But I don't stop. I can't stop until I have vomited up the entire contents of my stomach onto the ground beneath my feet.

PART 2

KRISTA
(NÉE WHITNEY CROSS)

Don't worry. They both deserved it.

CHAPTER 45

EIGHT MONTHS BEFORE

Becky and I are having lunch at Cosmo's Diner.

Becky is a good person to have as a friend. Whenever I meet a prospective friend, I evaluate their positive and negative qualities. Becky is incredibly loyal—the sort of friend who might someday help me bury a dead body, if such a thing were required, which, historically, it has been for me. Also, she is far less attractive than I am, so she does not serve as a temptation for my significant other. For that reason, I have cultivated the friendship since my permanent return to this country from Portugal. I even convinced Blake to find her loser husband a job at his company.

"So have you and Blake set a wedding date yet?" she asks as she drags a french fry through the blob of ranch on her plate. "I definitely think fall is the best time to get married. Everybody thinks it's the summer, but early fall is *so* much nicer."

"Blake has been so busy at work," I say. "We've barely had time to celebrate."

"Oh, I bet you've celebrated." She winks at me. "He can barely keep his hands off you. And he's so *hot*. You're so lucky, Krista."

I already know Becky thinks Blake is hot, based on the shameless way she flirts with him. But she's right—I do feel lucky. Blake is, after all, the whole package. He is intelligent, and on top of that, he's motivated and successful. If I start a family with him, he will provide for us, which will be nice considering I've been just barely scraping by on my salary from the dry cleaner. He's nice but not so nice that people walk all over him. He's loyal—I never catch him checking out other women. And he has a sweet side, even though he'd never admit it. He gives the best hugs of anyone I've known, and when his arms wrap around me, I feel the love emanating from his body.

I can't wait to marry him and spend the rest of my life with him.

Our waitress approaches our table. She's very pretty in a fresh-faced sort of way, like I am, and the thought crosses my mind that she is the sort of girl that Blake could have fallen for if he didn't have me. Too bad for her.

And then I read her name off the tag pinned to her shirt:

Whitney.

My old name. I loved my name when I was younger, and I hate that I had to start over with a new one. But I couldn't take a risk—Jordan Gallo's family was not messing around. Still, I feel a flash of nostalgia every time I meet somebody named Whitney. I've always thought that in the future, I would be able to go back to being Whitney Cross someday, when things cooled off.

"Can I get you some dessert?" the new Whitney asks us.

Becky raises an eyebrow at me, but I shake my head. "Just the check, please."

"You got it!" Whitney says.

I applaud her enthusiasm. I've worked as a waitress, and it can be exhausting. She's got a lot of customers, yet she keeps a smile on her face. Although I wonder if she'll keep up her good spirits now that the manager seems to be coming our way with a sour expression on his face.

"Miss Cross," he says in a humorless voice. "A word for a moment, please?"

Miss *Cross*?

What?

The girl flashes us an apologetic smile. "Sorry, just a moment, and I'll be back with your check."

She rushes off, and Becky is saying something to me, but I can't even focus. Because the manager just referred to her as Miss Cross. Her name is Whitney Cross.

That's *my* name.

And it's not a common one. As far as I know, I was the only one out there. Yet here is a second one. Not only that, but she is approximately my age. My height and build. She even looks like me if you don't look too closely, and her hair is the color mine was before I started coloring it.

That's...interesting.

"Krista?" Becky is saying my name. Well, not my name, but the other name I took when I could no longer be Whitney. "Are you okay? You seem totally spaced out."

"Huh?" I force myself to turn my attention back to Becky's round face. "Sorry. I just have a lot on my mind."

"And you're going to have so much more on your

mind when you're planning your wedding with Blake," she teases me.

But I can't even focus on this conversation anymore. I need to know who this girl is. I need to know if she stole my name.

And for that, I need Elijah.

CHAPTER 46

Even though I haven't spoken to Elijah Myers in over a year, when I tell him I want to meet, he is available within the hour.

We end up meeting at our usual location: a relatively quiet park in downtown Manhattan that is nowhere near where either of us lives. I've never been to Elijah's apartment, but I know he lives in Brooklyn. When we meet, he takes the D train into the city.

Elijah is waiting on a park bench, wearing the same Linux baseball cap with a penguin on it that he's had since high school, which now looks like it has seen better days. His goatee is trimmed a bit better than the last time I saw him, but other than that, he looks exactly the same as always. He's barely even put on any weight since high school.

He stands up when I arrive, his eyes lighting up the way they always do when we see each other after a long time. "Whitney!" he says.

"Krista," I correct him, even though I secretly love it when he calls me Whitney. He's the only person who does anymore.

"Of course, sorry," he says quickly. "It's just…it's so good to see you."

He looks like he wants to give me a hug, but he doesn't, and I'm glad. Elijah and I don't have that kind of relationship, although I strongly suspect he would like it if we did. He isn't deluded though. He knows this is not a social call.

We sit together on the bench, and Elijah tugs on the collar of his Carnegie Mellon T-shirt. He peers at me curiously through his wire-rimmed glasses. "So what's going on?" he asks me. "What do you need?"

"Do you think," I say in the quietest voice I can, "there's a chance that somebody has started using my name?"

"No way," he says. "When I got the ID for Krista Marshall, it was clean. I checked and double-checked. Nobody else is going to be using it."

When I first left home at age seventeen, Elijah was the one who helped me get the new ID. He was the biggest tech nerd at our high school, and there were rumors around school about his hacking skills. We met in computer science class during junior year, back when I thought I would go to college and have a career in the field. So much for that. But I met Elijah, and it was the most important connection I had ever made.

"No," I say. "I mean Whitney Cross. Could someone be using my old identity?"

That question gives him pause. I appreciate that he's not just shrugging off my concerns. Elijah is thoughtful in that way.

"It's possible," he admits. "Whitney Cross was listed as a missing person, and you haven't used the name in a long time. And I scrubbed the internet of all mentions of you and Jordan. If somebody else was searching for an alternate identity, it would be up for grabs."

That's not the answer I want to hear. "Oh."

He frowns. "Why do you ask? Is there someone you think has been using the name?"

I hesitate, not wanting to share more than I have to. Elijah has a tendency to ask too many questions. "Maybe."

"I could look into it for you," he offers. When I start to protest, he adds, "I wouldn't charge you anything."

He never does. He only charges me for the materials themselves, like the cost of the new passport for Krista Marshall. And even then, I'm pretty sure he footed some of the cost.

"Okay," I agree. "Look into it."

"Will do." He leans back against the park bench. "So how is…uh…Blake? Still together?"

For some reason, it doesn't surprise me that he remembers my boyfriend's name from over a year ago. But I'm surprised he didn't notice the giant diamond on my left fourth finger. I reach for the ring instinctively and fiddle with the large stone, twisting it counterclockwise.

"Yes," I say. "We're engaged, actually."

"Oh," he says. "Good. Good for you."

He has to know that even if Blake weren't in my life, he and I would not be together. But those are not words I have ever said to him.

"How about you?" I ask politely. "Anyone special?"

His cheeks color slightly. "No. Not really."

"Well…" I glance over my shoulder. A street performer

has set up shop behind us and is simultaneously playing an acoustic guitar and a harmonica. A small crowd has formed that is tossing money into his open guitar case. "I better get going. I really appreciate this, Elijah."

"No problem."

When I stand, he stands too. He's always been short—he's about the same height I am in my heels, which means he's roughly five foot five. That isn't the reason he and I will never be together. But it doesn't help.

"Bye, Whit—er, Krista," he says. "I'll call you when I get any information."

"Thank you, Elijah," I say.

CHAPTER 47

I try to wait up for Blake at night, but it's hard when he gets home at close to midnight.

It's worth it though. When he gets home and sees me sitting on the couch, waiting for him, maybe with a plate full of freshly baked cookies, he looks so happy. The bright smile that spreads across his face makes my knees weak, even after nearly two years. Like I said, I can't wait to be his wife.

I really loved Jordan. I thought that he and I would get married someday, although I now recognize that high school relationships aren't meant to last. When I found out he was cheating on me, it *destroyed* me. He broke me.

That's why I had to do what I did. I'm not some homicidal sociopath. I simply knew that I could not be happy while Jordan was still alive and existing in this world.

So I *fixed* it.

Blake is the first man I have loved since Jordan. The first time he showed up to get his suit dry-cleaned, I knew that he was the one. That's why I kept giving him fake discounts on the dry cleaning until he asked me out. It certainly took him long enough! He was so clearly interested, so when he didn't ask, I investigated to see what was going on.

After camping out at the address Blake listed on his dry-cleaning slip, I discovered he was dating a skinny girl with white-blond hair who smoked like a chimney—*such* a disgusting habit. When they were at a restaurant together, I paid a waitress to alert his girlfriend that he'd been at the same place only a few days early with another girl, acting hot and heavy. She did it while Blake was in the bathroom, and the look on the girlfriend's face was exactly what I'd been hoping for. A few days later, Blake asked me out.

That other girl would never have made him happy in the long run. I did him a huge favor.

Tonight, it's closer to one when Blake's keys turn in the door to the brownstone we moved into together a few months ago. It has three bedrooms, and I knew Blake was going to pop the question soon when he mentioned that the middle one would be perfect as a nursery. It was so sweet when he suggested getting a fish to practice for when we're parents together, and I've been taking my fish mom responsibilities very seriously in order to prove myself to him. And I try to be understanding about his work, because I know this promotion is important to him, but it's hard.

I try my best though. I try to be the wife he wants me to be.

I rise from the sofa just as Blake stumbles into the foyer. His brown hair is slightly disheveled, and his tie is hanging loose around his neck. I take a second just to gaze at him. He's very handsome, but he barely seems aware of it. Maybe that's why he's not as self-involved as other good-looking men I've dated. Lately he's been talking more about how he wants to give me all the things that his father wasn't wealthy enough to give his mother before she died. He's focused on the big picture.

As he comes into the living room and sees me standing there, I expect to see that familiar pleased smile spread across his face. But instead, he just looks surprised.

"Krista," he says. "I didn't know you would be awake. It's almost one in the morning."

"I waited up," I say proudly.

"Oh."

"And I made you cookies."

That ought to get a reaction out of him. He loves the cookies that I bake—they always put a smile on his face. But instead, he pats his stomach. "Better not. I'm starting to get a gut."

He isn't—at all. On top of work, he religiously goes to the gym twice a week, and he's closer to a six-pack than a gut. And also, when has he ever cared about that? Who does he need to impress? After all, I'm already in love with him.

Blake comes closer to give me a kiss, and I expect it to be one of our usual long, lingering kisses that often leads to the bedroom. But instead, it's a peck on the lips. The sort you give your wife of forty years.

And when he pulls away, I notice something else:

His shirt is buttoned wrong.

I'm going to wager that there is no way Blake went through his entire sixteen-hour day with his shirt missing a button. At some point, he unbuttoned his shirt. And then hastily buttoned it again before coming home.

Also, I smell perfume.

But no, I'm being paranoid. Blake wouldn't cheat on me. He is a good guy, unlike Jordan. He wants to spend his life with me. He wants to fill the bedrooms upstairs with children. He loves me.

And yet...

I run my fingers down his chest. "You know," I say playfully. "I'm not very tired. Any chance you want to have a little fun?"

"Krista." He looks at me in astonishment. "It's one in the morning!"

That has never stopped him before. We have had sex at all hours of the night. He is *always* in the mood if I am.

Except right now, apparently.

He leans in to peck my lips again. "Sorry, I'm just beat tonight. That Henderson campaign is kicking my ass. But tomorrow..." He manages a tiny smile. "I'm going to rock your world, okay? Rain check?"

"Uh-huh," I say, crestfallen.

He looks at me for a moment, then surprises me by pulling me in tight for a hug. "I love you, Krista. So much. I can't wait to marry you, babe."

"I love you too," I say back.

I do love him. So much.

But I don't trust him.

CHAPTER 48

Blake snores.

It's not loud enough to be intolerable. It's a soft sound, somewhere between heavy breathing and an outright snore. Occasionally, it's annoying, but mostly I think it's sort of cute. You know that you like a guy when you're into his snoring.

But the important thing is that if he's snoring, that means he is asleep.

I creep around the side of the bed, watching his face to make sure he doesn't wake up. When I get to his nightstand, I pick up his phone where it's charging. Blake has been talking about getting a new phone for a while, but he hasn't gotten around to it because he's been working nonstop. And now I'm glad, because his old phone still has fingerprint recognition.

As gently as I can, I take Blake's thumb and press it into the pad of the phone. Right away, he notices something has disturbed him. He lets out a groan, then flips over in bed, mumbling something in his sleep. I hold my breath, expecting his eyes to fly open.

But they don't. He's still asleep. And a second later, he starts snoring again.

Blake's phone is now unlocked. Which means I have access to his emails, his photographs, and his text messages. I can look at whatever I want.

Some people would say this is a violation of privacy. But if the two of us are going to be married, if we're starting a whole new life together, there should be no secrets between us. What is mine is his and what's his is mine. And since this phone is his, then it is actually mine. And I have every right to look at it.

I think it's extremely unlikely that there are any incriminating emails or photographs, so I go straight for his text messages. It's the expected mix of texts from his work colleagues and way too many from his boss. For the most part, it's reassuringly uninteresting. There's only one name that stands out to me.

Stacie.

Stacie is Blake's boss's assistant, and it's my understanding that she also often serves as the assistant to the entire office. I met her at the Christmas party last year, and she was outright stunning in a low-cut dress that left very little to the imagination. Yet not the slightest bit out of Blake's league.

He wouldn't.

Would he?

I open up their text conversation. Most of it is benign office stuff, but the last text from Stacie was sent at one thirty in the morning, which is a very suspicious time to be sending a message. And what is even worse is the contents of the message:

> I had a great time tonight. If you ever change your mind about doing it again, you know where to find me.

Well, that's that.

Of course, I can't stop myself from scrolling through the rest of their text messages, although I'm sorry after I've done it. Some of it is business, but much of it is flirting. Granted, she's flirting with him more than he reciprocates, but he's plenty guilty too. I scroll through the messages leading up to tonight.

> Are you still here, Porter?
>
> Ugh, yeah. Late night. What are you still doing here?
>
> Forgot my purse. Just came to grab it, then I'm out of here.
>
> Lucky you.
>
> You should take a little break. Want some company?
>
> Sure.

That's the last communication they had before her message about having fun and how they should do it again. And then he stumbles home at one in the morning wearing her perfume, his shirt buttoned incorrectly. It doesn't take a rocket scientist to figure out that one.

That bastard. He told me he *loved* me. He told me he wanted to marry me. He gave me a ring. He pretended to be a good guy. And all along, he's been cheating on me. *Lying* to me.

I replace Blake's phone on the nightstand. He is still sound asleep, blowing air from between his lips. He has that dark shadow on his jaw that he always has until he shaves in the morning. He's sexy. I know exactly what she sees in him.

I imagine what would happen if I went downstairs to the kitchen and boiled some water, then brought it up here and threw it in his face. That would change his life forever. The burns he would sustain would be permanent—his face would be scarred for the rest of his life. He might lose his vision.

He'd never cheat on me again, that's for sure.

I consider it. I *strongly* consider it. But ultimately, I decide against it. First of all, the consequences of deliberately burning someone would be considerable. I might go to jail. And if I got arrested, the police would surely figure out that I am Whitney Cross, and then I would really be in trouble.

I thought Blake was the one. I loved him.

Why did he have to be a cheating bastard like all the others?

CHAPTER 49

I toss and turn for much of the night after discovering those messages on Blake's phone.

When I discovered Jordan was cheating on me, I was still in high school, living with my parents. I can't say I had the best relationship with my parents—that's an understatement. They always blamed me for some stupid accident that happened when I was a kid. Who holds a grudge against a *child*? My father called me a sociopath, even though I was only seven years old and had no idea what that meant. Anyway, Joey was fine. It was just a broken arm. It's not like he had brain damage. It didn't keep their golden boy from getting that fancy schmancy investment banker job.

My relationship with my father was never the same after that incident, but I never cared what he thought. And now he's dead anyway.

Is it such an awful thing to want retribution against people who have wronged you? When I was in middle school and my best friend Ashley Cerutti decided I was no longer cool enough to hang out in our friend group, should I have just shrugged and said "no problem"? Stood by as she took all my friends away from me? Anyway, if she didn't want her hair to catch fire, she shouldn't have worn so much hair spray.

After the whole school found out that Jordan was cheating on me, I ran home to my mother to tell her what had happened. She was in the kitchen, peeling potatoes for dinner, when I came into the room sobbing.

Her brow wrinkled. "What's wrong, Whitney?"

"Jordan cheated on me!" I wailed.

She could have taken me in her arms and held me, which was what I'd been hoping she'd do. I wanted to cry my guts out while she stroked my hair and told me that Jordan was a dirtbag and that I'd find someone a million times better. Then we'd eat cookie dough together—my favorite thing.

But instead, she looked at me and said, "Maybe if you didn't act so crazy, he wouldn't have done it."

And then she went back to peeling potatoes.

I ate cookie dough alone that night in my bedroom while I sobbed into my pillow and plotted a way to make Jordan pay.

So in the end, it was good that my mother blew me off when I told her about Jordan. Because if she hadn't, he never would have realized the error in his ways. He never would have acknowledged what he did to me, especially while sobbing and begging me to make it right again—as if he could! I'm sure he would have grown up to be a terrible person who would have hurt many other women. I did the world a favor.

When Blake and I were getting serious and he introduced me to his father, I knew I had to reciprocate. Early in our relationship, I'd told him about my father's heart attack but admitted that my mother was still living. I should have told him they were both dead, because now he expected to meet my alleged mother.

Blake meeting my real mother was out of the question, of course. But I located a performance school in the East Village, and I approached one of the teachers to ask if there were any middle-aged students who might be interested in a little work on the side.

That's how I met Wanda.

Wanda was fifty-two years old, and she was *perfect*. My own mother bears more of a resemblance to me, but Wanda was close enough with her dyed blond hair and fair skin. When we got coffee together at a small coffee shop by Washington Square Park with little outdoor tables, we talked about the part I wanted her to play.

"I love to bake," I explained to Wanda. "So maybe you can tell him how we used to bake cookies all the time when I was little."

My real mother used to bake cookies a lot, but we rarely did it together after Joey's accident. She didn't seem to want to spend much time with me after that.

"I'm not much of a baker," Wanda admitted. "I don't think I've ever baked cookies in my life!"

"It's easy," I told her. "The secret is in the butter."

I then explained to her how I always use high-quality butter that I let sit at room temperature for exactly fifteen minutes—no more, no less. Wanda nodded, taking notes on a scrap of paper.

"He sounds like a good guy, this Blake," she said after

I'd explained in detail how to make the perfect snickerdoodle cookies and how much he likes them. "Sounds like you really like him."

"Oh, I do."

She frowned at me over her cappuccino. "Then why don't you tell him the truth about your mom? I bet he'd understand. I mean, I don't want to talk myself out of a job, but it seems like the truth is the best policy."

At that moment, I desperately wished I could introduce Blake to my real mother. I wished I had a normal family where we could drive out to Jersey together, and she'd pepper him with lots of nosy questions, and he'd act annoyed later, but then we'd laugh about it.

But I couldn't tell him the truth. I couldn't tell him that my mother didn't like me because she thought I was a sociopath and didn't even know my name anymore and probably thought I was dead—no, she was *hoping* I was dead.

"No," I said. "He wouldn't understand."

I ended up hiring Wanda, and she played the part to perfection. She was sweet but not *too* sweet, and she even gave him a good-natured grilling about his intentions toward me. I loved the way he answered those questions. She joined us for a few pleasant meals before I regretfully told him she was returning to her home in Idaho. I had imagined she'd join us again for the wedding, but it doesn't look like that will be happening now.

No, Blake and I are done.

I finally give up on sleep at four in the morning. I roll out of bed, creeping across our bedroom to the closet. I pull out a shoebox stuffed all the way in the back, which I bring with me down to the living room.

Blake is utterly uninterested in my shoes, so I have no worries that he will go through my shoeboxes. I sit down on the sofa and take the lid off the box, which is packed with unmailed handwritten letters on white printer paper, folded into thirds. I remove one of the letters—dated one month ago—from the pile and start reading:

Dear Mom,

Blake surprised me today. It wasn't any special occasion, but there's a flower shop on his way home from the subway station, and he bought me a single red rose. I wish more than anything that you could be at our wedding, because I want you to see that I'm a good person.

You and Daddy were wrong about me. All I needed was the right man to make me happy.

I fold up the letter, unable to go on. It's painful to read my words from back when I believed Blake and I would have a happy ending together. It's all fallen apart now. Maybe I was right—maybe I am a good person, and all I need is the right man to make me happy, but Blake isn't that man. Maybe he doesn't exist.

I think back to the role Wanda played as my mother when we all went out to dinner together. Even though it wasn't real, it was the most affection I'd received from a maternal figure in years. When it was over, I ached for my own mother.

But I can't see my mother. I can't see her because I can't return to Telmont, and she probably thinks I'm dead anyway. And even if I could see her, she wouldn't give me the comfort I need. She wouldn't stroke my hair and eat cookie dough with me. She would tell me to buck up and that if Blake cheated on me, it's all my fault.

No wonder Blake doesn't love me. Even my own mother couldn't love me.

Even so, writing to her has become a habit over the last fifteen years. So I get out a piece of paper and compose yet another letter I will never send.

Dear Mom,

Well, it happened again. The man I love has betrayed me in the most horrible way.

I know you don't think I am capable of being loved, and maybe you're right. You don't think I deserve a happy life with a decent man. I thought Blake was the one who would prove you wrong, but instead, he made a fool out of me.

How could he do that, Mom? How could he tell me he loves me and that he wants to marry me, then treat me this way?

You always said to let it go. What you really meant is that I should let him get away with it.

But I'm not going to let that happen. I won't let Blake get away with what he's done to me.

I'm going to make him pay. Just like Jordan. Just like the rest of them.

Love,
Whitney

CHAPTER 50

The next day, I meet Elijah in the park again.

It would be easier to talk on the phone, but he has always been paranoid about phones. Or at least that's what he claims. Part of me thinks he just wants to see me.

Once again, he has arrived first. Unlike yesterday, he stands up when I arrive, grinning at the sight of me. "Hey," he says.

"Hey," I say flatly.

He frowns. "Everything okay?"

I haven't told anyone what I found out last night. But I have a feeling that out of everyone I know, Elijah can keep a secret. "I found out that Blake is cheating on me."

"Holy crap," he blurts out. "What an idiot."

"Yeah," I mumble.

"How are you doing?"

I don't entirely know how to answer that question. I am so hurt and disappointed, I can barely think straight.

But at least I have ensured that I will get something out of this. When I went downstairs to the living room last night, I found a flash drive that Blake keeps in his briefcase. He likes to keep a backup of all his files. He's always so dependable. I copied all his clients' records onto my own flash drive. I intend to sell everything I can to the competition. Not only will I make a pretty penny doing this, enough to rebuild my life, but when his boss catches wind of it, he will never work in this industry again.

I mean, it's not as good as pushing him off the roof, but it's something.

"I'll be okay," I finally say. "So…what did you find out about that waitress?"

"This information was *not* easy to find." Elijah's expression is grim. "But it turns out you were right. She's using your name and your Social Security number."

Even though I had suspected it, this news fills me with rage, even worse than when I found out Blake was cheating on me. She stole my identity. She stole my name. It wasn't hers to take, but she took it anyway. That *bitch*.

"Her real name is Amanda Lenhart," he goes on. "She was a PhD candidate in biology."

She gave up a life as a biologist and now she's waiting tables. Whatever prompted her to steal my name, it must have been really bad.

"Do you know why she needed a new identity?" I ask.

He shakes his head. It's frustrating that he doesn't know, because Elijah seems to know everything.

"There are no criminal charges against Amanda Lenhart," he says. "So I'm guessing there was somebody after her. Somebody who might've hurt her if they found her."

Somehow, it doesn't matter to me at all that she might have had a good reason. The fact that she stole my identity feels like the worst kind of violation there is. Is it worse than what Blake did?

I don't know. They both deserve to be punished.

I fiddle with my engagement ring, and a jab of sadness hits me. In the near future, I'll be returning this beautiful ring to Blake permanently. And that's when I get a brilliant idea. I had intended to tell Blake today that it was all over, but now I think I'll wait. I think there's a way to punish both of them and come off scot-free myself.

Plus, once Whitney/Amanda is dead, I can take my name back.

"Elijah," I say. "I need your help with one more thing."

He leans forward eagerly. "Anything."

I am going to teach Blake a lesson. I'm going to teach both of them a lesson.

CHAPTER 51

Blake is losing his mind.

It's been over two months since he lost his job after I tipped off his boss about the files that were sold to their competitor. It worked even better than I expected. Wayne Vincent didn't even bother to listen to Blake's side of things and made sure his name was mud around town. Now he can't find another job. He is obsessively exercising all day, and when he's not working out, he's playing games on his computer. And he's awake all night.

I have also been on his laptop, and I know exactly how little money he has left. When I brought up the idea of taking in a tenant, I knew he would have to agree.

As for Amanda, the bitch who stole my identity, she has been evicted from her apartment. It was actually very easy. I just sent Elijah over to her apartment building looking disheveled and had him knock on a few doors, trying to find "that girl Whitney who sells crack." They threw her out, and now she is sleeping on a friend's couch. A day after I posted the advertisement at Cosmo's for the cheap room, she gave me a call.

I've had to take steps to make sure she is the only candidate we are seriously considering. For that reason, I have used some of the money I earned selling the contents of Blake's flash drive to hire a few more actors from that performance college to pose as truly horrible prospective roommates. Elijah even did his part as well—Blake was close to throwing up his hands after Elijah got out that drill and tried to make a hole in the wall.

Amanda will be coming to look at the room tomorrow, and I'm sure her pretty face and clean-cut appearance will be all it takes to persuade Blake to let her move in. Yet I'm not entirely sure. I'd like one more piece of insurance.

While I'm walking home from work, I pass a flickering neon sign that says *Psychic Readings*. A light bulb goes on in my head. There is nothing that Blake thumbs his nose at more than stuff like that. On one of our early dates, I jokingly suggested to him that we should get readings done, and he looked at me like I had said the moon was made of green cheese and I was melting it onto a sandwich.

This will be perfect.

I push through the small glass door to get into the storefront. The entire store is very tiny and reeks of incense. It's even smaller than that place on Seventy-Sixth Street with the really good tacos. The primary lighting comes from a purple lamp hanging from the ceiling, which illuminates a small table in the center of the room. The table is covered in a night-sky-blue tablecloth with drawings of stars, the sun, and the moon.

A woman is sitting at the table, sorting through a large deck of cards. The table is otherwise bare except for what looks like a crystal ball in the center. She appears to be in her sixties, with long silver hair that seems almost glittery in the light of the room. She looks up at me, and her face cracks into a smile.

"Hello, my dear," she says. "My name is Quillizabeth. What is your name?"

Quillizabeth? Wow, this is even more perfect than I imagined. "Krista."

"Krista." There is a note of skepticism in her voice. "You don't look like a Krista."

She's right, and that's part of why I need to take care of the situation with Amanda. I am Whitney Cross, and someday I will be myself again. But I'm not going to get into all that right now. "Well, I am a Krista."

She seems to reluctantly accept this. "So how can I help you…Krista?"

"Well," I say, "this might sound a little weird, but…"

"Please, sit." Quillizabeth gestures at the chair across from her. "Have you ever had a psychic reading before?"

I settle down into the chair across from her. "No, I haven't."

"I recommend a palm reading to start," she says. "It's the best thing to ease you into the experience. But next time, I can do a deeper reading."

I am interested in none of that. I share Blake's skepticism about otherworldly things, although it's good for a laugh.

"Actually," I say, "I need your help with something else. I'll pay you, of course. Whatever you want."

The older woman raises her eyebrows. I recognize now that she is wearing multiple robes. Oh Lord, Blake is going to hate this.

"I need you to pretend to be interested in a room my boyfriend and I are renting out," I explain. "Just, like, come see the room, then say a bunch of scary psychic things."

Quillizabeth's lips set into a straight line so that they nearly disappear into her mouth. "I cannot just say a bunch of 'psychic things' if I don't feel them. This is not a *game*."

"No, of course not," I say quickly. Boy, this woman is something else. "I just think it would be good for my boyfriend to hear a psychic's perspective on the room, you know? So we can know in advance if there are any…like, spiritual issues before we rent it out."

She takes a moment to consider this. "You want me to lie to your boyfriend."

"Not lie, exactly. But I definitely think it's important for the house to be spiritually clear, and he won't go for it unless we say you are looking to rent the room."

I watch her face, wondering if she'll buy it. Whatever else I can say about this woman, she takes her trade very seriously.

"I do not approve of deception," she says. "But I sympathize with your desire to neutralize your house spiritually. I will come. And when I come, I will give you my recommendations."

"That would be wonderful," I say. "Thank you so much."

I had a whole script in my head for this woman to say, but now I think whatever she comes up with on her own will be so much better. I can't wait.

CHAPTER 52

Blake is now deep in conversation with Quillizabeth.

Right after I put the cookies on a plate, I sprinkled some flour on my shirt to give myself an excuse to leave the room so Blake could be alone with Quillizabeth. When I return to the living room, his eyes are bulging out, and he seems like he's counting the seconds before he can get her out of our house.

I sweep into the room to pretend to introduce myself to the woman that I met yesterday. Despite her reluctance to be deceptive, Quillizabeth does an excellent job pretending we just met. She holds out her hand to me, and I shake it.

And then, as our hands make contact, she jerks away. Her eyes go wide as she takes a step back.

"I..." The older woman's voice is hoarse. "I actually have to go. This place...it's too small. I won't be renting it after all."

Blake looks so relieved, it's almost hilarious. "Okay, it was nice meeting you," he says a bit too brightly.

I feign concern. "Is everything okay?"

Quillizabeth shifts her gaze to look at Blake. If I didn't know this was all an act, I'd say she was absolutely terrified. She then turns to me and says in an urgent voice, "Could I...speak to you outside, Krista dear?"

Outside? I don't think so. I want Blake to hear every part of this performance. "What is it?" I press her.

Quillizabeth takes another step back. "Outside. *Please*."

"Look...Quillizabeth." Blake sounds utterly exasperated. "We have another prospective tenant coming soon, so..."

"He's going to kill you," she blurts out. "Blake is going to kill you, Krista. You have to get away from here."

Oh my God. This woman deserves an Emmy. She really missed her calling.

"He's going to stab you with a kitchen knife." Quillizabeth points to the floor beneath our feet. "It's going to happen right *here*."

Blake looks a bit panicked. At the very least, he wants her out of here. He places a hand on her back, and she leaps away from him like he just scalded her.

"Please believe me, Krista." Quillizabeth is reaching out for me now with a gnarled hand. "Be careful. My visions...they are never wrong."

I'm the one who finally has to walk Quillizabeth outside, because she insists that she has to talk to me. That's fine. I want to give her a tip anyway. She was amazing. Amanda will be showing up soon, and the contrast will be stunning. She'll be moved in by the end of the week.

But when we get outside, Quillizabeth clings to my arm and doesn't want to leave. "You must listen to me, Krista. That man—Blake—he's dangerous."

"Blake?" I laugh, pulling a few bills out of my wallet. "No, I don't think so. And he can't hear you anymore, so we can stop the performance. You were great though."

"Performance!" she bursts out. "That was not a performance. I *saw* it. I saw him crouched over your dead body. I saw the blood all over the floor."

Despite how grateful I am to her, I'm starting to get annoyed. "Blake is not going to kill me. You don't need to worry about that."

"I saw it!" she insists. "I...I haven't had a psychic vision that strong in years. But it was clear as day." She reaches out to grip my wrist, her fingers biting into my skin. "He's going to kill you, Krista. You need to get out. *Now.*"

I get a chill down my spine. I don't believe in any of this crap, but there is something about the certainty in the old woman's face that is creeping me out. She genuinely thinks that Blake is going to kill me. She thinks he's going to stab me to death in my own living room.

Which is ridiculous.

I manage to wrench my hand away from her. "Okay, *enough.*"

"Krista..."

"No," I say firmly. "I'm fine. Whatever this is... You don't have to worry about me. I promise."

Quillizabeth is very reluctant to leave, and for a moment, I'm worried I'll have to call the police. But then she gives me one last fearful look, and she ambles down the street. I stand there, watching her, making sure she doesn't linger on our block. Or, God forbid, try to come back.

I always thought that psychic stuff was bullshit, but it seems like Quillizabeth might really have the gift. Because something terrible is going to happen in that house. Except it won't be Blake standing over my dead body.

It will be me, standing over him.

CHAPTER 53

Amanda has been living with us for a week.

I have already caught Blake and Amanda sitting together on the sofa in the middle of the night, a little bit too close, watching television together. If they're left alone, it's only a matter of time before something would happen between the two of them—once a cheater, always a cheater.

But that's not in the cards. Because by tomorrow, Blake and Amanda will despise each other.

I wake up very early this morning, while Blake is still sound asleep in bed. I wanted to make sure he slept through the night, so I baked him some cookies yesterday laced with sedatives. I got them last week when I convinced my doctor to prescribe me by making up a story about sleep problems. It wasn't hard—I've lost some sleep since realizing I was engaged to a cheater anyway. I tried a cookie, and if you're really looking for it, there is a bit of a bitter aftertaste, but it's barely noticeable. Blake didn't notice when he ate three of them last night.

I wanted to make sure he was asleep, because there's a lot I need to do.

I overheard him offering to let Amanda partake in his Frosted Flakes. Of course he would be nice to the pretty girl. Well, Amanda is about to take advantage of his kindness. I grab the box of Frosted Flakes off the counter, which is nearly half full. Then I pour the contents down the garbage disposal.

My next move is to take two of the apples on the counter and place them in a small paper bag. I climb up on the counter and stick it on the top shelf in the cabinet. It will take a little while, but those apples will rot. We already have a tendency to get fruit flies here, and with a little encouragement and a food source, they will be everywhere. Blake is a sucker for cleanliness, and this will drive him out of his mind.

My next stop is the bathroom, where I systematically empty his soap and his shampoo as well as most of his toothpaste. I leave my own products alone. He can use them if he wants, although he mentioned how much he hates "smelling like a girl."

Lastly, I retrieve a bottle of laundry detergent that I purchased and hid in the hall closet. Blake is highly allergic to any fragranced detergent, especially ones containing a chemical called limonene. I found that out early in our relationship when I decided to wash some of his clothes to be a good girlfriend, and he freaked out because I used a detergent with limonene. *I get the worst rash from even a small amount.* As it turned out, that was a very useful piece of information.

I carefully pour about one tablespoon of my own detergent into Blake's hypoallergenic bottle. I close the bottle and shake it to distribute the limonene. I open it up again and take a sniff. I don't smell the citrus, but it will get all over his clothes the next time he does a wash.

He won't suspect me of any of this. After all, he and I have been living together for months. Amanda is the only one new to the equation.

Pretty soon, they won't be flirting with each other anymore. They're going to hate each other.

And this is only the beginning.

CHAPTER 54

Blake is already in bed that night when Amanda comes home from working at the diner. He's scrolling through his phone, so he doesn't seem to notice when the door slams.

I wonder if he still talks to Stacie. I haven't checked, because it doesn't really matter. What's going to happen to him will happen either way.

"I'm going to go downstairs and get some water," I tell him. "Want anything?"

He shakes his head no. Maybe he's texting with Stacie. Or some other woman.

When I get downstairs, Amanda is in the kitchen, drinking water from one of our glasses. Despite the fact that we told her it was okay to do so, I feel a surge of irritation that she is using our stuff. It's one more thing that she has borrowed from me and that I will soon take back.

"Hi, Whitney!" I say cheerfully. The name feels like acid on my tongue.

She lifts her eyes, which are slightly red-rimmed. "Oh. Hey, Krista."

I join her in the kitchen, leaning against the counter in a position I hope seems friendly enough. "Everything okay?"

"Sort of." She manages a lopsided smile. "Blake is pissed off at me for eating his cereal, even though he told me it was fine."

"Did he say he was pissed?"

Her jaw twitches. "He came to the diner and yelled at me while I was working."

Oh, Blake. I almost burst out laughing. It's not like him at all, but he's been under a lot of stress lately and barely sleeping. "I'm so sorry he did that to you. That is not acceptable."

"I didn't even eat that much cereal," she says. "Hardly any!"

"Blake is..." I choose my words carefully. "He's difficult. He's not an easy man to get along with, and he likes everything just so. I have to be honest with you. He wasn't excited to have a tenant move in, but he agreed because money has been tight since he lost his job."

Amanda nods in understanding. "I got a feeling he was fired..."

"Oh, he was," I confirm. "There was... well, there was an *incident*. And now, of course, he's having trouble finding something else."

I can't give her all the gory details, but I can hint at Blake's wrongdoing. It will be enough to get the wheels turning in her brain.

"Look," I say. "I like having you live here, Whitney. I'll make sure Blake doesn't bother you, but it might be a good idea to stay out of his way. No point in poking the dragon."

She rubs her face with her palms. She looks tired. "Yeah. I have definitely learned my lesson. Honestly, I thought we would become friends. He seems like such a nice guy."

From the look on her face, I'm pretty sure that's not all she was thinking about him. I saw how close she sat next to him on the couch when they were alone that night. Nice guy or nice in bed? She didn't want to be his friend. She wanted *him*.

That's about to change completely.

CHAPTER 55

Blake and I don't go out to dinner much anymore.

We don't have much money, so eating out is a luxury we can't afford. Fortunately, I like to cook, and I love to bake, so it's not a major sacrifice for me.

But tonight is Friday night, so we decided to go out. We went to this cheap, hole-in-the-wall Mexican restaurant that is known for smothering their food in spicy and delicious sauces. Technically, it's more of a takeout place, because you order at a counter. But they have seats, and after you place your order, they bring your food to you. And if you order a margarita, it comes with a little umbrella in it.

Blake is sitting across from me while we wait for our food. He got a steak burrito, and I got the burrito bowl to avoid the carbs—after all, I will be single again very soon. He's wearing a T-shirt and scratching absently at his arm. He has a horrendous rash from the small amounts of fragranced detergent I have been mixing with his hypoallergenic one. The rash itself makes his skin red and bumpy, and he's got angry scratch marks running up the length of his arm because it's intensely itchy.

He also has dark hollows under his eyes from not sleeping well. He was already suffering from insomnia since losing his job, but I got the brilliant idea to blast a soundtrack of ominous thumping noises on my phone in the middle of the night. I hide the phone at the top of our closet so it sounds like it's coming from above us, and then the second Blake leaves the room to confront Amanda, I shut it off. I doubt he's gotten one decent night of sleep in the last month. It's easy to drive someone out of their mind when you know them well enough.

I almost feel sorry for him.

Almost.

He and Amanda hate each other now. I have helped things along considerably by leaving little sticky notes from Blake inside her door. The notes say things like "stop leaving the light on in the kitchen" or "please request permission twenty-four hours in advance before using our television," and all of them are signed with Blake's name. When the two of them are together, she looks like she wants to strangle him with her bare hands. If she had anywhere else to go, she would be gone. But since her last landlord thinks she's a drug dealer, she doesn't have a lot of options.

"I'm thinking about selling the brownstone," he blurts out.

My heart sinks. If he sells the brownstone, Amanda will have to move out. It will all be over. "What? You love our house."

"I do," he admits. "But, Krista, I can't afford it anymore.

I can't make the mortgage payments. I'll find something else cheaper, maybe in Queens or something."

"Queens? Oh God, we're both going to have a horrible commute."

"I know." He rakes a hand through his hair, which makes it stand up a bit. He used to be the most put-together guy I ever knew, and now he's a mess. "But what do you want me to do? I can't pay the mortgage."

"What about Whitney?"

He makes a face like he always does when I mention her. "What about her?"

"We already spent the two months' rent she gave us plus the deposit. We'll have to pay her back."

"Yeah…"

We get interrupted by a server coming over with our baskets of food. Blake looks down at his burrito like he couldn't be less interested in eating it. He scratches his arm again.

"I don't know," he says finally. "I don't see any other way."

I've got to figure out a way to get him to hold off on selling, at least for a little bit longer. But I get distracted when a familiar face comes inside the restaurant, walks up to the front, and gets in line behind a family of four.

It's Elijah.

What on earth is he doing here?

Blake tosses a glance over his shoulder. "Hey, isn't that guy one of the people who was looking at a room?"

I blink at him. "What guy?"

"The short squirrelly guy with the beard and penguin hat?" He takes another look. "I remember that stupid hat. Don't you?"

I shake my head slowly. "I don't know. There were so many people. Maybe he looks familiar..."

Damn it, Elijah. Now that Blake has focused his attention back on me, Elijah is looking this way. It's no coincidence that he's here. He lives in Brooklyn. He wouldn't just randomly be at the same Mexican restaurant as us on a Friday night.

Is he *following* me?

"Excuse me," I say to Blake. "I have to run to the bathroom."

I grab my purse and hurry to the single bathroom, which turns out to have an out-of-order sign on the door. But the knob turns, and I push my way inside, closing the door behind me. The toilet bowl is drowning with paper towels—unusable—but that's not why I came in here. I lock myself inside and find Elijah's number in my phone. He picks up on the second ring.

"What are you doing here?" I hiss into the phone before he even has a chance to say hello. "Are you following me?"

"No," he says quickly.

"Elijah..."

"Fine, okay. A little." He clears his throat. "I'm worried about you, Whitney."

"*Krista.*"

"Blake doesn't look good," he goes on. "He looks... unhinged."

The lights flicker in the bathroom. "Yes, that's the whole freaking point."

"Yeah, but... Are you safe with him? What if he really does have a breakdown?"

"Blake isn't going to hurt me."

"But what if he does? What about what that psychic said?"

I roll my eyes. I cannot *believe* he is bringing that up. I only told him about it because I thought it was so ridiculously funny and I wanted to share it with somebody. Well, I shared it with Becky and Malcolm, but when I told them, I had to act like I really believed it.

"Blake is not violent," I assure him. "I promise you, he's not going to hurt me. I don't think he's ever even thrown a punch in his entire life."

"I'm just worried about you…"

I feel like a jerk yelling at Elijah when that's what this is all about. He's worried about me.

"You need to stop following me," I tell him. "Blake recognized you just now. If you keep doing it, he's going to notice, and he's going to freak out."

"Okay." That finally seems to get through to him. "I'll stop. I'm sorry."

It's beginning to occur to me that while Elijah has been my greatest asset since I left home, he is also becoming quite a liability. He knows too much, and he worries too much. That's a problem.

But it's a problem that I need to put a pin in for now. I have other things to worry about.

CHAPTER 56

I'm in the living room, on the phone with Becky, and we are discussing what has become a favorite topic: Blake and whether he is losing his mind.

"I'm just worried about you, Krista," Becky says.

But she's not worried about me in the same way that Elijah is worried. She's worried about me in exactly the way I want her to be worried about me.

"You shouldn't worry." I say it in a way that sounds like I'm reassuring her even though I'm actually worried. "Blake is…well, he's definitely going through something, but he'll be okay. He hasn't… I mean, he isn't threatening me. He's never hit me."

"Do you really want to wait for that to happen though?" Becky presses me.

Amanda comes in through the front door. She looks exhausted from work. She gives me a half-hearted wave, then stumbles up the steps to the second floor.

"If you want," Becky says, "you are welcome to stay

with me and Malcolm for as long as you want. We've got that extra bedroom…"

"That's very sweet," I tell her, "but you don't need to do that. I'll be fine."

"Don't you remember what that psychic said though? What if he really does stab you to death?"

I almost laugh out loud. "That won't happen, Becky."

Except I say it with a nervous edge to my voice. Like I think there's a chance that Blake might hurt me.

Becky says something else, but I don't hear it, because an ear-splitting scream suddenly rips through the air. I grip the phone tighter, looking up at the ceiling.

"Becky," I say. "I have to go."

"Okay," she agrees. "But if Blake does anything violent, you get out of there ASAP. Malcolm has the car, and we can be over there to pick you up in five minutes."

"Thank you," I say tearfully. "You are a good friend, Becky."

I hang up and then start up the steps to the third floor. Amanda hasn't screamed again, but when I get closer to her room, I can hear her sobbing. What now?

I knock gently on the door. "Aman—er, Whitney?"

There's a long pause before she answers, "What?"

"It's Krista. Is everything okay?"

She yanks open the door. Her pretty face is streaked with tears, her eyes red and puffy.

"Whitney, what's wrong?" I ask.

"Blake threw rotted fruit covered with maggots all over my bed," she manages in a whimper. "That's what your boyfriend did."

My eyebrows shoot up to my hairline. *Blake* did that? Wow, he really is losing it.

Maybe he's not as harmless as I thought.

I clasp a hand over my mouth. "Oh my God, how awful! Do you have any idea why he would do that?"

"Because he's out of his mind!" she sobs. "He's *horrible*. He's always leaving me these nasty notes, and he looks at me like he wishes I were dead." She looks over her shoulder at the bed, where there are indeed rotting apples covered with writhing maggots all over her blanket, which will probably now need to be thrown away. I never thought he'd *do anything* once he found the fruit bag. "I don't think I can take much more of this. I…I might have to move."

This is not good. Amanda wants to leave, and Blake has been talking about selling the brownstone. I'm going to have to accelerate the timeline.

"Where will you go?" I ask her.

"I don't know," she says helplessly. "I burned out all my friends staying on their couches before I moved in here. I feel like I can't ask again. And…I don't have much money."

Amanda is confiding in me. This might be a good time to admit what I know to her. I want her to be able to trust me, and this is an important step. But most importantly, I need her to admit what she did. Because I have to be 100 percent sure.

"Listen." I slip into her room and close the door behind me so that we're alone. "I wanted you to know that…I know."

Fear flickers in her eyes, but she tries to maintain her composure. "What do you know? What do you mean?"

"You know what I mean…Amanda."

She gasps and takes a step back. "I…I don't…"

"I have a friend in IT who told me your driver's license

looked fake, so he did some digging," I say. "But don't worry. Blake doesn't know. I didn't tell anyone."

Her brows scrunch together. "You didn't tell *anyone*?"

Bingo.

"Not a soul."

Amanda drops down onto the edge of the bed, avoiding the apple and the maggots. She buries her face in her hands. "I don't know how this happened. How did my life become *this*?"

"If you want to talk about it…"

She raises her face from her palms. "You swear you won't tell anyone?"

"I swear on my life."

And that part is entirely true.

She squeezes her eyes shut, and a pair of twin tears roll down either cheek. "My mother had cancer. Stomach cancer. The prognosis was horrible, especially without treatment. But the treatment… It wasn't cheap, and her insurance didn't cover it."

"Oh," I murmur.

"It's not the kind of thing where you can go to a bank and get a loan for chemotherapy," she murmurs, not meeting my eyes. "So I borrowed it from somebody else. Somebody who didn't ask too many questions."

"I see."

I had assumed Amanda was on the run for nefarious reasons. Instead, it's because she was trying to raise money to pay for her mother's cancer treatment. Somehow this irritates me even more. She had a mother who loved her enough that she would do anything to keep her alive. That's a hell of a lot more than I ever had.

"And then, of course, she died anyway." Amanda

laughs mirthlessly. "All that money and the chemo port and the vomiting and the hair falling out, and she didn't even live as long as her prognosis without treatment. And then I was on the hook for all that money." She winces. "It's not the sort of thing where you can declare bankruptcy, you know? If I didn't come up with it, they were going to kill me."

"So you changed your name..."

"I used what little money I had to buy a new identity," she explains. "Whitney Cross was some teenager who disappeared a while back, probably murdered or something. She wasn't using her identity, and I needed it."

I grit my teeth. I wasn't *murdered*, for God's sake. As if! I simply wasn't using my identity for a little while. But that didn't give her the right to *take* it. The fact that nothing has happened to her since becoming Whitney Cross means that it would have been safe for me to slip back into my old identity.

That is, if she hadn't *stolen* it.

"So that's my whole pathetic story," she says. "If you tell anyone, I'm obviously dead. So I hope you don't."

I sit down beside her on the edge of the bed. "Your secret is safe," I reassure her. "In fact, I think it's wonderful how you tried to help your mother."

"For nothing," she says. "She was furious about how I got the money for her treatment. She didn't want this for me. She worked so hard for me to get an education, and now..."

Oh, cry me a river. She borrowed money from a loan shark, and it backfired. What did she expect?

"Listen," I say, "now that you've shared this with me, I'd like to tell you a little secret of my own."

She looks at me with interest. "What?"

"I'm thinking about leaving Blake."

Her mouth drops open. "Seriously?"

"Does that surprise you so much? You think he's a psychopath."

"Of course I do. But..."

"He didn't used to be like this. He's scaring me more and more lately." I shudder. "I need to get away from him before something terrible happens. I'm worried that he might...might hurt me."

Amanda reaches out to take my hand. I let her do it, even though I want to slap her.

"I need more time though," I say. "I don't have much savings, so I want to make sure that I have enough money and that I have a place to go."

"I totally understand that," Amanda says.

"Maybe," I say, "the two of us can get an apartment together and share the rent."

For the first time since she came home and saw what Blake did, her face brightens. "That would be great, Krista. I would really like that."

I force myself to return her smile, even though it feels like plastic on my face. "Take a look at apartments. If you find something, let me know."

She nods eagerly. "I bet you five bucks we can find a place as big as this for a quarter of the price in Staten Island."

Staten Island? Is she *kidding*? "Come on. Let's get this mess cleaned up."

I help Amanda clean up her sheets. For the record, I am so angry at Blake for doing this. What the hell is wrong with him? Why couldn't he throw the maggot-ridden apples in the garbage like a normal person? It seems like the stress of everything is making his behavior a bit more unpredictable than I expected. Now I have to clean up another one of his messes.

It takes us a few trips and a lot of laundry detergent, but we end up getting everything clean. I rinse the last of the disgusting apple off my hands in the kitchen sink while Amanda is spraying her room with my air freshener.

After I dry off my hands, I wander into the living room, where Goldy is swimming around in her little fishbowl. Blake and I bought Goldy when we first moved in. She was our starter pet. We imagined that someday we would upgrade to an animal that required more responsibility and love, like a cat. And then maybe a dog. And someday, a child.

But none of that is going to happen. Not anymore.

Thanks to Blake.

I get close to Goldy's bowl. I tap on it gently, and she looks up at me. She's a good fish. She's provided us with a lot of entertainment in the time that we've had her, although that time is quickly coming to an end. Faster than I thought it would.

"Goodbye, Goldy," I say sadly. "I'm sorry about this, but you should know that it's Blake's fault."

Goldy was a symbol of the life we were starting together. It only makes sense that now that our future is going down the toilet, she should be the first to go.

CHAPTER 57

We are in the bedroom, and Blake is staring at the bottle of bleach I've got in my hand. The same bottle I stashed there after Goldy went belly-up.

"What's this doing in our closet?" I demand to know.

Blake has a baffled look on his face. As much as I hate him, part of me almost wants to reach out and give him a level ten hug, because he truly looks like he needs it. He can't figure out how his phone ended up in Amanda's bed or how her lipstick ended up on his collar. He has no choice but to blame her for everything. He's lost.

"I have no idea," he gulps.

"Did you kill Goldy to frame Whitney?"

He looks like he's about to be sick. "No. Christ, of course not. You can't possibly think…"

This gives me the chance to start ticking off his sins. All the strange things he's done lately, although many aren't things he has actually done. He listens to me, wanting to protest but knowing in his gut that I won't believe him. All the while, I'm packing my clothes.

"That psychic woman was right," I conclude. "If I stay long enough, God knows what you'll do."

"No. *No.*" He looks almost like he's about to burst into tears. "I would never cheat on you, and I would never hurt you."

Well, that's a load of bullshit. I zip up my suitcase. "I think I better go."

And then he stands in front of me, blocking my exit from the room. "Blake, get out of my way right now," I say.

He doesn't budge. The tension builds. And for a split second, I am scared that I have pushed him too far. That my mild-mannered fiancé might have really snapped. And maybe somebody really is going to find my body on the first floor in a pool of blood.

But then he steps out of the way.

He's not done though. He follows me down the stairs to the first floor, pleading with me the whole time. He doesn't realize his night's going to get even worse if he eats the leftover Chinese food for dinner tonight. I grabbed a handful of Amanda's hair from the brush she left in the bathroom and stirred it into his noodles as a little something extra. He *never* takes them out of the container or heats them up before eating them.

Blake is still begging and pleading when I get to the front door, and he doesn't stop as I'm putting on my jacket and my sneakers. He even follows me outside.

"I love you, Krista," he says.

Yeah. Right.

Blake seems surprised by the taxi that shows up at our front door because they're relatively rare on our street. He doesn't realize I called for one, and the timing is impeccable. I step inside, relieved I don't have to listen to more of his lies.

As the taxi is pulling away, I turn to look through the rear window. Blake is still standing there, watching from the street. I notice Mr. Zimmerly coming out of his house, and again, the timing is incredible. At the worst possible moment, he starts yelling at Blake, probably to take in his garbage cans—I can't hear them, but that seems to be all he ever talks about. Just for fun, I've been adding a little fuel to the flame by pulling the bins back out after Blake puts them away. I've caught Blake staring at the bins he's sure he put away and scratching his head. It really is the little things. As we turn the corner, Blake has started yelling back at Mr. Zimmerly.

Blake hates Mr. Zimmerly. I know it, and everyone else on the block knows it. If anything ever happened to him, Blake would be the first suspect.

And that gives me an idea.

CHAPTER 58

Stacie Parker follows the same schedule every Saturday night. I've been watching, so I know.

Between 8:00 and 8:30, she comes out of her apartment building, teetering in a pair of stiletto heels and a dress that is embarrassingly short. She waits for a minute or two, and then she climbs into an Uber. The Uber then brings her to a bar or club, where she wastes the rest of her night drinking and flirting with men.

I can't believe Blake liked her. I can't believe he threw away everything we had for that woman.

One thing I have to say for him, he's not giving up easily. Since I moved out, he has been calling and texting me nonstop. Becky has been trying to convince me to block him, but I like watching him suffer. I especially liked the messages he sent me when he discovered Mr. Zimmerly was dead.

That must have been quite the shock for him. Mr. Zimmerly was shocked too when I hit him on the head. I wasn't sure what to use but landed on that antique clock we bought at that flea market. Blake's fingerprints would definitely be on it, and it felt like a good way to say goodbye to our life together. It's only a matter of time before the police figure it out.

Right now, I am sitting in Malcolm's car, across the street from Stacie's building. I didn't ask his permission to borrow it, but I knew they were staying in and he wouldn't miss it. I need a car to do what I need to do next.

At just after eight o'clock, Stacie stumbles out of her building, looking like she's already slightly drunk. That's good. It will make this next part so much easier.

She doesn't even have a jacket on, and she's shivering in the November night air. I'm sure she has already called an Uber, so I need to be quick. I pull up in front of her building. I roll down the window before she can check my license plate, although she doesn't seem like the cautious sort of person who would do that.

"Stacie? You called for an Uber?"

She smiles at me. "Yes, thank you."

And then she climbs in, closing the door behind her. There's another car turning onto the same street, and I zoom away before it can arrive.

"I've got water bottles in the back if you want it," I tell Stacie.

"Oh, thanks!" she says. "Female Uber drivers are so much more considerate! I'll definitely give you five stars."

The water in the back serves two purposes. First, it will distract her from her phone so she won't notice that the Uber she called is not the same car that has picked her up. Second, I used a very fine needle to inject something into her drink.

"So," I say casually, "doing anything fun tonight?"

"Always," Stacie giggles. "Just hanging out with the girls tonight."

"No boyfriend?"

"No, not at the moment, sadly."

I check in the rearview mirror, and she is drinking from the water bottle. Good. It won't take long now before she starts to get drowsy. I used more of the sedative on her than what I used in the cookies that knocked Blake out before I swiped his phone and hid it in Amanda's room.

Blake kept a photo of me on his desk at work, so in the back of my mind, I was a bit worried Stacie might recognize me. That's why I bought a cheap wig, and I got a little creative with makeup. But I shouldn't have worried. Stacie doesn't seem the slightest bit interested in me, and anyway, she's mostly looking at the back of my head. I've also got a pop music station playing loudly, on the off chance that she might recognize my voice.

"It's hard to believe you're single," I comment. "I mean, if *you* don't have a boyfriend, what hope do the rest of us have?"

Stacie laughs. "You would be surprised. It's harder than you think, even for me. All the good ones are taken."

My jaw tightens. "Oh yeah?"

"Yes. Trust me."

"What about at your work? I've heard that's a good place to meet people. Not that I would know." I laugh good-naturedly.

"Oh no." In the rearview mirror, I can see her shaking her head emphatically. "I tried that once, and it did *not* work out."

"That sounds like an interesting story."

I'm hoping Stacie is the sort of person who enjoys talking about herself. She certainly seems like she is.

"Not that interesting," she says. "There was this guy... not exactly my boss, but worked right under my boss. Anyway, he was *so* hot. I was really into him."

"Hard to imagine he didn't like you back."

"Oh, he did," she assures me, and I want to strangle her right now. But no, too soon. Wait for the sedatives to kick in. "But he was engaged to some other girl—a real Mary Jane type. I thought I could lure him away from her. And I came pretty damn close."

"Oh? Did you hook up?"

"Once. In his office." She giggles again. "It was super hot."

And there it is. Confirmation that Blake cheated on me with Stacie. I was 99 percent sure it was true, but now I have my 100 percent confirmation.

That bastard really cheated on me. I loved him with all my heart, and I believed he loved me just as much. We were supposed to spend the rest of our lives together. He ruined *everything*.

And now I don't have to feel bad about what's about to happen.

"So what went wrong?" I ask. "Why didn't he leave his fiancée?"

I glance back in the mirror in time to catch her rolling her eyes. "After we hooked up, he got all ridiculous. He kept talking about what a huge mistake it was, and it could never happen again, and how much he loved his fiancée, blah blah blah. It was pretty pathetic. I lost a lot of respect for him after that."

Me too.

Stacie lets out a loud yawn, head lolling against the window. "God, why am I so *tired*? It's only eight o'clock. I'm turning into an old person."

"If you want to close your eyes, I'll wake you up when we get there."

She smiles sleepily. "Thanks. You're a doll."

A few minutes later, she is completely passed out in the back seat. Which is good, because by now she might have noticed that we are nowhere near wherever she is meeting her friends for drinks.

But the sedatives won't last forever. That's why I also have a bottle of chloroform next to me. That will knock her out long enough for me to bind her wrists and ankles with duct tape when we get to our final destination—a patch of woods not too far from where I used to live in Telmont, New Jersey.

And then Stacie Parker and I are going to have some fun. Well, I'll have fun at least. And when the fun is over, I'm going to bring Blake a little souvenir for the kitchen. I think he'll really enjoy it.

CHAPTER 59

"I need to move out," Amanda tells me over the phone. "Blake has become intolerable. I can't deal with him anymore."

I got the call from Amanda right after I got out of the D train station in Brooklyn. Apparently, Blake has been terrorizing her since I moved out. He wants her to leave, and she wants to leave. I'm not sure what prompted this. I can imagine that hair in the Chinese food might have pushed him over the edge. He's squeamish.

I doubt anyone has found the little gift I left in the kitchen yet—I'd know if the fingers had surfaced. And I'm even more doubtful that Blake discovered Stacie's blood on the floorboards of the living room. I saved the blood after I killed her and spilled it right in the center of the room to make it easy for the police to find, in case they are completely incompetent. I don't think it will be hard for them to believe Blake killed Stacie though, especially since he won't be alive to defend himself.

"I understand if you can't live with him," I say. "I mean, that's why I left. I couldn't take it anymore either."

"I never thought so before"—Amanda's voice trembles—"but I'm beginning to worry he could be dangerous."

I still don't believe Blake is capable of hurting anyone. He doesn't have it in him. Take it from a woman who knows.

"What if we talk tomorrow?" I suggest. "I can come over before Blake gets home from work, and we can talk about finding a new place together." When she hesitates, I add, "I mean, it's not like you're going to move out this second, right?"

"I guess," Amanda says, although she sounds doubtful.

"Listen," I say. "You scope out some apartment listings. We'll make plans to check them out."

The plan seems to placate Amanda. She agrees to meet at the brownstone tomorrow, early evening.

That means I don't have much time. Whatever is going to happen must happen tomorrow.

So it's a good thing I'm here in Brooklyn, a block away from Elijah's apartment. He's got a few things for me, and he didn't want to carry them around. One especially.

Elijah lives in a four-story walk-up, and of course he's on the fourth floor. The street is relatively deserted except for a man lying on the sidewalk, clutching a drink in a brown paper bag. Several storefronts are shut down and boarded up, with the wooden planks covered in obscene graffiti. It's not exactly prime real estate, like our brownstone on the Upper West Side, and I find myself clutching my purse closer to my chest. With Elijah's brains, he could be incredibly successful, but he lacks Blake's ambition, and

I get the feeling he'd rather spend his free hours playing video games than climbing the corporate ladder. Plus, his social skills are severely lacking.

I walk up to the intercom and hit the button for apartment 4A. Almost instantly, the buzzer sounds, and I'm able to go inside.

I huff and puff my way up the stairs to the fourth floor. I don't know how he manages to live here, although I can just imagine Elijah dashing up all those stairs every day. He probably enjoys it.

When I get to apartment 4A, I have to take a second to catch my breath before I ring the doorbell. Again, Elijah answers almost immediately like he's been waiting just behind the door, and his face lights up at the sight of me standing there red-faced.

"Whitney." He grins. "Come in."

I don't bother to correct him this time. It's not like anybody important is going to overhear in this hellhole.

I slip inside Elijah's small apartment and take off my jacket. It's the first time I've ever been here, and I'm surprised by how clean it is. I don't know what I was expecting, exactly. I had imagined dirty pizza boxes and lots of bottles of Mountain Dew. Maybe he cleaned because he knew I was coming. The furniture is sparse—a sofa, a wide-screen TV, a bookcase constructed from cinder blocks, and a coffee table with a game controller abandoned on it.

As for Elijah, he looks about the same as always. He's wearing another old T-shirt with a pair of jeans, and even though we're indoors, he's wearing his white Linux baseball cap with the penguin on it. I've only seen him without it a handful of times, and his thinning sand-colored hair was always plastered to his skull, like a case of chronic hat hair.

"Nice place," I comment.

He beams at me. "Thanks."

Okay, enough small talk. "You got everything?"

The smile drops off his face. He usually seems proud to help me with everything I ask him for, but not this time. "I do."

"Let's have it then."

"Whitney." He looks down at his dirty sneakers. "I'm just not sure about this…"

"I can give you more money if that's the issue."

He jerks his head up. "That's not the issue. At *all*."

I frown. "You said you could help me. Are you going to help me or not?"

He lets out a long sigh. "Just a minute."

I wait in the living room while Elijah disappears into another room. I wait for a good few minutes, too antsy to even look at my phone, and then finally he comes back out carrying a paper sack. I note that it's the perfect size to hold a couple of apples…or a couple of fingers. Talk about versatility.

Elijah thrusts the paper bag in my direction. "Here."

I check inside. Sure enough, it's everything I wanted. A Social Security card and passport for a new identity—something I hope not to need, but you never know what will happen after everything goes down tomorrow. I hadn't predicted how things would go south with Jordan after all.

And there's one other thing in the bag. A very small bottle filled with a clear liquid.

"Is this it?" I ask. "The tetrodotoxin?"

I was reading up on toxins, and I decided that tetrodotoxin—the poison in blowfish—was my best bet. I wanted something lethal that wouldn't work instantly.

"Yes," he says. "That's it."

"Perfect. Thank you."

Elijah's eyes look big behind his glasses. "This will kill him, you know."

"Yes, that's the point."

Elijah already knows that I killed Jordan. He also knows about that bitch who stole Jordan from me. Like I said, he knows a little too much.

"Well," I say with finality. "Thank you for everything."

His face fills with panic. "Listen, Whitney, you don't have to do this."

I drop the bottle of tetrodotoxin back in the paper bag with my new passport and Social Security card. "Yes. I do."

"You don't," he insists. "I mean, yes, Blake is an asshole who cheated on you. But who cares? He's an idiot. He doesn't even deserve you. You can just walk away from this."

Elijah doesn't know about what I did to Mr. Zimmerly and Stacie Parker. If he knew about that, he wouldn't be telling me to walk away. He would know it's far too late.

"I can't let it go," I say tightly. "How would you feel if the person you loved was having sex with somebody else?"

He gives me a sad look. "Believe me, I know exactly how that feels."

It's no revelation that Elijah loves me. It's a fact that I have known for a very long time. I have used it to my advantage for many years, but now it's gone too far. His infatuation with me has become annoying, and it's starting to interfere with my plans.

"Elijah," I begin in a patient voice that I have used before with him.

"I know, I know," he sniffs. "I realize you don't feel that way about me. But, Whitney, I would be so good to you. I would worship you every day, and I would never, *ever* cheat on you like he did."

I wish I could love Elijah. It would be so much easier if I did.

"I would treat you like a queen," he continues. "I'd wake up every morning thinking how lucky I am just to be with you."

"Elijah…"

The longing is plain on his face. For a moment, I wonder if he's still a virgin. It doesn't seem outside the realm of possibility. If he is, it is partially my fault. He has been pining over me since we were teenagers. He's a nice enough guy, but his unrequited love for me has ruined his life. He would have been so much better off if he'd never met me.

"Forget Blake," he says. "I love you, Whitney. Please let me show you how much."

And then he leans in to kiss me.

It's an okay kiss. It's not like the first kiss that Blake and I shared, which made fireworks go off in my entire body—the kind of kiss that was still lingering on my lips hours later as I fell asleep alone in bed because he was too much of a gentleman to take me to bed that first night. But when we separate, I can tell it was that kind of fireworks kiss for Elijah.

"Wow," he breathes. And even though it wasn't an amazing kiss, the look on his face makes up for it.

"Let's go to the bedroom," I say.

CHAPTER 60

Technically, it wasn't cheating on Blake.

Blake and I are on a break, and tomorrow morning, Malcolm will return my ring to him. Also, he cheated first, so I am allowed at least one freebie. Plus, this was basically pity sex, so I'm not even sure it counts.

It was extremely average, or a bit worse than average, if I'm being completely honest. Elijah didn't quite know what to do, and the foreplay was nonexistent, but it was enthusiastic and about what I expected. He loved it, so there's that.

Now it's an hour later, and it's time for me to go. I slip back into the short, clingy green dress that Blake used to compliment me on—I remember him running his fingers along the small of my back and telling me how sexy I looked in it. He always loved it when I dressed up.

After I'm fully clothed, I check out my appearance in the bathroom mirror. I look tired but still good. I have a lot of decent years ahead of me before I start to look old.

There's a splotch of dark red on my chin, and I scrub at it with soap until it's gone. I take my hair out of the bun and fix it atop my head so instead of being sloppy, it looks stylishly messy, the way Blake likes it.

When I am satisfied, I come out of the bathroom and return to the bedroom to say goodbye to Elijah.

He's lying on the bed, a hint of a satisfied smile on his lips. It was average for me, but it was a wild ride for him. He thanked me when it was over, which was actually very sweet. His arms are lying on either side of him, very still.

And also, his throat has been split by a bloody gash.

I felt bad about it. I truly did. But Elijah knew far too much about me, and his crush on me was bordering on unhealthy. It's better this way.

Anyway, I'm not a terrible person. I gave Elijah a good time before I cut his throat open. He literally went out with a bang. And I waited until he was very sleepy and satisfied to do it. It was all over in a split second—he barely even knew he was dying.

Tomorrow is going to be a very busy day, and I don't want to have to worry about Elijah fretting over me like a mother hen. I've gotten what I need from him.

"Goodbye, Elijah," I tell him.

He doesn't answer.

I'm not leaving immediately. I'm going to wipe down everything in the apartment that I touched. I have to wait until the coast is clear to leave, not that anyone here will recognize me. And I get the feeling Elijah doesn't have many friends. There's nothing to connect the two of us.

It feels satisfying to check off the boxes. First Mr. Zimmerly, then Stacie, now Elijah. Only two left. By tomorrow, I will have set everything right.

CHAPTER 61

Amanda is cutting out from her shift early and tells me she'll be home by seven, so I arrive at the brownstone an hour before that to give myself time.

This morning, I gave Blake a bag of cookies laced with tetrodotoxin. It's not clear how quickly the toxin will work, but it won't kill him right away. I dosed it low enough that I calculated he won't die for at least four to six hours after eating the cookies I gave him. But he very well might not have eaten them right away.

The timing is crucial. He needs to be alive or recently deceased when Amanda comes home. Because if he is dead, there's no way the police will think he stabbed her to death. And they need to think that he killed her, then committed suicide. I'll stash the rest of the bottle of toxin in the drawer of his bedroom.

Death from tetrodotoxin usually occurs from respiratory failure. Over the course of several hours, Blake will have increased difficulty swallowing and speaking, with significant confusion, seizures, and irregular heartbeats. Of course, there's a chance he might go to the hospital, but considering he has no health insurance, he will consider that a last resort. I'm hoping that he will chalk it up to a flu-like illness and try to sleep it off. I expect to find him lying on the sofa or in his bed, either dead or in significant respiratory distress.

All this is the expected outcome, but as I unlock the door to my old home, I feel an unexpected wave of sadness wash over me.

Blake might be dead.

I didn't feel bad about killing Elijah. He had such a pathetic life, it almost felt like I was putting him out of his misery. And then there was Stacie, who was a cheating bitch. And Mr. Zimmerly, who was old and unhappy. Even Jordan felt different. I loved Jordan, but in that immature, teenage way.

It's different with Blake. I loved him with all my heart. I had imagined a life with him in a very concrete way. I wore his ring. I imagined starting a family with him. And I had believed he felt the same way.

And now…

It will be hard to look at him lying on our shared bed, dead or unconscious, and knowing for sure that the future we dreamed of is gone forever.

Why did you cheat, Blake? Why couldn't you have been a good guy like I thought you were? Why couldn't you have meant it when you said you loved me and only me?

My heart is pounding as I walk into the house. I make a beeline for the sofa, bracing myself for what I might find there. But no. He's not there. He must be upstairs, in bed.

I walk up the steps to the second floor, knowing that

this is it. He will be lying in bed, very likely as dead as Elijah. I walk as slowly as I can, not wanting to see it. But then when I get to the bedroom...

He's not here either.

Dammit. Where is he?

Maybe he really did go to the emergency room. I had been banking on the fact that he wouldn't do that, but maybe I misjudged him. And if that's the case, the jig is up. The doctors in the emergency room will surely know that he was poisoned, and it won't be hard for them to put two and two together. Especially when they find that note I slipped into his pocket.

I take my phone out of my purse, trying to figure out my next move. Then I notice I have a missed call from him as well as a text message. I read the text, and then I listen to the message.

Okay. *Interesting*.

This might work out after all.

PART 3

CHAPTER 62

BLAKE

I throw up onto the sidewalk until my ribs hurt.

By the end, I'm dry heaving, but I don't want to stop. Not until I'm sure that every trace of those cookies is out of me.

When I'm pretty sure my stomach is empty, I get to my feet unsteadily. I close my eyes, trying to remember exactly when I ate the cookies. It hasn't even been an hour. How long does it take for something you eat to get into your bloodstream? I don't know the answer to that. I've emptied my stomach, but it could be too late.

I feel awful, but mostly because I've been throwing up. Are my fingers tingling, or am I just imagining it? I can't tell.

Mostly, I can't keep my thoughts from racing. Krista—the woman I loved—is not who I thought she was. She is... Well, if the things her mother was saying are true, she's a psychopath. She killed her boyfriend. She killed the girl her boyfriend was cheating with. She probably killed Mr. Zimmerly and Stacie.

Oh God, Stacie... It's all my fault.

I take stock of my body. I feel...okay. I have a headache, and I'm mildly nauseous, but I can chalk that up to the fact that I've been throwing up for several minutes. I think I got all the poison out of my system before it started working, whatever it was.

Krista poisoned me. She tried to *kill* me.

I don't quite understand what happened or who Whitney really is, but there is no doubt in my mind that Krista is the daughter of that woman I just met. Aside from the resemblance, everything sounded familiar. Telmont sounded familiar because Krista mentioned it before. And now that I think about it, she also mentioned once that she spent time in Braga, plus she loves that wine from Porto. That's why it rang a bell for me. I've sure never been there.

Krista lied to me about her whole life. She claimed she was from Idaho and moved to the city with a friend after high school—a lie. I don't know who that middle-aged woman we had dinner with was, the one who waxed nostalgic about Krista's childhood. She clearly wasn't her mother—another lie. She told the truth about her father having a heart attack, although she failed to tell me it was the stress of all the awful things she did that caused it.

Now what?

I think back to the suicide note Krista wrote on my behalf. The whole thing is horrifying, but there's one sentence in particular that keeps tugging at me:

After all the lives I've taken, I can't go on.

She clearly wants me to take the fall for the murders of Mr. Zimmerly and Stacie, but is that all? The note was so nonspecific. She's not going to want the police to have any doubt about what I've done.

After all the lives I've taken...

She's going to kill Whitney.

A sudden certainty comes to me—that's her plan. She is going to murder Whitney in my home so there will be no doubt about what I've done. But now I've taken a trip to New Jersey and put the kibosh on her plans.

Or have I?

If Krista assumes I'm going to eat the cookies either way—which is a pretty good bet considering my weakness for her snickerdoodles—she might decide to kill Whitney anyway. After all, the suicide note is in my pocket.

I've got to call the police.

I take my phone out of my pocket. I start to dial 911, but before I reach the third digit, I hear the story in my head and realize how ridiculous and convoluted it sounds. Nobody is going to take me seriously if I tell them the whole story. I'm even having trouble wrapping my head around it. They'll have me committed before they believe it. Or worse—they'll think I made it up to take suspicion off myself for Zimmerly's murder.

I've got to talk to Krista. If she knows I'm alive and threw up the cookies, maybe she won't do anything stupid.

Maybe.

I select Krista's number—the first on my list of contacts, because I call her more than anyone else I know. The phone rings on the other line, again and again. She's not picking up.

This is Krista... Leave a message!

I clear my throat. "Hey, uh, Krista? It's Blake. Look, I'm...I'm in Telmont because... Well, you know why. And I've been... I talked to Whitney's mother—I mean, *your* mother—and I...I just... Can you please call me back? Please, Krista? I need to talk to you. I still... I just want to see you. I'm so sorry about everything, and... Look, I'm driving back to the city now and...just wait for me. Please."

It's a long, rambling message, and by the time I finish speaking, I wish I hadn't left a message at all. Krista might be the woman I love, but I need to remember that she tried to kill me. She wants me dead.

I type a text message that's a little more succinct:

Call me.

I check my watch. If I leave now, I'll be back in the city by about seven, depending on traffic. I'll be going in the reverse direction of traffic, so hopefully the highway won't be a parking lot. Maybe I can stop anything bad from happening.

A voice in the back of my head tells me that I should call the police right now. Even if they think it's a wild story, they might still send a patrol car over.

But Whitney is rarely home before ten or eleven, and I'll be back in the city in two hours. I can make it back in time to stop anything bad from happening.

CHAPTER 63

KRISTA

As promised, Amanda is home by seven.

She's very prompt. She's also clean and gives us rent on time, and she's relatively quiet. She is, in many ways, the perfect tenant.

And I hate her with every fiber of my being.

Amanda is dressed in her usual blue jeans and T-shirt from the diner, and the vague scent of grilled beef still clings to her. Aside from that dark red lipstick I gave her, which she tried once and said wasn't her style, she never wears any makeup. If she dolled herself up, she would be just as gorgeous as Stacie was, but she chooses not to do that.

Although to be fair, Stacie wasn't very pretty at the end. I sliced up her face pretty good before ending it all. After about forty minutes, she was begging me to kill her. So really, it was an act of mercy.

Amanda is surprised to see me in the living room. "I didn't realize you were already here."

"Well, I've still got the key."

"True." She plops down on the sofa, letting her head fall back against the cushions. "I'm just glad it wasn't Blake. He's been so impossible lately. What an asshole."

I feel a surge of irritation. Blake is not an asshole. He's a decent guy—one of the few I've met. Okay, he did cheat on me, and I did try to kill him. I'm still going to kill him. But still. She doesn't have the right to talk about him like that. She hardly knows him.

I sit down beside her on the sofa. "He's not so bad."

Amanda rolls her head to the side to look at me. "What are you talking about? You just broke up with him."

"I know, but..." I'm not sure how to articulate what I want to say, and I'm not sure I want to say it to her. None of this is any of her business anyway. "So did you look at any apartments?"

She sits up straighter on the sofa. "Yeah, there are a few in our price range, and more if you don't mind living outside Manhattan."

"I'm okay with it," I lie. I do *not* want to live outside Manhattan, but we need to kill some time until Blake gets back.

"Great!"

Amanda digs her phone out of her purse and brings up one of the rental websites. While she's doing that, my gaze strays to the coffee table in front of us. Blake is usually anal about keeping the coffee table free of any clutter, but right now, there are a few pieces of mail strewn across it as well as some magazines and catalogs, which speaks to his state of mind when he took off. The clutter on the table hasn't attracted Amanda's attention, and I'm glad.

Because underneath one of those magazines is an extremely sharp knife.

CHAPTER 64

BLAKE

Right after I get onto Riverside Drive, my vision goes double.

At first, I think it's because I've been driving for four hours. I blink a few times, and it goes back to normal, which confirms my theory. At first. But then a few minutes later, it happens again. I'm looking up at the stoplight, and even though I know there should only be one, somehow there are two of them. I blink, and the red lights swirl.

Shit.

I had hoped I threw up everything that was in my stomach. But apparently, some of it was absorbed. That probably also explains why my headache has kicked up several notches, and so has the nausea that has been with me since Telmont.

I don't know what to do. I'm about ten minutes away from the brownstone. I definitely shouldn't be driving like this, but I don't have time to waste. The double vision seems to go in and out, so while it's not ideal, it could be worse. I mean, I could be *blind*.

At least it's not dark out. I can still see. I can still navigate, although I have to admit, if a pedestrian walked in front of me, I wouldn't be able to stop in time. I am gripping the steering wheel with both hands, trying to make it those last few minutes back home. I let out a shaky breath.

I could pull over. I could call 911 and explain the situation. I have a feeling that whatever Krista gave me, I should be at the hospital. Not that I can afford the hospital since I don't have health insurance, but what's a little debt (okay, a lot of debt) if I'm dying?

Am I dying? No, I couldn't be. I threw up most of those cookies.

The GPS has become useless because I can't even see it anymore. Well, I can see it, but there are two of them, which makes it very hard to follow. I'm just going based on memory, praying I don't accidentally go the wrong way on a one-way street. I turn onto Columbus Avenue, and now I'm almost back. Just a little farther.

I had been hoping I got it wrong. I had been hoping maybe Krista didn't poison the cookies after all. Maybe the whole thing was somehow a big misunderstanding and she doesn't actually want me dead.

But I'm not wrong. I don't know what she gave me, but it's killing me.

I make the final turn onto the block for the brownstone, and the car jumps the curb when I try to park it, but I don't even have the energy to try to fix it. I'll just have to park on the curb. I didn't run anyone down, so that's the important thing. And it's not like Mr. Zimmerly is going to complain.

Poor Mr. Zimmerly. It's my fault he's dead. The whole damn thing is my fault. Well, in a more direct way, it's Krista's fault, but if I hadn't had that moment of weakness with Stacie, none of this would be happening. The second it was over—hell, even before that—I regretted it. I felt awful about it for weeks and nearly broke down and told her a hundred times. I don't cheat—I'm not that guy. I loved Krista and couldn't believe I had done something so stupid to jeopardize what we had together.

But then after a month or so went by, the guilt started to fade. It was the worst thing I'd ever done, and I wanted to put it behind me. Krista never found out—or so I thought—and there was no reason to wreck what we had over one stupid night.

Little did I know she *had* found out and was making plans to burn it all to the ground.

My vision is swimming, and my head won't stop throbbing. I fumble to grab my phone from the mount on the dashboard, nearly dropping it. I have to call 911. I don't even have a choice anymore. There's no time to talk Krista out of slashing Whitney's throat. I'll be dead before that happens.

Except when I look down at the screen of my phone, I can't even focus on it. It becomes two phones, then three, then it's one again.

Okay, I'm in really bad shape.

I manage to shove the driver's side door open, and with much effort, I make it to my feet. The double vision is the worst part, because it makes me feel nauseatingly dizzy, but I can walk. If I'm holding on to something.

I need to get inside. The lights are on, which means Whitney is home, and she can help me call for an ambulance.

Unless, of course, I got the whole thing wrong and Whitney is in on it too. But I don't believe that. Or at least I have to hope it's not true.

It's touch and go until I make it to the steps of the brownstone. Then I've got the railing to hold on to, and I make it to the front door. It feels like a miracle, but when I pull my keys out of my pocket, I realize that it's extremely hard to unlock a door when the lock won't stop moving. I never realized how tiny that lock was.

Why do they make locks so small? This is impossible…

Finally, I give up and press my finger against the doorbell. The chimes echo throughout the house, and I stand at the door, swaying as I wait for somebody to answer. If somebody doesn't come soon, I'm not sure I'm going to make it. I need help.

Anybody…

CHAPTER 65

KRISTA

"This apartment could be perfect," Amanda is saying.

I am so utterly bored. I am sick of looking at apartments with Amanda and pretending to be excited about them when I know I will never live in any of them. I recognize that she doesn't know that, but I just don't care.

Where is Blake? Why isn't he home yet? Did he die on the way back?

"It's a walk-up but only on the second floor," she says. "And it's pretty close to the subway line."

"Let's put it in the Maybe pile."

"Do you like it better than the apartment in Park Slope?"

I don't remember the other apartment, but she is looking at me expectantly, so I say, "Yes. This one is definitely better."

"Okay." She nods thoughtfully. "By the way, I'm so glad we're doing this together, Krista. On my own, I'm not sure I could even find a place to live."

I glance down at my watch, then back up at her. "I'm happy to be there for you, Amanda."

She flashes me an uncomfortable smile. "You shouldn't call me that."

"Why not?" I'm trying to mask my irritation, but I'm failing. "It's your name, isn't it?"

"Yes, but..." She squirms. "If anyone found out my real name, it would be bad. Really bad."

I know that, of course, because I'm not an idiot. "I don't blame you. Whitney is a nice name."

"You think?" She makes a face. "I hate it, actually. It's like the name of some bitchy popular girl in high school who torments the girls who aren't as pretty as she is. You know the type, right?"

What does *that* mean? "I guess so..."

"Anyway, it definitely doesn't feel like me."

It's not enough that she stole my name, but she doesn't even *like* it? The nerve of this girl! I would love to take my time doing what I want to do to her like I did with Stacie, but I can't. It's got to happen fast, right when Blake gets home.

Where is he anyway?

"I would do anything to get my old identity back," she sighs, leaning back into the cushions.

"What if you had a choice?"

She puts down her phone and looks at me curiously. "A choice?"

"Right. What if somebody said that you could either get your old identity back or have your mother back, alive and well?"

She gives me a funny look. "I'd want my mother. Obviously."

That's not the decision I would make. If I had a choice between getting to be Whitney again and never seeing my mother again, it would be an easy choice. When there is a choice, I always choose myself. I don't care to see my mother again anyway. We never got along, especially after Joey broke his arm. She hated me after that.

"It all just sounds a little ungrateful," I say.

She frowns. "Ungrateful?"

"Yes. Here you are, using somebody else's name, and you don't even *want* it. It's an inconvenience to you." I give her a pointed look. "A lot of people would be *thrilled* with what you've been given, you know."

Amanda squirms on the sofa. "You know," she says, "I'm just thinking…we're having such a hard time agreeing on a place…maybe it's not such a great idea for the two of us to live together."

"No?"

"I mean, I like you and all," she says quickly.

Yeah, right.

"But given all the stuff with Blake, maybe it's not such a great idea."

Stuff with Blake? What is she talking about? My heart ratchets up a notch. "Did you *sleep* with him?" I blurt out. If she slept with him, I'm going for the face. I don't care about the time crunch.

"What? No!" Her eyes fly wide open, but I'm not sure if it's because I caught her or just surprised her. "I just meant that he and I didn't get along. I would never…" She grabs her purse from the floor and drops her phone back into it. "Look, maybe I should just get going."

She stands up from the sofa, and I rise to my feet as well. She wants to leave, but I can't let her. It's now or never. I reach for the magazines on the coffee table and wrap my fingers around the handle of the knife.

And that's when the doorbell rings.

Amanda's attention is distracted by the sound of the chimes. Which makes it that much easier to jam the blade of the knife deep into her belly.

CHAPTER 66

BLAKE

Please open the door, Whitney. Please...

I am fading fast. I can barely even stand up anymore without holding on to the doorframe. I have too much saliva in my mouth, yet I can't seem to swallow it. None of this is good.

I hope the hospital has an antidote to whatever it was that Krista gave me. I don't even know what the hell it was.

Just as I'm about to ring the doorbell again, the door swings open. I expected to see Whitney standing there, but instead, it's Krista. Oh no, it's too late. But on the plus side, I only see one Krista. At least I think it's Krista. Maybe I'm starting to hallucinate.

"Blake." She reaches out to grab my arm. "Come inside. Where have you been?"

I follow her, trying to do my best to hide the fact that I am actively dying. "I was...driving."

Shit, are my words starting to slur? Not good.

"Driving? Where did you go?"

"I told you. I went to Telmont." I wipe some drool out of the corner of my mouth because I can't seem to swallow right anymore. "I...I went to talk to Whitney's mother. And she told me..."

Krista arches an eyebrow. For a second, there are two of her, but then she's back to being one again. "She told you I'm Whitney."

"No, I saw the photo, and..." I wipe my lips again with the back of my hand. "I don't understand. If you're Whitney, then who is..."

A dark shadow passes over Krista's face. "An impostor. A girl who stole my name while I wasn't using it. You can see why she needed to pay the price."

"Pay the..."

And that's when I catch sight of the living room sofa. The girl I knew as Whitney Cross is lying slumped down, her midsection drenched in blood, which has leaked all over the fabric of the couch.

I'm too late. I couldn't stop her.

I step into the living room, trying to get a closer look, but I can't walk right anymore. I almost fall, but Krista catches me at the last second before I go down. She supports me for a moment; then I grab on to the wall to help me stay upright.

"Oh Christ." I rub my temple with my other hand. "Krista..."

"Don't be such a soft touch," she snaps at me. "She *deserved* it. Just like you deserve it for what you did. You and Stacie."

"That was *nothing*." I do my best to get the words out clearly. She needs to know this. "It was a onetime thing, and I regretted it immediately. I felt awful about it. I didn't care about Stacie. I cared about *you*. I loved *you*."

Her lips twist into a grimace. "Do you still?"

I don't know how to answer that question. How can I tell her that I love her after everything she's done? I don't even know who she is. And on top of that…

"You tried to kill me," I point out.

"Tried?" She smirks. "It looks like I'm doing a pretty good job of it, actually." Her gaze rakes over me. "How are you feeling right now, Blake?"

She knows I ate the cookies. Of course she knows—I practically fell on my face two seconds ago. I was kidding myself thinking that I could hide this from anyone. My speech is slurring, I can't walk a straight line, and I'm back to seeing two of her.

"It was tetrodotoxin," she informs me. "You know, the stuff that's in blowfish that's supposed to be so toxic? Usually, death results from respiratory failure within four to six hours." She looks at me curiously. "How long since you ate the cookies, Blake?"

I don't even know. I think it's been about three or four hours. And now that she mentions it, it does feel a little difficult to breathe all of a sudden. I am leaning against the wall now to keep from collapsing, and even that is not going to be enough in a few minutes.

"There's no suicide note," I manage.

"What did you say?" She bats her eyes at me. "You're slurring your words quite a lot."

I try again, enunciating every word: "I. Ripped. Up. The. Suicide. Note."

"Oh." She waves a hand. "No problem there. I'll write another one. I am very good at those."

I fall to my knees, knowing that I won't be able to get back up. This is it. I am not going to be able to survive this. I don't want it to end right here, right now, but what can I do? I can't call 911. I can't even work my fingers anymore.

I can't believe Krista did this to me. I *loved* her. I wanted her to be my wife.

And now she's standing over me, watching me die.

Except a second later, she's not standing over me anymore. She's on the floor next to me. Our eyes meet, and suddenly, the front of her white tank top turns bright red. She opens her mouth to say something, and blood drips from her lips.

"Krista?" I gasp.

I look up, and Whitney is standing over us, swaying on her feet, gripping a knife so tightly that her blood-speckled knuckles are white.

"Krista!" I do my best to crawl over to her. I'm not doing so hot myself, but she looks even worse than I do. She is literally choking on her own blood, which is now coming out of her mouth and out of her back, soaking the floor beneath us. "Krista…"

"I'm calling 911," Whitney says in a shaky voice, clutching her blood-soaked abdomen.

I crouch over Krista, watching the life drain out of her. I don't understand how she could've watched me dying a few minutes ago and felt nothing. Because this is the hardest thing I've ever had to watch. Even harder than when my mother died. Because I never expected to have my mother forever, but I thought I would grow old with Krista.

"Please don't die, Krista." Despite everything she did to me, my eyes fill with tears. "I love you."

Her lips crack open, and a bubble of blood forms at her lips. "You…don't…even…know me."

"I do," I insist. "I know you. Come on, Krista. Hang in there."

As Whitney talks on the phone to the 911 dispatcher, I pick up Krista's hand. It's cold and clammy. Her eyes are still cracked open though—she's still alive and conscious but barely.

"I love you," I say again. "I know who you are, and I love you. Please…"

For a split second, a ghost of a smile touches her lips. But then her eyes flutter closed, and suddenly, her body becomes very still. My gaze drifts down to her chest. Is it still rising and falling? Has she stopped breathing?

"We have to do CPR," I tell Whitney.

She hangs up with 911, and she looks at me like I've lost my mind. "CPR? Blake, you can barely breathe. And I've got a stab wound."

"I know, but…"

She's right. Even if I could remember the right ratio of breaths to compression, I don't have it in me. I can't breathe for another person when I can barely breathe for myself.

Krista is going to die. The life is draining out of her before my very eyes.

And the truth is it's exactly what she deserves.

CHAPTER 67

KRISTA

I knew I should have stabbed Amanda one more time to make sure she was dead.

I knew I should have added more tetrodotoxin to those cookies.

I knew I should never have trusted Blake.

I knew I'd never live happily ever after. My mother was right.

I knew it.

I…

CHAPTER 68

BLAKE

I'm still alive.

It's been one week since...well, since everything. One week since Krista tried to kill me. One week since she died on the floor of our living room, with me crouching over her bloody body in tears. One week since I was carried away to the emergency room, where I had to be sedated and intubated. (I don't remember much of that last part.) Apparently, there's no antidote to tetrodotoxin, but if you live through the first twenty-four hours, you have a good chance of not dying.

And now I have been pronounced (mostly) recovered, which means I get to go home from the hospital.

My father closed the hardware store and flew out to the city to be with me, but he went back home yesterday when it was obvious that I was out of the woods. I told him to go—I know he's short on help at the store, and I didn't want him to lose his business because of me. But it meant that I didn't have anyone to pick me up today, when I'm being discharged.

So I asked Amanda.

It still feels strange to call her that. For the whole time she was living with us, she was always Whitney. But actually, she seems more like an Amanda.

She told me why she changed her identity—about how she needed the money to pay for her mother's chemo and that she got it from the wrong people. The story broke my heart a little bit, especially because my own mother died of cancer, and I also know what it's like to be desperate for cash. But what astonishes me most is that Krista heard that story and still wanted Amanda dead. Krista was right—I really didn't know her.

I get dressed on my own in anticipation of going home. Even though I'm able to do all the motions of dressing myself, my body feels like it went through a battle, and when I'm done dressing, I feel like I need a nap to recover. I'm beyond exhausted.

Ingesting a lethal toxin? Not recommended.

The nurse who went through my discharge paperwork with me today comes by with a wheelchair. "I don't need that," I tell her, which isn't entirely true, because I'm still pretty shaky on my feet. Still, I can make it out of the building.

"Hospital rules," she says. "We don't want anything to happen to you—at least not until you leave!"

I don't want to make trouble, so I obediently climb into the chair. She pushes me down the hallway to the elevator. After an interminably long elevator ride, we arrive at the lobby. As promised, Amanda is sitting in the lobby waiting for me. She rises to her feet when she sees me.

"Is that your girlfriend?" the nurse asks me.

A split second after the question leaves her lips, her face turns pink. Because she knows—of course she does. Everyone knows I'm in the hospital because my girlfriend tried to kill me. And if that weren't enough, it's all over the news. The whole *city* knows.

Krista is famous now. The *New York Times* had a big splashy article about all the dead bodies left in her wake. It's more than I even knew about—more than just Stacie and Mr. Zimmerly. My ex-fiancée had a bad habit of dealing with her problems with murder.

"Hi, Blake," Amanda says as she gets closer to me. "You look like shit."

"Hey, thanks."

After her own wound was deemed nonserious and she was released from the hospital the next morning, Amanda has been back to visit me several times. And right now, she helps me get out of the wheelchair and steady myself on my feet.

"I can't catch you if you fall, you know," she says.

"I'll be fine."

There are taxis waiting outside the hospital, and I would have been perfectly fine to hop into one of them on my own, but I'm glad Amanda is here with me, and also, it was the hospital rule that someone had to pick me up. She opens the taxi door for me and then climbs inside behind me.

"But the ride is on me," I tell her. "Don't say no."

"Why would I say no?" she retorts. "I saved your life after all. The least you can do is pay for the ride."

That is very true. The doctor told me that if I hadn't come to the hospital and been intubated, I would have been dead within the hour. Krista wasn't going to call for an ambulance. If Amanda hadn't stabbed her from behind, she would have let me die right in front of her.

"I've got all my stuff packed by the way," Amanda tells me as the taxi shoots up First Avenue. "My friend from the diner told me I can crash on her couch for a while."

I look at her in surprise. "Why would you move out?"

"Um, because you told me to move out. You *ordered* me to."

I did do that. I banged on her door and told her she had thirty days to get the hell out of my home. But a lot has changed since then. I don't want to kick Amanda out and make her live on a friend's sofa when I've got a whole house that's practically empty.

"I want you to stay," I say. "I mean, if you want to."

Her eyebrows shoot up. "You sure about that?"

"Very sure." She looks hesitant, and I add, "And you can eat all the cereal you want."

Her face relaxes into a smile. "Well, I won't turn down a decent mattress over a lumpy sofa."

Even just the brief conversation with Amanda has exhausted me, so I lean my head back against the headrest so I can rest. But every time I shut my eyes, I see Krista standing over me, watching me die. I still can't wrap my head around what she did to me or the fact that she killed so many people in her lifetime…until Amanda finally put an end to it. It's no exaggeration to say that Krista was a psychopath. Hell, you could go ahead and call her a monster.

Is it terrible to say I miss her?

EPILOGUE

FOUR MONTHS LATER

BLAKE

My car is loaded up with everything I own.

Well, not everything. I couldn't bring furniture, and a few boxes have already been shipped to my father's house in Ohio. But I have filled every spot in the trunk and back seat of the used Kia that I purchased last week. It's ready to go.

And so am I.

Amanda joins me in the living room as I take one last look around the brownstone, which gave me some of my happiest and worst memories of living in New York City. Now that the particularly snowy winter has come to a close, I've decided to start the process of trying to sell it, which was one of the easiest decisions I've ever had to make. If I never see this place again, it will be too soon.

Thankfully, it won't be hard to sell. While recovering from being poisoned, I spent a little time fixing up the brownstone using all the home repair skills my father taught me when I was younger, because I was worried that nobody would be interested after...well, everything that happened here. But believe it or not, there are plenty of people eager to own the former home of a now notorious murderer. It looks like there's going to be a bidding war.

"So this is it," I say to Amanda.

She flashes me a sad smile. She's been helping me pack and load up my car. And after I leave, she is going to facilitate the sale of the brownstone in exchange for living here rent-free for a little bit longer. I managed to make my mortgage payments after a few paid interviews about Krista, but the whole thing left a bad taste in my mouth. A publisher offered me an extremely lucrative book deal, and I turned them down outright.

"I'm going to miss you, Blake," she says.

I'll miss her too. After spending so long hating her, Amanda and I have bonded a lot over the last few months. I don't know what I would've done without her to talk to about everything that happened.

"I bet you five bucks you'll be bored to tears in six months and want to come back to New York," she says.

"I'm never coming back," I say, and I mean it. "You can always come visit me in Cleveland though. Open invitation."

"I might take you up on that." She grins. "I want to come visit your store."

Yes, I am taking over my father's hardware store. After it was discovered that Krista had been the one who got into my files and sold our marketing campaign, Wayne Vincent called me personally to offer me the VP job again. Apparently, Malcolm wasn't able to keep up with the workload, and they were planning to let him go. *Nobody could handle this job better than you, Blake.* But after the way he threw me out on my ass after all those years without even giving me the benefit of the doubt…well, I couldn't imagine ever going back there. I hadn't realized how toxic Coble & Roy was, even when my predecessor tried to hurl himself out the window. (Truthfully, there's a part of me that still wonders if Krista was somehow behind that, but now that she's gone, I'll never know.)

Anyway, my father is over the moon excited about me taking over the store, and it feels like the right thing to do. This city has nothing left to offer me, and it will be good to continue the family business. Plus, I miss my dad, and he won't be around forever. I can't wait to get home to Cleveland.

Now the only thing left to do is get on the road.

Amanda and I face each other, and for a moment, it's a little awkward trying to figure out exactly how to say goodbye. A week ago, she and I hooked up—once. It wasn't something either of us planned, but we've been spending so much time together and having such intimate conversations, it just…happened.

When it was over, I felt disgusted with myself. Krista was barely dead, and everything that happened was still fresh in my mind. But also, sleeping with a woman who saved your life did seem like a good antidote to your girlfriend trying to kill you.

Amanda and I end up giving each other a hug, which feels right. Amanda is so different from Krista—the sort of woman I'd always imagined ending up with. I only wish I had met her earlier, because Krista has screwed me up for a long time to come.

"Are you going to be okay?" I ask her.

She hesitates for a moment, then nods. "Yes."

"Because if you need to borrow any money from me…"

"It's okay. I've worked something out."

One thing I was very concerned about was that with all the publicity around Krista, Amanda's identity was outed. But she told me that with some of the money she has earned, she's working out a payment plan. So it's all going to be fine, or so she says. I'm still a little worried. You don't want to mess with a pissed-off loan shark. I made her promise that if she is in any trouble, she'll let me know. If this brownstone sells for what I think it will, I should have plenty of money to lend her.

"All right," I say. "I guess this is it."

Amanda walks me to my car, and we hug one last time. I've lived in this city for over a decade now. I'll be sad to leave it behind, but I'm also happy for a fresh start. Everything happens for a reason, and it feels like this is my fate.

I can't wait to start my new life.

AMANDA

I feel a bit sad as I watch Blake drive away in his new used car. It was nice spending time with him for the last few months, but he'll be happier back in Ohio. He was making it work for a little while, but he's too much of a Midwest boy. He was always going to end up back there, even if Krista hadn't ruined his life.

I will miss him though. He's a nice guy, very easy on the eyes, and a great kisser. I can see why Krista was so possessive of him.

I also love how he believed every word I told him.

He's worried about me. I could see it all over his face. He's worried that the loan sharks will come after me. If he knew the truth, he wouldn't be worried. He also wouldn't let me stay in his house or offer me money. And he definitely would not have gone to bed with me last week. But what he doesn't know won't hurt him.

It all happened one month before Krista was killed. I was working the late shift at the diner, dreading going home to the brownstone, and I noticed a gruff-looking man at one of the tables who was making me very nervous. As the rest of the customers emptied out, he stayed behind, nursing the same cup of coffee. It wasn't until the place was practically empty that he grabbed my arm while I was walking by his table.

"Take a break, Amanda," he told me. "I want to talk to you out back."

He called me by my real name. I thought about running for it, but I knew that was suicide.

I met him next to the dumpster behind the diner. He introduced himself as Frank Gallo. He told me that he knew I owed one of his colleagues a lot of money, and he wanted to help me clear my debt.

I was sure whatever he was going to ask me to do was going to be something terrible, but I was so tired of running. I was tired of living in shitty apartments with asshole landlords who accused me of eating too much cereal and using the wrong kind of laundry detergent. I was willing to do just about anything to put an end to all this. "What do you want?" I asked.

"You're living with a woman named Krista Marshall," Frank Gallo said. "She killed my nephew, Jordan, and got away with it. Like you, she thought she could hide, but she couldn't. We always catch up sooner or later. Ironically, it was you who helped me locate her."

I didn't know what he meant by that, but his words were enough to make me shiver in the back alley. "What do you want me to do?"

"You kill Krista Marshall," he said, "and we'll forget about all your gambling debts."

Yes, of course they were gambling debts. Does anyone really borrow money from a loan shark to pay for their *mother's chemotherapy*? Give me a break. I'm not Pollyanna. Anyway, my mother is an alcoholic who barely looked at me through my entire childhood, and if she got cancer, I would happily watch it eat away at her until she died.

I've done a lot of rotten things in my life—call it bad upbringing. But I'd never killed anyone before. Still, I wanted my life back. And it didn't feel like I had much of a choice.

"Fine," I told him. "I'll do it."

Ironically, the night Krista stabbed me, I had planned to kill her. Like Krista, I was thinking that Blake would go down for it. I didn't like him much back then, and anyone could see that he was falling apart. I had already pegged him as the one who killed Mr. Zimmerly next door. None of it happened the way I expected, but in the end, I was the one who killed Krista. I did exactly what Frank Gallo asked me to do, and he has assured me that my debt has been paid.

So you see, when I stabbed Krista that night, I wasn't saving Blake's life.

I was saving my own.

I bet you five bucks Krista never saw that coming.

Keep reading for a look at another Freida McFadden thriller, *The Surrogate Mother*!

CHAPTER 1

At this moment in time, my life is just about perfect.

A couple of years ago, I couldn't have said that. A couple of years ago, I would have rather slit my wrists than stood up in front of a room full of executives from Cuddles, "the new name in diapers," and presented them with a new ad campaign filled with dozens of pictures of cherubic babies with halos on their heads and the tagline: "Because your little angel is worth it." I would have done the presentation, of course, but the smile on my face wouldn't have been genuine, the way it is today.

But right now, everything is exactly the way I want it to be. Well, not *exactly*, but very close. I have the job I always wanted. I'm married to a wonderful man. And in a few short weeks (depending on the whims of the Labor Gods), I'm going to become a mother for the very first time.

You might say I have a glow about me.

"This new campaign," I say, as I gesture at the projected

image on the screen, "has the potential to propel Cuddles into the same league as Huggies and Pampers."

I turn my gaze to Jed Cofield, the executive VP of marketing at Cuddles. Jed is in his forties with thick, chestnut hair, penetrating dark eyes, and a suit from Hugo Boss. Even though he wears a gold band on his left hand, in the two years I've worked with him, he always stands a bit closer than he needs to when we talk—close enough that I can accurately identify what he ate for his last meal. Even now—even with my impending motherhood—I notice his eyes traveling down the length of my body.

Back before I was promoted to my current position as Director of Content Strategy at Stewart Advertising, I learned a lot about how to appear confident. Eye contact is key. So I lock eyes with Jed, straighten my posture, and throw my shoulders back.

I have every reason to be confident. I know my campaign is fantastic. I worked my butt off making sure of that.

"How did this campaign perform with the twenty-five to thirty-four female demographic?" Cofield asks.

It's an excellent question. In the diaper market, twenty-five to thirty-four females are essentially *the* demographic, as far as Cuddles is concerned. Few sixty-year-old men buy diapers for babies, no matter how compelling our commercials are. Of course, I've aged out of this key demographic, yet I've got a package of newborn diapers stuffed in the closet, but no need to point that out.

Denise Holt, the Chief Marketing Officer and also my boss, opens her mouth to answer the question. Three years ago, I might have let her. But part of being confident is you don't let your boss answer questions for you.

"They love the campaign, Jed," I say before Denise can

get a word out. I click on a button on my remote, bringing up a screen of data. "After viewing our campaign, they were fifty-three percent more likely to choose Cuddles over the other leading brands." I watch his eyebrows raise and add, "And in addition to your original target group, this campaign also resonated deeply with women aged thirty-five to forty-four. As you know, older mothers contribute at least thirty percent to the diaper-purchasing market."

Cofield nods, impressed. "Very true."

I make eye contact with him again. "We're going to crush it."

Cofield is smiling now, but Denise isn't. I've known Denise Holt for a long time, and I know she doesn't enjoy being upstaged. Denise was the one who hired me way back when—over a decade ago now. I still remember stumbling into her office and being terrified by her ice-blue eyes and blond hair swept back into a perfect French knot. I fiddled with my suit jacket collar as I fumbled through my rehearsed list of reasons why I wanted to work for Stewart Advertising and specifically for the infamous Denise Holt.

She hired me. Then she taught me everything I know, including how to tie my jet black hair into a French knot, which is apparently called a *chignon*. (Who knew?) It wasn't until she found out I was trying for a baby that our relationship deteriorated.

"They love it, huh?" Cofield says.

I nod. "They do."

His smile broadens. "Well, so do I. I love it. It's brilliant."

Outwardly, I remain calm, but inside, I'm doing

cartwheels. *The VP of Cuddles loves my idea. He loves it! He says it's brilliant!*

I can't help but flash a triumphant smile at Denise, who has been nothing but negative during the entire time I've been working on this campaign. As recently as yesterday, she was urging me to postpone this meeting because "it's not nearly ready." When I insisted on going forward, she accused me of having "baby on the brain."

Denise has chosen to remain free from maternal obligations. When I started out as her assistant, she drilled into me time and again that nothing wrecked a career faster than popping out a couple of rugrats. Denise's career means everything to her, and she's been extremely successful. Back then, I thought my career meant everything to me. Then Sam came along and convinced me otherwise.

I have no regrets. Everything is working out perfectly for me.

"Tell me, Abby." Cofield raises his eyebrows at me. "Will you be purchasing Cuddles for your baby?"

"Of course," I lie. "I want the best."

Yeah, there's no way I'm putting those shoddy diapers on my own child.

We iron out a few more details, then shake hands all around. Jed Cofield winks at me when we shake, and I squeeze his fingers firmly in the way Denise instructed me years ago. His warm fingers linger on mine for a beat longer than necessary. Cofield has been my biggest fan since I started working on the Cuddles campaign, so I won't begrudge him a handshake that lasts a second or two longer than I'd like.

But if he thinks he's getting anything more out of me, he's sorely mistaken.

"Congratulations," he tells me.

I'm not sure if he's referring to my successful pitch or impending motherhood, but I simply smile and say, "Thank you."

As Cofield and his associates clear out of the room, Denise and I are left alone. There was a time when I got a thrill out of any chance to be alone with my role model, but these days, I avoid it like the plague. Given how well everything went in the presentation, it would be appropriate for Denise to say something positive or even *complimentary*, but there's a sour look on her face that tells me I will not be receiving any praise today.

"I've been meaning to speak with you, Abigail," she says.

Denise is the only person at work who calls me "Abigail" rather than "Abby." I used to like it—the name made me sound like an executive, rather than a girl at the playground with freckles and pigtails. (I used to have freckles and pigtails.) I tried to get everyone at work to call me Abigail for a while, but it didn't stick. Now the sound of that name on her lips makes my skin crawl.

"What about?" I ask. I plaster on that fake smile I now use when I talk to my boss, although it gets harder every day. One day, I will be speaking to Denise and simply won't be able to smile. It will be physically impossible.

Denise eyes my outfit. My suit jacket and skirt are from Armani. In the month I made the purchase, Sam came to me with the credit card statement and a horrified look on his face. "Someone stole our credit card, right?" he said. "We didn't *actually* spend this much, right?"

I had to tell him that yes, we did. I absolutely did spend that much on a single outfit, and it was *worth it*. Sam claims his suits from Men's Wearhouse look identical to anything he'd get at Armani or Prada, but he's wrong. Maybe there's no difference across a lecture hall, which is all that matters to him—but close up, anyone worth their salt can tell an expensive suit from a cheap knock-off. And the executives I pitch to respect someone who dresses well—in that sense, my clothes pay for themselves.

Another lesson I learned from Denise.

"How are you doing?" she asks.

"Good," I say cautiously, because anything more positive than that is a cue for Denise to make my life worse.

"Wonderful, wonderful." Denise taps a dark red manicured finger against her chin. "Remind me how long you're planning to take for your family leave? Eight weeks?"

A muscle twitches in my jaw. "Twelve weeks."

"Twelve weeks?" Denise's eyes widen in astonishment, despite the fact that we've had this exact conversation nearly a dozen times. "That long?"

The muscle twitches again. I had my first migraine earlier this year following a particularly tense discussion with Denise—I can't let her get to me.

"Twelve weeks is allowed as family leave," I say.

"I realize that." Denise's ice-blue eyes narrow at me. "But that doesn't mean you *must* take twelve weeks, does it? It seems like an awfully long time. Your clients will be disappointed."

"I can do some of my work from home during the last month," I say. That's a compromise we've worked out. "Everyone is going to take on some of my workload. And of course, my assistant Monica will be around to help out."

"*Monica will be around to help,*" she repeats in a vaguely

mocking tone. She blinks a few times. "Well then, perhaps we should give *Monica* your position?"

If I slugged her in the face, I'd get fired. I have to remind myself of that. Again and again.

"I'm just kidding," Denise says, even though she's not smiling. "Of course, you are entitled to your twelve weeks, Abigail. I was just hoping you might reconsider."

I will not reconsider. I love my career, but I have thought long and hard about my priorities. I will not rush back to work. I don't care if Denise hates me because of it. And let's face it—she wouldn't hate me any less if I took four weeks.

"Anyway." Denise pats her flawless chignon, which makes my hand go automatically to my own French knot. I feel a strand has come loose and I quickly tuck it behind my ear. Denise must use a bottle of hairspray each day to keep hers intact, but it doesn't appear that way. Her hair looks silky and perfect. "I believe Shelley has planned some sort of...*party* for you in the break room."

I'm well aware that my best friend Shelley has scheduled a baby shower for me to follow this meeting—she would have preferred to surprise me, but given my tight schedule, that was impossible. It's sweet of her, but after fifteen minutes, I'll definitely have to make my excuses and slip away. My afternoon is packed—as it is, I won't get home till eight or nine tonight.

"I'm afraid I won't be able to make it," Denise tells me, which is no surprise. She's made no secret of the fact that she does not approve of events that "waste everyone's time" such as baby showers. "But please make sure you clear away all the trash from the room when you're done."

I bite my tongue to keep from reminding her that I am

no longer her assistant, and she can't tell me to clean up garbage anymore. But I keep my mouth shut, because I'm happy. I've impressed the Cuddles people, and I'm about to go to a baby shower in my honor. A *baby shower*. For *me*.

In the time I have worked at Stewart Advertising, I have made an appearance at roughly two million baby showers. Okay, that could be a slight exaggeration. It's possible I've only been to one million baby showers. Maybe three-quarters of a million. Definitely no less than half a million.

But now, for the first time, the shower is for me. Not for Elsa in reception, who has had at least a dozen children in her time working here. Not for Shelley, who has had a more respectable two. This shower is for *me*. The finger sandwiches that will be piled in the corner will have been brought in *my* honor. The presents stacked neatly in the corner of the room will be for *me*. The first piece of chocolate hazelnut cake will be handed to *me*.

There's only one thing different about this baby shower from all other baby showers thrown for the other women in my company:

I'm not pregnant.

READING GROUP GUIDE

1. Why do you think Freida McFadden chose to include a male POV when she so often focuses on women?

2. Why open the novel with someone's attempted suicide? Looking back, did that give you a clue as to what was to come?

3. What did you think of Blake and Krista's relationship at the beginning of the novel? Did you see the twist coming?

4. What was Whitney's role in everything that went down with Krista and Blake? How do you feel about her final revelation? Does that change things?

5. There is a lot of focus on living in Manhattan: Blake tries to keep has brownstone no matter what, and Krista judges Whitney for looking at renting in Staten

Island. How is the city portrayed, and what role might it play in the novel?

6. Did you think Blake would ever do anything to harm Krista? Were there moments you didn't trust him?

7. At its heart, this is a revenge story. Do you think Blake had it coming?

8. Did you believe what Whitney said about her background? Would you let her be your tenant?

9. What did Krista do to Jordan? To Stacie? Do you think she did that to anyone else?

10. It is known that Krista bakes delicious cookies from the very beginning of the novel. Looking back, why might that be? What might the cookies represent?

11. What was your reaction to Blake going back home? Why did he leave New York, and do you think he'll come back?

ACKNOWLEDGMENTS

The Tenant is one of the only books I've written that include the point of view of a man. With that in mind, I have to thank my husband, who read through the first few chapters and confidently told me, "Nope, a man would never say that." So helpful!

As always, I want to thank my mother for loving this book from the very start. I'm sure I sound like a broken record if you read all my acknowledgments, but I am very grateful to my agent, Christina Hogrebe, and the entire JRA team for your support and feedback. Thank you to Jenna Jankowski for your remarkably detailed and insightful comments as well as to everyone else behind the scenes at Sourcebooks. Thank you to Mandy Chahal for your superhuman marketing efforts.

Thank you to my many beta readers: Jenna, Maura, Pam, Kate, and Emily, who provided some amazing feedback. Thank you to Red Adept Editing for your feedback. Thank you to Val for the help with proofreading.

I always have to give a huge thank-you to my readers, both online and the ones who don't even own a computer. I am so grateful for your support!

ABOUT THE AUTHOR

#1 *New York Times*, *USA Today*, *Washington Post*, *Publishers Weekly*, and *Sunday Times* internationally bestselling author Freida McFadden is a practicing physician specializing in brain injury. Freida is the winner of both the International Thriller Writer Award for Best Paperback Original and the Goodreads Choice Award for Best Thriller. Her novels have been translated into over forty languages. Freida lives with her family and black cat in a centuries-old three-story home overlooking the ocean.